DAVID GERROLD

I0562870

For Malcolm Kroh
with love

Cover design by Glenn Hauman
Interior design by Arwen Rosenbaum
for ComicMix Pro Services
www.comicmix.com/pro-services

ISBN 978-1-958482-17-9 hardcover
ISBN 978-1-958482-18-6 paperback

For information address
David Gerrold at his official website:
www.gerrold.com

Contents

Introduction

At any given moment, half the world is dark.

The planet turns and we hunker down in our caves, huddling by our fires, listening uneasily to the noises of the night.

This night, our caves are made of steel and glass, and our fires are harsh and electric, but still we hunker down against the darkness, sometimes only with the phosphor glow of our devices.

When we venture out, we take our fires with us. We hold back the night, lighting our cities with walls of brightness, with incandescence and neon and sometimes even arcs of lightning.

Thus we challenge the dark to take us, to drag us down into the gloom, down into the fears that still lurk under our ancient beds. Because we bring our fires with us, we tell ourselves there are no monsters.

But we're wrong.

We are still the frightened huddling apes. We listen warily, we wrap ourselves in the illusions of warmth, but still we cast fearful glances at the windows, always on the lookout for the unknown things that live *out there*.

Sometimes...we find them.

Sometimes...they find us.
And sometimes, sometimes...*we are the monsters.*
The dark reveals that as well.
Here are five stories of night and monsters.
Shudder and enjoy.

All Of Them
Were Empty—

In a city of night and neon. She had puppy-soft eyes and an old army coat. I had a sweatshirt and levis and an acid-laced joint. We watched the colors smear.

We sheared our eyes on the slashing lights and let them bleed into the streets. The lights. Glowworm letters and gray crumbling walls.

My blood was copper, hers was gold; I was strong and red, she was soft and malleable.

She had sucking eyes. They could eat you up, or they could tease. Black whirlpool pupils, large and moist.

I moved like stone down the hollow deathwalk, the tall night above, the close city around. The unreal-colored neon flashed us messages of EAT, DRINK and JESUS SAVES. She moved with me like a wraith, a shadow of a girl suspended in air, attached to my jacket, following ghostlike and effortless. "Deet?" she said, and her voice was like that first big hit—painful, elusive and narcotic.

"Deet?" she asked again. "Let's go home, huh?"

A shake of my head. "Not yet, Wooze. Not yet." Wooze, short for Woozle.

"But I'm tired, Deet. It's my period and I don't feel good."

"Then go."

"I don't want to go alone."

"Then don't go."

"Deet..." she said plaintively. I looked at her; she was using that tone of voice again. She shut.

"Nobody asked you to come," I said.

"I don't like to be by myself. I want to stay with you."

"Okay, then stay. But if you're going to talk about going home, I'm gonna ditch you."

"You wouldn't."

"Want to find out?"

She didn't answer, instead pulled her coat tighter about her, shoved skinny hands into skinny pockets and cringed against the city. Cars like giant panthers prowled the night streets, rolling silent-rumbly through dark-lit intersections and wet gutter bottoms. Eyes glowing, they spotlit their prey in white-lined crosswalks and rushed eagerly toward them, only to be cheated when the lone figures vanished into the safety of the soft black buildings.

Doors like hungry mouths pulled at us. She half-ran, half-walked to keep up with me. "Deet? Where we going anyway?"

"To a place."

"You said that before, Deet. Which place? We going to Cannie's?"

I shook my head. "Not Cannie's. I don't like his stuff."

"You used to."

"Not any more. Got something new."

"A new place?"

"A new place, yeah." Hands in my pockets, tight-wrapped around a narrow roll of bills. Yeah, a new place. And new stuff.

And new people.

Got to get away from the old stuff. Clot your mind. Too many pills, your eyes turn to glass, shatter with the morning. Your stomach turns to liquid, bleeds away in the night.

Two ways to go. Up or down. Down, back into the bright-lit land of the straights—or up, into the pastel razorblade world of H. H for heavy stuff, for hard stuff.

Uh-uh, not me. Not H. H is for hooked. Seen the cold turkey once too often. Not H.

But still, two ways to go. Up or down.

Tried them all, speed, mesc, acid. Acid's okay and mesc is a people trip. But speed is the deathman. Speed kills, comes after you with the crystal knife shining.

Still, you got to make the choice, Deet; can't stand still—up or down?

—or why not out?

Why not a whole new direction? Hang a sudden left and leave them all. A whole new kick. Who said it had to be this or that? Why does it have to be either? Yeah, I had it. I had it now. I knew the way.

To hell with up or down. What's wrong with right and left and north and east and yesterday and Tuesday and Charlie and purple and?

I knew the way. All I had to do was find it. I didn't have the address though. All I had was a description of where it was, and I still had to go looking for it.

Woozle was woozy. She kept wiping her nose on her sleeve. It was red; so were her eyes. "You crying again?"

"Uh-uh, Deet. I wouldn't do that. Uh-uh. I got a cold, that's all. I told you, it's my period."

"That gives you a cold?"

"Yes. No. I don't know." She shrugged her baggy green coat around her shoulders. "Deet, I'm awfully tired. Could we sit down a minute?"

"We're almost there."

"Where? We aren't anywhere...."

"We're almost there. Don't worry about it."

She sat down anyway. All right; I stopped and waited. The streets shone in the dark. Like water. Dark puddles from the rain lapped at the curbs. I lit the last joint, inhaled deep, deep, deep, sharp pain, and deeper, deep hit. Acid-laced hit. Yeah.

I wanted to hallucinate. Another hit. I could feel it coming.

I offered Woozle the joint. She shook her head. "Uh-uh. Not any more, Deet. I'm afraid I'll go on a bad trip."

I already was. I took another. Yeah, that was it.

A car came floating down the street, cleaving water to either side of its bow, cleaving an inky wake. I was glad we were on this side of the street. I didn't want to swim the canal tonight. I wondered where the horses were.

Did they still put running lights on them? I wondered. On what, I asked, but I couldn't remember.

The joint disappeared back into a baggie, flame pinched out first, then into the underwear. Nestled tight, a nice place to keep things.

The door was where I had left it. Knocked.

No answer. Knocked it again.

An eye, red like the cherry on a copcar, peeked out. "Yeah?"

"Deet. My name's Deet."

"Yeah? So what?"

"Told to come by."

"By who?" the eye demanded, floating behind a black wall

"You did. Somebody did. Said something about a new kick or something."

"What'd you say your name was?"

"Deet."

The eye swiveled around to look at the Woozle. "What's that?"

"She's with me."

"She okay?"

"I said, she's with me."

"Who sent you?"

"I don't know his name. Their names."

"Who's they?"

"A guy—no, two guys. And a girl. Strange girl. Pale eyes."

"Tamra?"

"That could be it. Yeah, that's it. That's who it was. Tamra."

"Uh-uh—no Tamra. We got no Tamra." The eye started to close.

"Hey!"

It opened again.

"Hey, man—what is this? You guys told me to come by here—"

"Where'd we tell you?"

"Here!"

"No, where were we when we told you?"

"Cannie's."

"Where's that?"

I told him.

"Wait." The eye closed.

We waited.

Night waited. The street lights seeped and sucked at the dark. It sucked back. Somewhere a thing splashed through the waves.

The eye opened. "All right."

We went in. It was red-lit, like the churchman's Hell. A naked red bulb sat on top of the room, not bright enough to light, dim enough to be painful. Everything was a red blur.

Woozle took one look and groaned. She covered her eyes and grabbed at my jacket with an unsteady hand. She hung onto me all the while, following with one hand over her eyes. Well, she'd asked to come; it wasn't my fault.

The guy—yeah, it was a guy—had hair of barbed-wire brillo, a dark scraggly bush. Eyes like a prowl car. Heavy. He was wearing only shapeless underwear and a paint-stained blanket-poncho. It didn't cover much.

"This way," he said.

We pad-padded down a long corridor. The place was one of those narrow apartments that shows only a door to the street and stretches forever inland. Narrow rooms, narrow rooms, one after the other, open and empty. Some mattresses, an old box, a blanket, the remains of a shirt, scraps of paper, floors and walls. Nothing more. And everything red-lit.

We went all the way to the back. One or two of the doors were closed, with sounds seeping out around the edges—once the sound of surf. But the ones I could see into were empty. A record player tinkered with sounds and darkness.

The last room was like all the rest. Except something smelled funny. Like dusty orange. Two or three mattresses lay dirty on the floor. Four people in the room: two guys, two girls. They all had tombstone eyes. I didn't like the looks, but I'd heard about the new kick and I wanted to try it.

"This's Deet," grunted the brillo-head.

Casual glances, nothing more.

"That's Woozle," I said, nodding at the Wooze. She was still covering her eyes.

"Sit." One of the girls shrugged. I sat. Woozle, putting one hand behind her, lowered herself. The mattresses had no soft; they were flat and dusty-slimy.

The two guys were off to one side, sitting-leaning up against the wall and looking at each other. Okay, none of my business. It was the girls who held my attention. They had pale eyes, pink in the red-lit room.

"Who are you?" one asked.

"Deet. I'm Deet. He just told you—" I pointed at brillo-hair, but he wasn't there anymore.

"Uh-uh," she shook her head. "Who are you?"

Shrug. "I'm me. That's all."

"Okay. Who's she?"

"She's Woozle. She goes where I go."

"Everywhere?"

"Just about."

"You like that?" Her voice was like an empty room. It echoed.

"Yeah, it's okay, I guess."

"You don't like it?"

"I don't know," I shrugged again. "I'm used to it."

"You want to change it?"

"Why should I?"

"Yes. Why should you?"

I wasn't sure what she was talking about any more. I shrugged. "Why do you want to know?"

This time, she shrugged. "Need to know. That's all."

Woozle tugged at my arm then. I ignored it.

The other girl now, "Where're you headed?"

"Nowhere now. We're here."

"This is where you want to be?"

Another tug at the arm. I shook it off and answered the pale-eyed question, "It's as good a place as any."

"Deet..." said Woozle, and she had that tone again. Plaintive. "Deet...!"

"Christ, you're a nuisance, Woozle, you know that? What do you want?"

She pushed hair back out of her eyes, looked at me, wetly. "Deet, I want to go home."

"Then go, dammit!"

"Uh-uh, Deet. Not without you. Deet, I'm scared." She lowered her voice to a point where she was almost mouthing the words. "Deet, these people scare me."

"It's all right, Wooze. I'm here."

"That's what I'm scared about. You're here. I don't think you should be."

"You starting that again?"

She lowered her eyes. "No. I'm sorry. It's just that—"

"Aw, look—" I knew she wanted me to touch her then, but I didn't. "Look, this'll only take a minute. Promise. Then we'll go. Okay?"

She looked up with tear streaks. "Promise?"

"Promise," I said, and touched her chin. "Just don't nag me, okay?"

"Okay, Deet. I'm sorry." She sniffed at her sleeve.

I looked back at the girls. They had long stringy hair; like they were hiding behind it. There was something funny about the shapes of their mouths too. I smiled, sort of, as if to excuse the Woozle.

They didn't smile back. Okay, I didn't care. They took up their questioning where they left off. Questioning? What was this anyway—a test? Why did I have to pass a test?

"Hey," I interrupted. "I didn't come to talk. I came for the kick."

"We know. You'll get it. But it's...uncool to just kick and run. You've got to talk to us first. We like to talk."

"I don't." I looked at their eyes.

"But we do," they answered patiently.

"Look, I got the cash for it—just give it to me and we'll go."

"Don't want cash," said one.

"Want you," said the other.

"Huh?" I said.

And, "Deet!" said Woozle. "Let's get out of here."

I ignored the voice at my sleeve. "What're you talking about?"

"We want you. To talk to. That's our price."

"Oh. I thought you meant something else."

"Uh-uh," she said.

"Good. That's not my bag.?'

"Not ours either." She rearranged herself on the mattress. They looked at me again. Hungry. Patient bitches, weren't they?

"What is your thing?" they asked.

"I don't know. Just being me, I guess."

"But who are you? Do you know?"

I shook my head. To clear it. It wasn?t making sense any more. If it ever did. "Hey, enough of this already. Where's the hit I came for?"

"We're giving it to you," said one.

"We're trying to give it to you," said the other.

"Right now," added the first.

"Uh-uh," I shook my head. "Uh-uh, rm not buying a shuck. I haven't smoked anything. I haven't dropped anything. So far, all we've done is talk—"

"Yes, yes," she had a voice like a movie geisha, all treble and no bass. "That's it. A communicating...thing."

"Huh? I don't...?' I mean, it doesn't."

She cocked her head, "It is essential that—"

Something was wrong, the whole thing was all tilty-slidy and kept creeping off at the edges. I tried to yank it back, but it wouldn't. Somehow I kept missing the undertones.

They were ignoring me. They were looking at each other and talking softly, words like, "...doesn't want...needs a tangible..."

The first one shook her head, as if in disagreement, "...does want..."

"...doesn't..."

"...does...just doesn't know that he..."

The second one shook her head now, "No...needs a tan gibble... trib won't work unless...must believe..."

The first one nodded at that, "Yes...is necessary...give something..."

The second one made a suggestion.

The first one glanced up sharply. "...not..."

The second one: "...what else...trib is trib...he wants...we give..."

"Trib is not trib...this bite is..."

"Bite is bite is bite..." snapped the second. "Want not hear about it..."

"Possibility for ickle-ickle-ickle..."

"Am aware...am aware...am aware..."

"Rather try communicor again..." insisted the first.

"Won't work...won't work...doesn't want...doesn't want..." The second one seemed to have the upper hand in whatever it was. At last, the first one gave in and they looked at me, "Okay. We give."

"Great. What do we do? Smoke it? Drink it? Eat it?"

"None of those," they shook their heads.

"Then how—?"

"Rub it on," said one. The other was burrowing around under the mattress. "Take off your clothes," she said.

"Huh?"

"Take off your clothes. That's what you have to do."

"You're not putting me on?"

"You want the hit?"

"Are you going to take one too?"

They shook their heads. "We're already on ours. We don't need yours."

"Oh." I still didn't move to drop my clothes.

They waited. "Are you shy?"

"No. It's just that—"

"Would you like us to take off our clothes too?" one asked. The other didn't wait for me to answer, but dropped her robe (how come I hadn't noticed that before?) to the floor. She was as sexless as an eight-year-old boy. Flat chested. I stared, yeah. No curves, nothing. What a bring-down. A super-bummer. A beautiful face like that and no bod. No hair, no nothing. The other was just the same, she'd dropped her robe too, only she was wearing black briefs. She didn't move to drop them. It wasn't necessary. My curiosity was dead.

"Well?" she asked.

"All right." I shrugged out of my shirt, started to fumble with my belt. "Hey, Wooze?"

"Yeah?"

"You coming?"

"Huh?"

"Take off your clothes..."

"Uh-uh, Deet. I don't want any. Thanks."

"Aw, come on. I don't want to go alone."

"No, Deet. All I want to do is go home."

"Don't be a drag, Woozle. Do it."

"I don't want to."

"But I want you to."

"Deet, I'll go anywhere you go, Deet. I'll never leave you alone. Promise. But please, don't ask me to take any more stuff, Deet. I don't like it."

"How do you know? You haven't tried it." I pulled her to her feet, started pulling her clothes off. She tried to resist at first, then realized it was useless. The army coat, the baggy jeans, the T-shirt and soiled underwear fell to the ioor. She stood there naked and wiped her nose on the back of her wrist. "Sit," I said. She sat.

I kicked off my shoes, then dropped my pants and underwear all in one motion. Sit, lift the legs and slide them off; one foot, then the other. The two of us sat naked on the mattress. Ready for action. Whatever the action was.

Woozle was clenched in on herself, arms folded across tight little breasts. I don't know why she was ashamed. She had more than these girls did. No matter, she kept her nose into her knee and sniffed, wiped it across her leg.

I turned to the chicks. (What happened to the two guys who were in the room? Where did they go?) "Okay, we're ready."

One of them stepped forward (there was that funny smell again) and held out a jar that looked like a cold cream thing. I didn't take it.

First, I asked, "How much?"

"Enough," she replied. "Enough for two."

"No. I mean, how much do I owe you?"

She cocked her head in puzzlement, "Nothing."

"Uh-uh," I started to pick up my pants. "No free rides. Not for this head."

They exchanged a confused glance, "Why?"

"Anything free's got a hook in it. Like the first jolt of H—and that's not my bag. Don't plan on getting hooked on anything."

They looked at each other again. "Okay. Twenty dollars."

"Twenty?"

"Two rides. One yours, one hers."

"Yeah," but I was still suspicious.

"You want it? Or not?"

I sniffed. That was the source of the funny odor, like old orange peels. So were the girls. "What is it?"

She shrugged, "No name. Just is."

"And I just rub it on."

She nodded. She held the jar in her two hands and waited.

"No hook in it?"

"If you don't want it, we don't put hook in. Okay?"

"Okay," I said slowly. "No hook." I still didn't like it, but I wanted to try it. The smell was getting deep, deeper. I wanted to feel what was at the bottom.

The decision was made. I pulled the twenty out of my pocket, creased it between my fingers to straighten it, and tossed it over. The jar was heavy in my hands and it had a slippery feel.

Okay, we'd do the number. Just once. See what it was and that'd be it. Course, that's what I'd said about acid the first time too. The top unscrewed greasy, and suddenly the funny smell was intense. It was sort of like ozone and sort of like flowers.

The girls were sitting again, hardly even watching. As if they'd lost all interest after making the connection. I turned to Wooze and offered the jar to her. She didn't look up. She didn't stand up.

"Just rub it in?" I asked.

"Uh huh," said one of the girls. I couldn't tell which, I wasn't looking at them. "All over. Cover everything you want to take with you."

"Except the soles of your feet," put in the other. "Unless you don't want to come back." And with that, they both laughed. I didn't get the joke. Perhaps I would later. I took some of the goop in my hand and smeared it across Woozle's chest. I had to go down on one knee and push her arms aside to do it. She didn't resist.

After a bit, I made her stand up and I made sure that I'd rubbed her all over—except for the soles of her feet. "What's it feel like, Wooze?"

"Notbing yet. Just slippery."

"Well, maybe it takes a little time. You do me now."

She did. Her hands were dull and lifeless and spread the goop with no more feeling than shovels. She did it mechanically and uncaring, but she was thorough. I helped her a little bit, but it wasn't necessary. She was like a machine, running sensors all up and down me as if to memorize my body for later.

Then I was covered with the goop all over and the smell of it was overpowering. "Now what?" I looked at the girls, but they weren't there.

"Hold hands," they replied. "That is, if you want to go together."

Yeah, that sounded right. This was the new kick. This was what I'd been promised in front of Cannie's—a trip you could share. No more one-man-alone numbers. I was tired of sitting around in a room watching everybody else going in a different direction. I wanted someone to share my direction. Yeah, I was ready for it. Now, you could go and take someone good along to share it with you—and you could share theirs. I reached out for Woozle's hand. It felt different somehow. Tinier. Yeah, if you were going to share it, you should at least be holding hands.

I could feel the stuff now. Or, that is, I couldn't feel it any more. I couldn't feel anything any more. I felt...disembodied(?)...no, that wasn't it either. Creeping cold warmth was seeping out around my edges, dilating into the not-quite.

My eyes, great multi-faceted things, grew till they spread around the top and sides of my head and I looked in all directions at once. Woozle's hand looked back at mine. We stood half an inch above the floor and listened to water burning our legs.

What it was, was this—I was a pillar of fire, taken fresh from the freezer, standing still in the lightless and examining things in the reflected glare of (myself) and all was timeless until the water drops spattered into steam upon the hot. That didn't make sense.

But who cared? I was tripping. And Woozle was too. She was with me. She always was. Oh, yeah. We were in a tiny red cubicle—red from the frozen flame?—just one cubicle out of millions of identical tiny red cubicles stacked one upon another, left and right and north and east and yesterday and Tuesday and purple and—

FLASH!

Woop? What was that? Now the top of the room hung below us. We looked down the long tube at ourselves still holding hands. The red light seeped and pulsed and permeated it all. We were above and looking down and sideways at the little honeycombed rednesses below. Little black insects scraped within.

The whole city of shining black was below us. We looked down at them from our hot two-hundredth-story window, noses pressed flat against the glass, trying to push through it so as to see our own selves from the outside. Cannie's was only ten floors below. We watched the black uniforms herding them out of the building and into the street where they shot them. What a joke. Why hadn't it been listed in TV Guide?

Ooh, that was almost a bummer. We hopped the up elevator at the top floor and kept going and—

FLASH!

-ed again. What was that? Wow—whatever it was, it was. A desert hung below us. Above us. "Oh, Wooze, look at that!"

She looked, "Yeah, Deet, I see it." Luminous flyspecks danced and skittered along a net of silver threads, in and out, patterns of streaking steel. Beyond it, the greater dark.

Another—

FLASH!

—and this time we're out in nothingness, looking at the whole marble. Why isn't it bigger? I thought it was bigger than that, didn't you? "Hey, Deet—I mean, Woozle, isn't that supposed to be bigger?"

"I don't know, Deet. I'm just following you. Wherever you want, Deet."

"Hey, don't be a bummer—this is...something."

Blue and white streaks, flat mottled brown patches, familiar shapes, but white streaks kept them from being too familiar and—

FLASH!

Now! I was starting to see the inside of it. It was like a whiteness, but with crystal blues and spidery blacks and all kinds of coldnesses creeping out from inside. An expanding—and a shrinking too.

"Deet! Please, slow down a bit. You're going too fast for me."

"No, I'm not. It's okay."

A greater darkness beyond, everything was scattered and speckled tiny this side of it. I wanted to expand to fill it. A glaring whiteness off to one side shouldn't have been that big. After all, it was really only very tiny and—

Hang on, Deet—here we go!

FLASH!

The glaring whiteness dwindled to be a speck like all the others. I marked it for future reference. In case we wanted to come back to it later.

A wash of bright stretched from one infinity to the other. All the yesterdays stacked against all the tomorrows. The thing had a structure, but I was too close to it to see what it was. I'd have to move back—and the greater darkness backdrop was still just as far away and—

"Deet! Can't we stop and rest for just a minute?"

"Oh, no, kitten! Come on, we're almost there! This is it! This is really it!"

And—

FLASH!

I grabbed her hand and we went. Yeah, this was it! I didn't have to say it any more. It wasn't necessary. I was convinced—because it really was it. IT! The trip—and it was still going!

A great wheel of spiraling sparkling dust turning against the ultimate velvet. Turning, turning. Oh wow, how big is that thing? How big?

FLASH!

Tiny—really very tiny. A myriad of them spin twinkly through the darkness. Like snowflakes, scattering in a wind, roiling ever outward. We dive back into and out of it. I want to keep going. Expand to fill the whole—

FLASH!

—little fireflies disappear into the hole. And—

FLASH!

FLASH!

FLASH!

And I still hadn't filled it.

FLASH!

But I was getting there! I was!

FLASH!

Oh, Woozle? Isn't this the greatest—

FLASH!

Almost, almost. Just once more, I think—and then we'll fill this tiny black cubicle, and then one more after that and we'll burst it and look down onto it from the outside and look down at all the row upon row of identical shiny black globes and—

FLASH!

Not yet!

FLASH!

Still not yet! Dammit! Once more. I want it, dammit! Let's go, Woozle. Once more.

FLASH!

And I throw my hands outstretched into the nevermore, always reaching and grasping, that elusive black wall remaining just ever so out of my reach and—

FLASH!

FLASH!

FLASH! DAMMIT!

Blackness, nothing but blackness and blackness beyond. Almost, almost. I almost made it, this time I almost made it...

FIASH!

But nothing.

Okay, so we don't do the big number this time around. We dive back into the wrong end of the microscope and shrink down into the other direction of infinity—inwardly.

Ping.

The little wheels reappear, spinning madly. I pick one at random and down we go, and—

Ping.

—it becomes a big wheel. I head for a spiral arm, zig-zag around the exploding core, and—

Ping.

—pop out at a here in the middle of empty brightness. Rocky nothingnesses whirl about it. The wrong one. Not mine. Try again. So—

Ping.

And this time, here is a blue and red binary, a pinpoint of bright and a bloated crimson vagueness. Streamers of blood-colored gas spiral outward from the giant. The lesser-sized one would have been lost among them if not for its brilliance. But— This one isn't mine either.

Ping.

Up and out again. An explosion, a never-ending one. Dazzling, sleeting, brighting, sheeting, flaring, flashing, glaring, shimmering, slashing intensity of light so thick you have to push at it to move. All around me. All around. We hung at the core of the supernova and—

FLASHED.

The wheel again, the great wheel. No, that's the wrong direction. I wanted to go the other way. My God, how big is that thing anyway? Immense. No, tiny—tiny, tiny, remember! I am immense. Remember the outer blackness, how big it is and how big I am and never fill it. That wheel is only a mote of dust in the hungry sucking dark. I am as big to the wheel as it is to me. I am small and vast and—

Ping.

I remember and dive back into it. Back to the home world, right Woozle?

Woozle?

Hey, Woozle—where are you?

Woozle...?

I'm alone in the vampire dark. Somewhere I've lost my—

"Woozle!!"

No answer.

I plunge through the night, carefully retracing. Where did I leave her? Where did I let go? She was with me here. Flash. Here. Flash. Here.

She was with me all the way. Or was she? She wasn't. She wasn't with me at all.

Flash/Ping.

Back down into the wheel. Back down. Home system, home sun, home planet. Yeah, that's it. Blue-white streaked disc. Dive into it.

I know what must have happened. She couldn't keep up. Yeah, that's right. She-couldn't keep up. So she went home without me. She went on home. Yeah, that's what she must have done. Yeah, that's it. She wouldn't just run off on her own.

Into the disc and down the long tunnel and the walls unstretch, become a room again, and I land on the floor and down.

The room is empty. And alone.

All of them were empty—

In The Quake Zone

The day after time collapsed, I had my shoes shined. They really needed it.

I didn't know that time had collapsed, wouldn't find out for years, decades—and several months of subjective time. I just thought it was another local timequake.

Picked up a newspaper—*The Los Angeles Mirror*, with its brown-tinted front page—and settled into one of the high-backed, leather chairs in the Hollywood Boulevard alcove. There were copies of the *Herald,* the *Examiner,* and the *Times* here as well, but the *Mirror* had Pogo Possum on the funny pages. "Mighty fine shoes, sir," Roy said, and went right to work. He didn't know me yet. I snapped the paper open.

I didn't have to check the papers for the date, this was late fifties, I already knew from the cars on the boulevard, an ample selection of Detroit heavy-iron: the inevitable Chevys and Fords, a few Buicks and Oldsmobiles, the occasional ostentatious Cadillac, a few

Mercurys, but also a nostalgic scattering of others, including DeSoto, Rambler, Packard, Oldsmobile, and Studebaker. Not a foreign car to be seen, just a bright M&M flow of chrome-lined monstrosities growling along, many of them two-toned. The newer models had nascent tailfins, the evocation of jet planes and rocket ships, giddy metal evolution, the hallmark of a decade's misguided futurism and an industrial dead-end.

The Mirror and *The Examiner* both disappeared late '58, maybe early '59, if I remembered correctly, the result of a covert deal by the publishers. Said Mr. Chandler to Mr. Hearst, I'll shut down my morning paper if you'll shut down your afternoon. "Let us fold our papers and go."

A new Edsel cruised by—right, this was '58. But I could already smell it. The Hollywood day felt gritty. The smog was thick enough to taste. The Hollywood Warner's theater had another Cinerama travelogue—the third or fourth, I'd lost track. I was tempted; not a lot of air conditioning in this time zone. A dark old theater, cooled by refrigeration, I could skip the sweltering zenith. But, no—I might not have enough time.

The papers reported that timefaults had opened up as far north as Porter Ranch, popping Desi and Lucy seven years back into the days of chocolate conveyer belts and Vita-meata-vegamin; as far east as Boyle Heights where ten years were lost and the diamond-bright DWP building disappeared from the downtown skyline, along with the world famous four-level freeway interchange; as far south as Watts, they only rattled off a couple years, but it set back the construction of Simon Rodilla's startling graceful towers; and all the way west to the Pacific Ocean. Several small boats and the Catalina Ferry had disappeared, but a sparkling new Coast Guard Cutter from 1963 had chugged into San Pedro. The big red Pacific Electric streetcars were still grinding out to the San Fernando Valley. I wondered if I'd have a chance to ride one before the aftershocks hit.

Caltech predicted several days of aftershocks and the mayor was advising folks to stay close to home if they could, to avoid further discontinuities. The Red Cross had set up shelters at several high

schools for those whose homes had disappeared or were now occu-
pied by previous or subsequent inhabitants.

Already the looters and collectors from tomorrow were flock-
ing to the boulevard. Most of them were obvious, dressed in jeans
and T-shirts, but they gave themselves away by their stare-gathering
unkempt haircuts and beards, their torn jeans and pornographic
T-shirts. They'd be stripping the racks at World Book and News,
buying every copy they could find of *Superman*, *Batman*, *Action*,
and especially *Walt Disney's Comics* with the work of legendary Carl
Barks. And Mad Magazine too; the issues with the Freas covers were
the most valuable. Later, they'd move west, hitting Collector's Books
and Pickwick's as well. The smart ones would have brought cash.
The smartest ones would have brought year-specific cash. The dumb
ones would have credit cards and checkbooks. Not a lot of places
took credit cards yet, none of them recognized Visa or Mastercard.
And nobody took checks anymore; not unless they were bank-dated;
most of the stores had learned from previous timequakes.

The Harris Agency—there was no Ted Harris, but he had an
agency—was just upstairs of the shoeshine stand; upstairs, turn left
and back all the way to the end of the hall, no name on the glass, no
glass. The door was solid pine, like a coffin-lid, and painted green
for no reason anyone could remember, except an old song, *"What's
that happenin' behind the green door...?"* The only identification was
a small card that said, "By appointment only." That wasn't true, but
it stopped the casual curiosity seekers. My key still worked, the locks
wouldn't be changed until 1972; there was no receptionist, the outer
office was filled with cardboard file boxes and stacks of unfiled folders. Two typists were cataloguing, they glanced up briefly. If I had a
key, I belonged here.

Georgia was still an intern, working afternoons; she'd started
when she was a student at Hollywood High, half a mile west and a
couple blocks south. Now she was taking evening courses in business
management at Los Angeles City College, over on Vermont, a block
south of Santa Monica Blvd. A few years from now, she'd be a beautiful honey-blonde, but she didn't know that yet and I wasn't going

to risk a bad first impression by speaking out of turn. I pretended I didn't know her. I didn't, not yet.

I brushed past, into the cubby we called a conference room. More old paper and two old women. Pinched-faced and withered, they might have been the losers in a Margaret Hamilton look-alike contest. Sooner or later, one of them was probably going to demand, "Who killed my sister? Was it you?!"

Opened my wallet, started to flash my card, but the dustier of the two waved it off. "I recognize you. Wait. Sit." But I didn't recognize her. I probably hadn't met her yet. Some younger iteration of her had known an older iteration of me. I wondered how well. I wondered if I would remember this meeting then. The other woman left the room without saying a word. Just as well; some folks get uncomfortable around time-travelers. Not travelers—*ravelers*. The folks who tend the tangled webs.

I sat. A dark mahogany table, thick and heavy. A leather chair, left over from the previous occupant of this office, someone who'd bellied up early in the thirties. She disappeared into a back room, I heard the scrape of a wooden footstool, the sound of boxes being moved on shelves, a muffled curse, very unladylike. A moment later, she came back, dropped a sealed manila envelope on the table in front of me. I slid it over, turned it around, and scanned the notations. Contract signed in 1971, backshifted to '57. Contract due date 1967. It had only been sitting here a year, and the due date was still nine years away.

A noise. I looked up. She'd put a bottle on the table and a stubby glass. I turned the bottle. It said Glenfiddich. I didn't recognize the name. I gave her the eyebrow. She said, "My name's Margaret. Today's the day you acquire this taste. You'll thank me for it later. Take as much time as you need to read the folder, but leave it here. Here's a notepad if you need to copy out anything. That contract's not due for 9 years, so the best you can do today is familiarize yourself, maybe do a little scouting. There's an aftershock due tomorrow morning, about 4:30 am; go to West Hollywood and it'll bounce you closer to the due date. Oh, wait—one more thing." She disappeared again, this time I heard the sounds of keys jingling on a ring. A drawer opened, stuff was shuffled around, the drawer was closed. She came back with a cash box and an old-fashioned checkbook. "I can only give you three hundred in time-specific cash, but it'll still be good in '67. There's a bank around the corner, you've got two hours until it closes, I'll give you a check for another seven hundred. You can pick up more in '67. But be careful, your account doesn't get fat for awhile. How's your ID?"

In the past, my personal past, I'd renewed my driver's license as quickly as I could after every quake, but a DL expires after three years, a passport is good for ten. The lines at the Federal Building were usually worse than the DMV, especially in a broken time-zone, but except for a gap of three years in the early 70's, I had valid passports from now until the mid-eighties.

"I'm good," I nodded. I signed my name and today's date to the next line on the outside of the envelope, then broke the wax seal. It was brittle; it had been sitting on the shelf for a year, waiting for today, and who knows how long before it got to this time zone. I didn't have a lot of curiosity, most of my cases were small-timers. The big stuff, the famous stuff, most of that went to the high-profile operations, the guys on Wilshire Boulevard, some downtown, some in Westwood. There was a lot of competition there—stop Sirhan from killing RFK, catch Manson before he and the family move into the Spahn movie ranch, apprehend the Hillside Stranglers, find out who killed the Black Dahlia, help O.J. find the killers of Ron and Nicole...and so on.

The thing about the high-profiles, those were easy cases. The victims were known, so were the perps. The big agencies had a pretty good idea of the movements of their targets long before the crimes occurred. But most of the laws had been written before time began unraveling and the justice system wasn't geared for prevention, only after-the-fact cleanup.

Then one hot night in an August that still hasn't happened, Charles "Tex" Watson gets out of the car up on Cielo Drive and someone puts a carbon-fiber crossbow bolt right through his neck, even before he gets the gun out of his jacket. The girls start shrieking and two more of them take bolts, one of them right through the sternum, Sexie Sadie gets one in the head. The third girl, the Kasabian kid, goes screaming down the hill, and some redheaded kid in a white Nash Rambler nearly runs her down, never knowing that the alternative was having his brains splashed across the front seat of his parents' car. I didn't do it, but I knew the contract, knew who'd paid for it. Approved the outcome.

That was the turning point. After that, the judicial system learned to accommodate itself to preventive warrants, and most of the worst perps will be safe in protective custody weeks or even months before they have a chance to commit their atrocities. The question of punishment becomes one of pre-rehabilitation—is it possible? When can we let these folks back out on the streets? If ever. Do we have the right to detain someone on the grounds that they represent potential harm to others, even if no crime has been committed? The ethical questions will be argued for three decades. I don't know yet how it resolves, only that an uneasy accommodation will finally be achieved—something to the effect that there are no second chances, it's too time-consuming, pun intended; a judicial review of the facts, a signed warrant, and no, they don't call it pre-punishment. It's terminal prevention.

Meanwhile, it's the big agencies that get the star cases—save Marilyn and Elvis, save James Dean and Buddy Holly, Natalie Wood, Sal Mineo, Mike Todd, Lenny Bruce, RFK and Jimmy Hoffa. Stop Ernest Hemingway from sucking the bullet out of his gun and keep Tennessee Williams from choking to death on a bottle cap. Save Mama Cass and Jimi Hendrix and Jim Morrison and Janis Joplin and John Lennon. And later on, Karina and Jo-Jo Ray. And Michael Zone. Kelly Breen. Some of those names don't mean anything yet, won't mean anything for years; the size of the up-front money says everything—but we don't get those cases. The last one we bid on was Ramon Novarro, beaten to death with his own dildo by a couple of hustler-boys, and we didn't get that job either; later on, after the Fatty Arbuckle thing, and that was a long reach back anyway, all of those cases went through the Hollywood Preservation Society, funded by the big studios who had investments to protect.

No, it's the *other* cases, the little ones, the unsolved ones that fall through the cracks—those are the ones that keep the little agencies going. Most families can't afford five or six figure retainers, so they come to the smaller agencies, pennies in hand, desperate for help. "My little girl disappeared in June of '61, we don't know what happened, nobody ever found a trace." "I want to stop the man who raped my sister." "My girl friend had a baby. She says it's mine. Can you stop the conception?" "My boy friend was shot next November, the police have no clue." "I was abused by my step-father when I was a child. Can you keep my Mom from ever meeting him?"

There were a lot of amateurs in this business—and more than a few do-it-yourself-ers too. But most folks don't like to go zone-hopping; it's not a round-trip. You don't want to end up someplace where you have no home, no family, no job. Just the same, some people try. Sometimes people clean up their own messes, sometimes they make bigger ones. Some things are better left to the professionals.

The Harris Agency had three or six or nine operatives, depending on when you asked. But some of them were the same operative, inadvertently (or maybe deliberately) time-folded. Eakins was a funny duck, all three of him, all ages. The Harris Agency didn't advertise, didn't have a sign on the door, didn't even have a phone, not a listed one anyway; you heard about it from a friend of a friend. We took the jobs that people didn't want to talk about, and sometimes we handled them in ways that even we didn't talk about.

You knocked on the door and if you knocked the right way, they'd let you in. Georgia would sit you down in the cubby we called a conference room, and if she liked your look, she'd offer you coffee or tea. If she didn't trust you, it would be water from the cooler. Or nothing. She conducted her interviews like a surgeon removing bullet fragments, methodically extracting details and information so skillfully you never knew you'd been incised. Most cases, she wouldn't promise anything, she'd spend the rest of the day, maybe two or three days, writing up a report, sending an intern down to the

Central Library or the *Times*' morgue to pull clippings. She'd pull pages out of phone directories, call over to the Wilcox station to get driver's license information (if available), and even scanned the personal ads in the *L.A. Free Press* a couple times. For the most part, a lot of what the outer office staff did was "clipping service"—pulling out data before, during, and after the events; the more complete the file, the easier the job. Working with Margaret, the jobs were usually easy. Usually, not always.

Georgia replaced Margaret in '61, right after Kennedy's election; Margaret retired to a date farm in Indio, as soon as she felt Georgia was ready; she'd managed the agency since '39, never missing a beat. She trained Georgia and she trained her well. The kid had been a good intern, the best, a quick-study; after graduation from Hollywood High, she stayed on full time while she picked up her degree at L.A.C.C. The work wasn't hard, but it was painstaking; Margaret had been disciplined, but Georgia was meticulous. She relished the challenge. Besides, the pay was good and the job was close enough to home that she could walk to work. And at the end of the day, she'd satisfied her spirit of adventure without mussing her hair.

The files demonstrated their differences in approach. Margaret never wrote anything she couldn't substantiate. She wasn't imaginative. But Georgia always added a page or two of advice and suggestions—her own feelings about the matter at hand. Margaret didn't disapprove. She'd learned to respect Georgia's intuition. I had too.

This envelope was thin, thinner than usual. Inside, there were notes from both, I recognized Margaret' crimped precise handwriting, Georgia's flowing hand. A disappearance. Jeremy Weiss. Skinny kid. Glasses. Dark curly hair. Dark eyes, round face, an unfinished look—not much sense yet what kind of adult he might be. A waiter, an accountant, an unsuccessful scriptwriter. Seventeen and a half. Good home. Good grades. No family problems. Disappears summer of '68, somewhere in West L.A. Not a runaway, the car was found parked on Melrose, near La Cienega. But no evidence of foul play either. Parents plaster the neighborhood with leaflets. Police ask the public for help. The synagogue posts a reward for information. Nothing. Case remains open and unsolved. No clues here. Nothing to go on. The file was a list of what we didn't know.

Two ways to proceed with this one—shadow the kid or intercept him. Shadowing is a bad risk. Sometimes, you're too late, the perp is too fast, and you end up a witness instead of a hero. Agents have been sued for negligence and malpractice, for not being fast enough or smart enough, for not stopping the murder. Interception is better. But that means keeping the vic from ever getting to his appointment in Samarra. And that means the perp never gets ID'd either.

The easiest interception is a flat tire or even an inconvenient fender-bender. That can delay a person anywhere from 15 to 45 minutes. That's usually enough to save a life. Most cases we get are events of opportunity. Take away the opportunity, the event doesn't happen—or it happens to someone else. That's the other problem with preventive interception. It doesn't always stop the bad luck, too often it just pushes it onto the next convenient opportunity. I don't like that.

Give me a case where the perp is known ahead of time, I can get a warrant. I don't have a problem taking down a known bad-boy. I don't have to be nice, I don't have to be neat. And there are times when I really don't want to be. But give me an unsolved case, it's like juggling hand grenades. Sometimes the victim is the real perp. It's messy. You can get hurt.

But this one—I listened for the internal alarm bells—they always go off when something smells wrong. This one felt different, I'm not sure why. There's a flavor. I had a hunch, a feeling, an intuition, call it whatever—a sense that this case was merely a loose unraveled thread of something else. Something worse. Like the red-headed kid who didn't die on August 9th was merely a sidebar.

Think about it for a minute. Hollywood is full of manboys. They fall off the buses, naïve and desperate. They're easy targets for all kinds of opportunists. Old enough to drive, but not old enough to be street smart. They come for the promise of excitement. Ostensibly, it's the glamour of the boulevard, where the widescreen movies wrap around the audience; it's the book stores rich with lore, shelves aching with volumes of forgotten years; it's the smoky jazz clubs and the fluorescent record stores and the gaudy lingerie displays; it's the little oddball places where you can find movie posters, scripts, leftover props, memorabilia, makeup, bits and pieces of costumery—they come in from all the surrounding suburbs, looking for the discarded fragments of excitement; sometimes they're looking for friends, for other young men like themselves, sometimes they're unashamedly looking for sex. With hookers, with hustlers, with each other. With whoever. A few years from now, they'll be looking for dope.

But what they're really looking for is themselves. Because they're unformed, unfinished. And there's nobody to give them a clue because nobody has a clue anymore. Whatever the world used to be, it hasn't finished collapsing, and whatever is going to replace it, it hasn't finished slouching toward Bethelehem. So if they're coming down here to the boulevard to look for themselves, because this looks like the center, because this looks like where it's happening, they're looking in the wrong place; because nobody ever found themselves in Hollywood, no. Much more often, they lose whatever self they had to start with.

You can't save Marilyn and Elvis because they don't exist, they never existed—all that existed was a shitload of other people's dreams dumped on a couple of poor souls who'd had the misfortune to end up in front of a camera or a microphone. And you can't save anyone from that. Hollywood needs a warning label. Like that pack of cigarettes I saw up the line. "Caution, this crap will kill you."

Jeremy Weiss wasn't a runaway. He didn't fit the profile. And he didn't end up in a dumpster somewhere, his body was never found. He wasn't a hustler or a druggie. I doubted suicide. I figured he was probably destined for an unmarked grave somewhere up above Sunset Boulevard, maybe in the side of a hill, one of those offshoots of Laurel Canyon that wind around forever, until they finally turn into one lane dirt scars. Someone he met, a casual pickup, I know where there's a party, or let's go to my place—

So yeah, I could probably save this kid from the Tuesday express, but that wouldn't necessarily stop him from lying down on the tracks again on Wednesday night. Or if not him, then maybe Steve from El Segundo or Jeffrey from Van Nuys. Most of the disappearances went unreported, unnoticed. Not this one, though.

Margaret sat down opposite me. She put a second glass on the table and poured herself a shot, poured one for me.

I knew Margaret only from her work—the files that Georgia had passed me, up the line. Margaret was compulsive; she annotated everything on every case, including newspaper clippings, police reports when she could get them, and occasionally witness interviews. Reading through a file, reading her notes, her advice, her suggestions, it was like having a six-foot invisible rabbit standing behind every moment.

But today was the first time I'd actually met Margaret, and I held my tongue, still gauging what to say. Should I thank her for the cases yet to solve? Did she want to know how these cases would play out? Would it affect her reports if she knew what leads were fruitless and which ones were pay-dirt? Do we advance to Go or do we go directly to jail? The real question—should we put warnings into the files? Watch out for Perry, a harmless little pisher, but an expensive one; stay away from Chuck Hunt, the chronovore; don't go near Conway, the bigger thief; and especially watch out for Maizlish, the destroyer.

Should I ask—?

"Don't talk," she said. "There's nothing you have to say that I need to hear. I've already heard it. I'll do the talking here because I have information that you need." She pushed the glass toward me.

I took a sniff. Not bad. Normally, I don't drink scotch. I prefer bourbon. But this was different, sharper, lighter. Okay, I can drink scotch.

"Something's happening," she said.

I waited for her to go on. There's this trick. Don't say anything. Just sit and wait. People can't stand silence. The longer you wait, the more unbearable it becomes. Pretty soon, they have to say something, just to break the silence. Leave an unanswered question in the air and wait, it'll get answered. Unless they're playing the same game. Except Margaret wasn't playing games.

She finished her scotch, neat, put the glass down, and stared across the table at me. "The perps are starting to figure it out." She let that sink in for a moment. "The timequakes. The perps are using public quake maps to avoid capture. Or to commit their crimes more carefully. Bouncing forward, back, sideways. They call it the under-time railway. LAPD has taken down the Manson clan three times now. Each time, earlier. Now they're talking about maybe legalizing preemptive abortion. Just stop them from being born. Nobody's sure yet. The judges are still arguing. The point is, you'll have to be careful. Especially with cases like this where we don't have any information. The perp always knows more about the crime than the investigator. The more the perp knows, the harder the job becomes. If the case gets any publicity, the perp gets dangerous.

"Here's the good news. Caltech has been mapping the time-quakes. They've been putting down probes all over the county for thirty years now. We have their most recent chart. The one they didn't make public. It cost us some big bucks and a couple of blow jobs." She unrolled a scroll across the table—it looked like the paperback edition of the Torah, smaller but no less detailed. "It stretches from 1906 all the way to 2111, so far. All of the big quakes and after-shocks are noted, those are the public ones, the ones the perps know. But all of the littler ones are in here too." She tapped the scroll. "*This* is your advantage.

"Most people don't notice the little tremors, the unnoticeable ones. You know that feeling when you keep thinking it's Monday when it's really Sunday? That's a dayquake. Or when you've been driving for an hour and you can't remember the last ten miles? Or when you've been at work 8 hours and you still have 7 hours to go? Or when you're out clubbing and suddenly the evening's over before it's really started? Those are all tremors so small you don't even feel them, or if you do notice, you figure it's just you. But Caltech has them charted, has the epicenters noted, can tell you almost to the second how far forward or back each quake bounces. See the arrows?

You can chart a time-trajectory from here to forever—well at least up to 2111, depending on which of the local trajectories you choose. They probably have even more complete charts uptime, but we can't get them yet. We expect Eakins to send back copies, but nothing's arrived yet, not this far back. But it should have reached '67 by now. So as soon as you get there, come back to this office. I won't be here, I'm already retired in '67, but Georgia will have what you need. We start bringing her up to speed right after Kennedy's election.

"The point is, this timeline gives you more maneuverability. Protect it like it's gold. If a perp gets it, it'd be a disaster. That's why it's on proof paper. It goes black after twenty minutes' exposure to UV." She rolled it up, slid it into a tube, capped it, and passed it over to me. "Right. Get to the bank, get yourself some dinner, then get out to the quake zone. You've got a reservation at the Farmer's Daughter Motel. That puts you half a block from the epicenter. You can get a good night's sleep. Georgia will see you here in '67."

Picked up some comics at the Las Palmas newsstand and shoved them into my briefcase, I do a little collecting myself, on the fringes, mostly just for my retirement. But not only comics. Barbie dolls, G.I. Joe, Hot Wheels cars, Pez boxes, stuff like that. And I'm saving up for a trip back to '38, I hope to pick up some IBM stock.

The Farmer's Daughter is better than it sounds. On Fairfax, walking distance from Farmer's Market. Of course, it isn't the Farmer's Daughter yet, but it will be in '67.

I check in, check the room, check the bed, think about a hooker, I have the number of an escort service, they'll be in business for another year or so; but it's not a good idea. There might be a foreshock. Almost certainly, there will be a foreshock. Not fair to the girl.

So I content myself with a nightcap in the bar. It's almost deserted. Just the bartender and me. His name is Hank. I ask him what time he gets off, he thinks I'm hitting on him, he gives me a big friendly grin, but I say, no thanks. Close up and go home. Timequake tonight, an aftershock. He shrugs. He's already been caught in two quakes. He won't even keep a cat now. Everything important, he keeps in a bag by the door. Just like me.

Not a lot of out-of-towners visit L.A. anymore; they don't want to risk the possibility of time-disruption, finding themselves a year or ten away from their families. But some folks deliberately come to L.A., hoping to ride a quake back so they can prevent some terrible event in their lives. Some succeed, some don't. Others have meticulous lists of sporting events and charts of stock fluctuations; they expect to get rich with their knowledge. Some do, some don't.

I fall asleep in front of the TV, watching Jack Paar on the tonight show. I wake up and it's the last week of April '67. The smog is the same, the cars are smaller and more teenage; on the plus side, the skirts are a lot shorter. But my old brown suit is out of style. And my car is visibly obsolete—a '56 Chevy. Obvious evidence that I'm a wandering time-raveler.

Caught breakfast in the market, fresh fruit, not too expensive yet, then headed back up to the boulevard. Santa Monica Boulevard was now a tawdry circus of adult bookstores, XXX theaters, and massage parlors. The buildings all looked like garish whores.

Hollywood Boulevard was worse. The stink of incense was almost strong enough to cover the smog. Clothing had turned into costumes, with teens of both sexes wearing tight pants and garish shirts—not quite hippies yet, but almost. The first bell-bottom jeans were showing, the Flower Children were just starting to bloom. The summer of love was about to begin.

Several store fronts had signs for time-tours and maps of the quake-zones; probably a better business than maps to the homes of the stars. I noticed several familiar faces—a small herd of comic book collectors—heading toward the newsstand on Cahuenga; they were probably the first customers of the quake-maps.

Roy was still shining shoes, twelve years older, but just as slick and just as fast. "Shoes look good, Mister Harris," he said, as I walked in. He called all of us Mister Harris. Nobody ever corrected him. Maybe it was his way of keeping track. He knew who we were, but he never asked questions, and he never offered advice. He kept his own counsel. But sometimes, he steered the right people to the office and sometimes he turned other folks away. "What you lookin' for ain't up those stairs, mister." Every so often, Georgia would march downstairs and hand him an envelope. She never said why. I assumed that was something else she'd learned from Margaret.

The office had been redecorated; it felt more like Georgia now. All of the typewriters were IBM Selectrics. New lateral filing cabinets, a Xerox photocopier, even a fax machine. The cubby had been painted light blue with white trim and the stacks of boxes and files had disappeared, replaced by dark oak bookshelves. Most of the files had moved into the offices next door, which we'd leased in '61, when the accountant finally died. It'd be another few decades before we would have all that information on hard drives and optical discs. The same heavy mahogany table and leather chairs remained in the center of the room, but looking a lot more worn.

Georgia was expecting me. She tossed the same manila envelope on the table, brought in another bottle of Glenfiddich, one glass, and a new pocket-Torah. I passed her the old one, as well as the few collectible treasures I'd picked up in '58. She'd put them in storage for me.

"Lose the brown suit," she said. "I bought you a new one, dark gray. It's in the closet. Already tailored. Read the file, there's some new information." She reached for the bottle.

"Not this early, thanks." I was already signing the envelope. The file had been accessed only three times in the last twelve years. Margaret twice, Georgia once. But it was significantly thicker.

This time there was a bundle of newspaper clippings. Not about Jeremy Weiss, but about a dozen *others*. I checked the dates first. June of '67 to September of '74. Georgia had typed up a chart. At least thirteen young men had disappeared. Jeremy Weiss was the third. The third that we knew about. I wasn't surprised. I'd had a hunch there were more.

We weren't obligated to investigate the disappearances of the others; Weiss was the only one we had a contract on. But if the disappearances were related...if they had a common author, then finding that author would not only save Weiss, but a dozen others as well. Preemptive action. But only if the disappearances were connected. We'd still have to monitor—*save*—Weiss. Just in case.

I read through the clippings, slowly, carefully. Three times. There was a depressing similarity. Georgia sent out for sandwiches. After lunch, she sat down next to me—she was wearing the Jasmine perfume again, or maybe still, or maybe for the first time—and walked me through the similarities she'd noticed. The youngest victim was fifteen, but big for his age; the oldest was twenty-three, but he looked eighteen.

Last item in the envelope was a map of West Los Angeles with a red X at the site of each vic's last known location; his apartment, his job, where his car was discovered, or the last person to see him alive. There were no X's north of Sunset, none south of Third. The farthest west was Doheny, the farthest east was just the other side of Vine Street. It was a pretty big target area, but at the same time fairly specific.

"I want you to notice something," she said. She pointed to the map, tracing an area outlined by a yellow highlighter. All of the red X's were inside, or very close to the border of the yellow defined region, except for the one east of Vine. "Look at this." She tapped the paper with her fingernail. "That's West Hollywood. Have you seen it?"

"Drove through it this morning."

"Ever hear of *Fanny Hill*?"

"Isn't that a park in Boston?"

"Not funny. Don't quit your day job. It's a book, by John Cleland. *Memoirs of a Woman of Pleasure*. It has redeeming social value. Now."

"Sorry, I'm not following."

"John Cleland was born in 1710. He worked for the East India Company, but he didn't make much money at it. He ended up in Fleet debtors' prison from 1748–1749. While there, he wrote or re-wrote a book called Fanny Hill. It's written as a series of letters from Fanny to another woman, and it is generally considered the first work of pornography written in English, its literary impact derives from its elaborate sexual metaphor and euphemistic language."

"And this is important because…?"

"Because last year—1966—the Supreme Court declared that it is not obscene." She didn't wait for me to look puzzled. "In 1957, in Roth versus the United States, the Supreme Court ruled that obscenity is not within the area of constitutionally protected freedom of speech or press, neither under the first amendment, nor under the due process clause of the fourteenth amendment. They sustained the conviction of a bookseller for selling and mailing an obscene book and obscene circulars and advertising.

"In 1966, in Cleland versus Massachusetts, the court revisited their earlier decision to clarify the definition of obscenity. Since the Roth ruling, for a work of literature to be declared obscene, a censor has to demonstrate that the work appeals to prurient interest, is patently offensive, and has no redeeming social value. It's that last one that's important, because it could not be demonstrated to the court that *Fanny Hill* has no redeeming social value. The case can be made that the book is an historical document, presenting an exaggerated and often satirical view of the mores of 18th century London, just as the *Satyricon* by Petronius presents an exaggerated and satirical view of ancient Rome; so a very strong case can be made that pornography represents a singular insight into the morality of its time. Thus, it has redeeming social value. Therefore, it cannot be prosecuted as obscene."

"Redeeming social value…."

"Right."

"Since the *Fanny Hill* ruling, pornography has become an industry. If a publisher can claim redeeming social value, the work is legal. A book of erotic pictures with a couple quotes from Shakespeare. A sex-film with a preface by a doctor—or an actor playing a doctor. It's a legal fan dance—you don't go to the fan dance to see the fan. The pornographers will be testing the limits of the law for years. The fans are going to get a lot smaller."

"Okay, so what does all this have to do with West Hollywood?"

"I'm getting to that. For the next decade, enforcement of obscenity laws will be left to local communities. There will be years of debate. Nothing will be clear or certain, because the definition of obscenity will be determined by local community standards. Until even that argument gets knocked down. At some point, the whole issue of redeeming social value becomes moot because it becomes unenforceable. How do you define it? And that'll be the end of anti-smut laws. But right now, today—it's all about local community standards."

"And West Hollywood is a local community...?"

"It's an *unincorporated* community," Georgia said. "It's not part of Los Angeles. It's not a city. It's a big hole in the middle of the city. L.A.P.D. has no authority inside this yellow area. There's no police coverage. The only enforcement is the L.A. County Sheriff Department. So there's no community and there are no standards. It's the wild west."

"Mm," I said.

"Right," she agreed. "None of the city ordinances apply. Only the county ones. And the county is a lot less specific on pornography. So you get bookstores. And more. The county doesn't have specific zoning restrictions or statutes to regulate massage parlors, sex stores, and other adult-oriented businesses. The whole area is crawling with lowlifes and opportunists. Here—" She pulled out another map. This one showing a corridor of red X's stretching the length of Santa Monica Boulevard, with a scattered few on Melrose.

"What's this?"

"A survey of sex-businesses in West Hollywood. Red for hetero, purple for homo, green for the bookstores. You get clusters. Here, all the way from La Brea to La Cienega, this used to be a quiet little neighborhood where seniors could sit in the sun at Plummer Park and play Pinochle. Now, there are male hustlers in hot pants, posing at the bus stops.

"Take a drive around the neighborhood. You'll see things like massage parlors advertising specific attention to love muscle stiffness—Greek, French, and English massage. Or sex-therapists who will help you work out your inhibitions with sex-fantasy role-playing. Here, here, and here, these are gay bars, this is a bath house, so is this. This place sells costumes, chains, things made of leather—and realistic prostheses."

"Prostheses—?" And then I got it. "Never mind."

"If you can imagine a sexual service, you'll find it here. This is the land of negotiable virtue. It's a sexual carnival, the fun zone, the zoo. This is the reservoir of licentiousness. This is where AIDS will start. You'll need to start carrying condoms. Anyway—" She stretched out the two maps side by side. "Notice the congruence? I'm going to make a guess—"

"These kids are horny?"

"And gay."

"Is that a hunch, or—?"

She didn't answer immediately. "Okay, I might be wrong. But if I'm right, then the police will be useless to us. Ditto the Sheriff's department. They don't care. Not here. They won't take this seriously. And we can't talk about this with any of the parents. And probably not even with the kids themselves. This is still the year of the closet...and will be until June of '69. Stonewall," she explained.

"I know about Stonewall. We bid on a contract to videotape it. The problem will be getting cameras onsite."

"Eakins is working on that. There's a thing called...never mind, I don't have time to explain it." She tapped the table. "Let's get back to this case. We've got six weeks until the first disappearance. This is as close as you can get by time-skipping. You'll have to live concurrently, but that'll be an advantage. You can familiarize yourself with the area, locate the victims, make yourself part of the landscape. Let your sideburns grow. We've found an apartment for you, heart of the district, corner of N. Kings Road and Santa Monica, second floor. Here, wait a minute—" She stepped out of the room for a second, came back with a cardboard filebox, and a set of keys. "We bought you a new car too. You can't drive a '56 Chevy around '67 L.A. It attracts too much attention."

"But I like the Chevy—"

"We bought you a '67 Mustang convertible. You'll be invisible. There are a hundred thousand of these ponies in California already. It's in the parking lot behind. Give me the keys to the Chevy. We'll restore it and put it in storage. Another forty years, it'll be worth enough to buy a retirement condo. A high-priced apartment."

She popped the top off the box. In it were another dozen envelopes of varying thicknesses. "Everything we've got on the other disappearances. Including pictures of the vics. It's the first two you want to focus on."

I sorted through the reports. "Okay, so we have an approximate geographical area and a pretty specific age range. Is there anything else to connect these victims?"

"Look at the pictures. They're all twinks."

"Twinks?"

"Pretty boys."

"And based on that, you think they're gay?"

"I think we're dealing with a serial killer. Someone who preys on teenage boys. Yeah, I know—lots of kids go missing every year just in L.A. County. They hop on a bus, they go to Mexico or Canada, they go underground to avoid the draft. Or maybe they just move without leaving a forwarding address. But these thirteen don't fit that profile. The only connection is that there's no other connection. I don't know. But that's what it smells like to me." She finished her drink. Neat. Just like Margaret. "I think if we find out what happened to the first victim, we unravel the whole string."

I finished my drink, pushed my glass away, empty. Put my hand over it in response to her questioning glance. One shot was enough. If she was right, this was big. Very.

Took a breath, let it out loudly, stared across at her. "Georgia, you've been working these streets long enough to know every gum spot by brand name. I won't bet against you." I gathered the separate files. "I'll check them out." I thought for a moment. "How old am I now?"

Georgia didn't even blink. "According to our tracking, you're 27." She squinted. "With a little bit of work, we could probably make you look 21 or 22. Put a little bleach in your hair, put you in a surfer shirt and shorts, you'll look like a summer-boy. What are you thinking? Bait?"

"Maybe. I'm thinking I might need to talk to some of these kids. The closer I am to the same age, the more likely I'll get honesty."

Something occurred to me. I turned the maps around and peered back and forth between them. Pulled the disappearance map closer.

"What are you looking for?"

"The dates. Which one of these was first?"

"This one, over here." She tapped the paper. The one east of Vine. "Why?"

"Just something I heard once about serial killers. Always look closest at the first vic. That's the one closest to home. That's more likely a crime of opportunity than premeditated. And sometimes that first vic and the perp—sometimes they know each other."

"You've never done a serial killer before," Georgia said.

"You're thinking about bringing in some help?"

"It might not be a bad idea."

Considered it. "Can't bring in L.A.P.D. They have no jurisdiction. And County isn't really set up for this."

"Bring in the Feds?"

I didn't like that idea either. "Not yet. We might embarrass ourselves. Let me do the groundwork first. I'll poke around for a few days, then we'll talk. See if you can get anything from uptime."

"I've already put a copy of the file in the long-safe. I'll add your notes next week. Then we'll look for a reply."

The long-safe was a kind of time capsule. It was a one-way box with a time-lock. You punch in a combination and a due date, a drawer opens and you put a manila envelope in. On the due date— ten or twenty or thirty years later—the drawer pops open, you take the file out and read it. Usually, the top page is a list of unanswered questions. Someone uptime does the research, looks up the answers, writes a report, puts it in another manila envelope, and hands it to a downtime courier—someone headed backwards, usually on a whole series of errands. The downtime courier rides the quakes until he or she reaches a point before the original memo was written. The courier delivers the envelope, and it goes into the long-safe, with a due date *after* the send date of the first file, the one with all the questions. This was one of the ways, not the only one, that we could ask the future for help with a case.

Sometimes we sent open-ended queries—what should we know about that we don't know yet to ask? Sometimes we got useful information, more often not. Uptime was sensitive about sending too much information back. Despite the various theories about the chronoplastic construction of the stress-field, there weren't a lot of folks who wanted to take chances. One theory had it that sending information downtime was one of the things that triggered time-quakes, because it disturbed the fault lines.

Maybe. I dunno. I'm not a theorist. I'm just a meat-and-potatoes guy. I roll up my sleeves and pick up the shovel. I prefer it that way. Let somebody else do the heavy thinking, I'll do the heavy lifting. It's a fair trade.

I didn't set out to be a time-raveler. It happened by accident. I was in the marines, got a promotion to sergeant, and re-upped for another two years. Spent eighteen months in Nam as an advisor, mostly in Saigon, but occasionally up-country and twice out into the Delta. The place was a fucking time-bomb. Victor Charlie wanted to give me an early retirement, but I had other plans. Rotated stateside the first opportunity.

Got off the plane in San Francisco, caught a Greyhound south, curled up to sleep, and the San Andreas time-fault let loose. It was the first big timequake and I woke up three years later. 1969. Just in time to see Neil Armstrong bounce down the ladder. Both Dad and the dog were dead. I had no one left, no home to return to. Someone at the Red Cross Relocation Center took my information, made some phone calls, came back and asked me if I had made any career plans. Not really, why? Because there's someone you should talk to. Why? Because you have the right set of skills and no close family connections. What kind of work? Hard work. Challenging, sometimes dangerous, but the money's good, you can carry a gun, and at the end of the day you're a hero. Oh, that kind of work. Okay. Sure, I'll meet him. Good, go to this address, second floor, upstairs from the shoeshine stand. Your appointment is at three, don't be late. And that was it.

My first few months, Georgia kept me local, bouncing up and down the early '70's, doing mostly easy stuff like downtime courier service. She needed to know that I wouldn't go off the rails. The only thing the agency has to sell is trust. But I wasn't going anywhere. The agency was all I had—they were a serendipitous liftoff from the drop zone of '69, and you don't frag the pilot. A lieutenant maybe, but never a pilot—or a corpsman.

I'd thought about corpsman training early, even gone so far as to sit down with the Sergeant. He just looked across the desk at me and shook his head. "There's more to it than stabbing morphine needles into screaming soldiers. You're better where you are." I didn't know how to take that, but I understood the first time mortar shells came dropping in around us and voices all around started screaming, "Medic! Medic!" I wouldn't have known which way to run. And I just wanted to keep my head down as low as possible until the whole damn business was over. It was only later, I got angry enough to start shooting back. But that was later.

After the courier bit became routine, Georgia started increasing my responsibilities. When you pass through '64, pick up mint-condition copies of these books and magazines. Pick up more if they're in good condition, but don't be greedy. Barbie dolls, assorted outfits (especially the specials), and Hot Wheels, always. Buy extras if they have them. Sometimes she just wanted me to go someplace and take pictures—of the street, the houses, the cars, the signs.

After a couple months, I told Georgia that the work didn't seem all that challenging. Georgia didn't blink. She told me that I had to learn the terrain, I had to get so comfortable with the shifting kaleidoscope of time that I couldn't be rattled. That's why the '60's and the '70's were such a good training ground. The nation went through six identifiable cultural transitions in the course of 16 years. But even though the '50's were supposed to be a lot quieter, she didn't think so. They weren't all that safer, it was just a different kind of danger. Georgia said she wanted to keep me out of that decade as much as possible. "You've got tombstones in your eyes," she said. "You'll scare the shit out of them. And frightened people are dangerous. Especially the ones with power. Later, after you've mellowed, we'll send you back. We'll see."

After a bit, she started passing me some of the little jobs, the ones where clients bought themselves a bit of protection, or closure, or prevention.

For instance, "Here, this file just came up. Here's fifty dollars. Go to this address, give it to this person. Find a way to make it legit, tell him you're a location manager for Warner Brothers, you're shooting a pilot, some TV series, a cop show, lots of location work like Dragnet, you want to measure the apartment, photograph the view from the balcony, and here's a few bucks for your trouble." That one was easy. A struggling young writer with no food in the house, desperate and waiting to find out if he'd sold his first book, all he needed was another week—his future self was giving him a lifeline.

Another one, "The mail carrier delivers the mail to this address between 1 and 2pm. Nobody will be home before 5. Open the mail box and remove any letters with this return address. Do this every day for the next two weeks." A fraternity at USC. That one didn't make sense until a year later when that same fraternity was thrown off campus for a hazing scandal. Somebody didn't get the invitation to rush, didn't pledge, didn't get injured, and didn't have his college career stained.

And a third, "Tomorrow afternoon, this little boy's pet dog gets out an open window and wanders away from the house. Nobody's home until three. Pick up the dog before it gets to the avenue, come back at seven, knock on the door, and ask if they know who the dog belongs to, you found it the next block over." Right. No mystery there.

"Tuesday evening, Lankershim boulevard, across the street from the El Portal theater. There's a blue Ford Falcon. Somebody sideswipes it, sometime between 6:45 and 9:30. Get the license number, leave a note on the windshield."

After those, I started getting the weird jobs. Some of them made no sense, there was no rational explanation; but the client doesn't always give reasons. Our rule is that we only take oddball cases on the condition that no physical or personal harm is intended.

Here's one, "Take this copy of *Popular Mechanics*, thumb through it so it looks used. Tomorrow afternoon, 1:30, go out to Van Nuys, 5355 Van Nuys Boulevard, Bobs #7. Sit at the counter near the front, near the go-order window. Order a Big Boy hamburger and a Coke. Read the magazine while you eat. Fold it so the ad on page 56 is visible. Leave a dollar tip. Leave the magazine on the table."

And another, "Friday night, just after the bars close, stand in front of the door at this address, like you're waiting for a ride. That's all. Nothing will happen. You can leave at 2:30."

And one more, "Take this package. No, don't open it. At 4:25, catch the 86 bus at Highland. Get off at Victory and Laurel Canyon. Cross the street and wait for the return bus. Leave the package on the bench."

And the weirdest, "Here's a white T-shirt, blue jeans, and a red jacket; right, the James Dean look. You've got the face for it. Tomorrow afternoon, Studio City, corner of Ventura and Laurel Canyon. When this kid comes out of the drugstore, you stop her and say, 'When you are ready to learn, the universe will provide a teacher. Even when you are not ready to learn, the universe will provide a teacher.' Hand her this paper. It has a poem by Emily Dickinson. Don't answer questions. Go into the drugstore, go all the way to the back and out to the parking lot, turn right and duck around the corner of the building, she won't follow, but she mustn't see you again. Walk west till you get to the ice cream store. You can park your car behind it."

Finally, when Georgia was satisfied that I could follow orders, she gave me a tough one. "Do you trust me? Good. Go to this address and kneecap this son of a bitch."

"Kneecap?"

"Slang term. Shoot him in the kneecap. Both kneecaps. We want him in a wheelchair for the rest of his life. Oh, and rip the phone off the wall. Wear these gloves, wear these shoes—use this gun, here's ammunition, here's a silencer, put everything in this plastic trash bag, bring it all back here for disposal."

"You're kidding."

"We don't joke about things like this."

"Shoot him in the kneecaps—y'know, that's a tricky shot. Especially if he's moving."

"If you can't manage it—"

"I can manage it."

"Would you rather just kill him?"

Thought about it for two or three seconds. "What'd he do?"

"You don't like being hired muscle, do you?"

"I just need to know—"

"It's righteous," she said. "He's a rapist. He rapes little girls. The youngest is six. And then he kills them. He goes off the rails tomorrow. Cripple him tonight and you'll save three lives that we know of, probably more if he starts time-walking."

"Can I ask you a question? Who makes these decisions?"

She shook her head. "It's a need-to-know thing." Then she added, "Think of it this way. The perps choose it when they choose to be perps. We try to provide permanent solutions. This guy tonight—he's a dangerous asshole. Do your job and tomorrow, he'll just be an asshole." She shrugged. "Or a corpse. Either is part of the contract. Whatever's easiest for you. Or most enjoyable. Your call."

"I'm not a psychopath."

"That's too bad. We really do need one. For the big jobs."

I let that pass. "Do we have a preemptive warrant?"

Georgia shook her head. "That law hasn't been passed yet. But we can't wait. Here, ease your conscience. After you do him, drop this envelope out of the plastic bag, leave it on the floor."

"What's in it? Cash?"

"Clippings. About how he'll torture his victims. Leave it for the cops, they'll get it. Don't touch anything, don't leave prints."

There were other jobs like that. They never got any easier.

In real life, you don't shoot the gun out of the bad guy's hand. The bad guys don't drop the gun, say ouch, and reach for the sky—no, they shoot back. With everything they've got, with bullets and mortars and mines that take your best buddy's legs off. They just keep coming at you, spraying blood and fire, hammering explosions, hailstorms of dirt and flesh and bone. You have to keep your head down and your helmet tight and hope you have a chance to lay down a carpet of fire, burn them alive and screaming, just to buy those moments of empty dreadful silence while you wait to see if it starts up again. In real life, you beat them senseless just to slow them down. And if that doesn't slow them down, you kill them, you blow them away, you turn them into greasy red gobbets.

On TV, everything is neat. Real life is messy, ugly, scabrous, squalid, festering, putrid, and painful. In real life, the bad guys don't think they're bad, they think they're good guys too, just doing their stuff because that's the stuff that a man's gotta do; but in real life, there are no good guys, just guys, doing each other until everybody's done. And then maybe afterwards, while you're picking up the pieces of your corporal or your radioman, you get a chance to sort it out. Maybe. And that's when it doesn't matter if anybody's a good guy, they're still dead.

Because in real life, there are no good guys. They don't exist and neither do you. That's the cold hard truth. You're not there, you're just another TV death, consumed like a TV dinner, until it's time to change the channel. You think you have a life? No. You're just the space where all this shit is happening. That cascade of experience—you don't own it, it owns you. You're the bug in the trap. The avalanche of time, the pummeling of a trillion quantum-instants, second after second, it pounds you down into the sand, and whatever you think you are, it's an illusion—you exist only as a timebinding hallucination of continuity. And after long enough, after you realize you can't endure anymore of this senseless pummeling—whether its mortar shells or rifle bullets or cosmic zingers so tiny you don't know you've taken one in the heart until you get to the third paragraph—you just continue anyway. Waiting. Sooner or later, the snipers will get your range.

You don't survive, you just take it a day at a time, a moment at a time. You pick your steps carefully, always watching for the one that might go click. And you don't think ahead, don't think about when it's going to be over, because it's never going to be over. You look, you listen, and you never move fast—until you have to. And when you do, you take the other guy down first, and keep him down, and you don't worry about nice and you don't worry about pretty; the whole idea is to keep him from ever getting up again. So you do what you do so he can't do what he does. And once in a while, somebody tells you it was worth it, but you know better, because you're still carrying the ruck through the hot zone, not them. In real life, real life stinks.

So I took him down. Him and the next three. And I learned to drink Glenfiddich straight from the bottle.

Until one morning, Georgia dragged me out of bed, still covered in vomit and stink, rolled me into a tub and filled it with cold water. Grabbed me by the hair, dunked me until I screamed, then poured cold black stale coffee down my throat until I was swearing in English again. My head hammering like a V-8 with a broken rod, she dressed me, drove me to the gym and handed me over to Gunter, the personal trainer. After that, 7am every day. In the afternoon, language classes at the Berlitz. Monday evenings, firing range—hands-on experience with weapons from here to flintlocks. Tuesday, world history class. Wednesday, Miss Grace's Academy of Deportment, I'm not kidding. Thursday, meeting—friends of Bill W. Friday, movie night. With Georgia. Not a date—cultural acclimatization. Saturday, assigned research and dinner at Georgia's. Not a date—a full report on the week. Sunday...breakfast with Georgia.

She didn't save my life. She made it worth enduring. Especially when we started sleeping together. Not at her place, not at mine, she wouldn't have that. We went to one of those little cardboard motels out on Cahuenga, where it turns into Ventura, halfway between here and the San Fernando Valley. She needed danger and I needed sex. So we rumpled the sheets like a war zone for three months regular, every Saturday night—until the next timequake and I had to go to Sylmar and bounce forward three years, and even though I was up for it, even thinking maybe I should buy her a ring, she'd already moved on, and that was the end of it. That was the zinger right through the heart.

I found something else to do on Thursday nights and let myself have one glass of scotch every time I finished a dirty job. Sometimes the clean jobs too. It didn't help. And I told her why.

No, it wasn't her. It was that other thing. The good-guy thing. I didn't feel like one. Killing for peace is like fucking for chastity. It doesn't work.

She offered to buy out my contract, send me off somewhere to retire, I'd certainly earned it. But no—I don't know why I said no. Maybe it was because there was still work to do. Maybe it was because I still wanted to believe there was something to believe in. What the hell. It was better than sitting on my ass and poisoning my liver.

So I took the envelope and left the bottle. Maybe someday I'd figure it out, but for now, I wasn't looking anymore.

Picked up the first vic at his job, tailed him to his place. Brad Boyd. He lived in a courtyard apartment on Romaine, just east of Vine. In two and a half months, the bitchy neighbor who hates his dog and his motorcycle will be the last person to see him. She'll scream at him about the bike being on the walk, in everybody's way; then she'll push it over. He'll pick it up, get on it, turn it away from her so both exhaust pipes are pointing in her direction, and rev it as loud as he can, belching out huge clouds of oil-smelling smoke; then he'll roar away. 9:30pm on a hot Thursday night in July. It's a blue Yamaha, two-stroke engine, 750cc, a mid-sized bike; it'll never be found. Left this vic at home, watching TV. The blue glow is visible from the street.

Headed out to the valley and drove past the Van Nuys home of the Weiss kid. He still lives with his mother, his dad died a year ago; he's in his last year at San Fernando Valley State College in

Northridge. His room is in the back of the house, I can't see any lights. But his car is in the driveway.

The fourth vic lives on Hyperion in the Silverlake area, catches the bus downtown, where he works for a bank. I ride the bus opposite him, sit where I'm not in his line of sight, and study him all the way to Hill Street. Randy something. Skinny little kid, very fair complexion, too pretty to be a boy; put a dress on him you can take him anywhere. They must have teased the hell out of him in school.

After that, I check the locations, the last known sightings. I'll start working on the other vics next week; I want to read the neighborhood first. Weiss's car will be found on Melrose Ave, two-three blocks east of the promising lights of La Cienega. Carefully parked, locked up tight. He went someplace, he never came back. I park across the street. I lean back against the warm fender of the Mustang and study the street. At first glance, it seems innocent enough.

This forgotten little pocket of West Hollywood is a time-zone unto itself, with most of its pieces left over from the twenties and thirties. In '67, Melrose is dotted with tacky little art galleries, interior decorators, and a scattering of furniture stores hoping to get trendy. It's a desolate avenue, even during the day.

At night, the street is dry and deserted, amber streetlights pockmark the gloom; a few blocks away, the bright bustle of life hurtles down La Cienega, but here emptiness, the buildings huddled dark and lonely against themselves, waiting for the return of day and the illusion of life. Bits of neon shine from darkened storefronts. Occasional redlit doorways hint at secret worlds.

Few cars cruise here, even fewer souls are seen on the sidewalks— only the occasional oasis of a sheltered restaurant, remaining open even after everyone else has fled; departing customers move quickly from bright doorways to the waiting safety of their automobiles, tuck a bill into the valet's hand, and whisper away into the night.

There's this thing they do in the movies, in a western, or a war picture, where someone says, "It's quiet, too quiet." Or: "Listen. Even the birds are silent." That's how they do it in the movies, but that's not how it works in the hot zone. In the zone, it's more like a little timequake. There's this sense, this feeling that you get—like the air doesn't taste quite right. And when you get that feeling, sometimes the little hairs on the back of your neck start tickling. You stop, you look around, you look for the reason why those little hairs are rising. Sometimes, it's just a shift in the wind and the way the grass ripples across the hillside, and as you watch the ripples, you realize that one of those ripples isn't like the others. And you wake up inside your own life in a way that makes the rest of the day feel like somnambulism.

Sometimes the feeling isn't anything at all. Sometimes the feeling is just too much coffee. But it's a real feeling and you learn to respect it anyway because you're out there in the hot and the guy who drew the pretty pictures on the chalkboard isn't. You hit the dirt—and the one time you hit the dirt and hear the round go past just over your head instead of through your gut—that one time makes up for all the times you hit the dirt and there's nothing overhead.

You learn to listen for the feeling. You never stop. Years later, even after the Delta has receded into time, you're still listening. You listen to the world like it's ticking off, counting down. You listen, not even knowing what you're listening for anymore.

Standing on Melrose, I got something. Not the same feeling, but a feeling. A sense there's something *else* here. Something that comes out, late at night. And good folks don't want to be here when it's up and about.

Get back in the car. Lean back and disappear into the shadows. Sit and wait, not for anything in particular. Just to see what comes out in the darkness. Picket duty. Eyes and ears open; mind catching forty. Watching. Reading the street.

The avenue has a vampiric life of its own. Every so often, motion. A manboy, sometimes two. Sometimes a girlboy. The children of the night climb out of their daytime coffins and drift singly through the shadows, flickering briefly into existence for a block or two, then disappearing just as ephemerally. It isn't immediately obvious what's happening here.

Finally, got out of the car and went for a walk. West, where Melrose angles in toward La Cienega. Where are the manboys going? Where are they coming from?

Ah.

Half a block east of the lights. A darkened art gallery with an unpaved parking lot. The lot is dark, unlit. At the back is a fenced-in covered patio. Discreet. Unobtrusive. Inconspicuous to the point of invisibility. You could drive by a thousand times and never notice, even if you were looking for it. It's furtive. Like Charlie. Things that hide are either frightened or stalking. Either way, dangerous.

Two-three teens standing in the lot, smoking, chatting. Only room for a few cars here. I fumble around in my pockets for a pack of cigarettes. I stopped smoking when Ed Murrow died, again when I left Da Nang, and a third time when I got off the plane in San Francisco; the third time it stuck; but it's still convenient to carry them. Pull one out of the pack, approach the girlboys, ask for a light, say thanks, nod, wait.

"You new?"

Shrug. "Back in town."

"Where were you?"

"Nam."

"Oh. I heard it's pretty bad."

"It is. And getting worse."

The boys have no real names. The tall thin one with straight black hair is "Mame." The shorter rounder one is "Peaches." The blond is "Snoopy."

"You got a name?"

"Solo."

"Napoleon?"

"Han."

"What'd you do in Nam?"

"Piloted a boat. Called The Maltese Falcon." Almost added, "Went upriver to kill a man named Kurtz." But I didn't. They wouldn't get it, not for twelve years anyway. I doubted any of them had ever read either Conrad or Chandler. Mame was more likely a

Bette Davis fan than Humphrey Bogart. The other two...hard to tell. Sean Cassidy probably.

"You goin' in?"

Took a puff on the cigarette. "In a minute." Hang back, listening. The girlboys are gossiping, overlapping dialog, about someone named Jerry and his unrequited crush on someone else named Dave, except Dave has a lover. Jerry has a secret too. Honey, don't we all? Oh, guess what? Speaking of secrets, Dennis' real age is 23, he's a chicken hawk, he's dating Marc. Marc? That's funny. Marc has the crabs, he got them from Lane. Lane? That sissy? Lane isn't even his real name. He's cheating on his sugar daddy, you know. Hey, have you met the new girl? With the southern accent? You mean, Miss Scarlett? More like Miss Thing. She's way over the top. She's just a sweet ole Georgia peach. I thought she said Alabama. Whatever. Do you believe her? Honey, I don't even believe me. She says she went in drag to her senior prom. In Alabama? Girl, I'll believe that when I hear it from Rock Hudson Jr.

Mame turns to me abruptly. "Getting an earful?"

Shrug again. "Doesn't mean anything to me. I don't know any of those people."

Satisfied, Mame turns back to the others. Did you hear about Duchess and Princess? I only know what you've told me. They were arrested—in drag—for stealing a car. Has anybody heard anything else? Not me. Have you ever seen them out of drag? No, have you? I have. Princess puts the ugh into ughly. Her and Duchess, it's Baby Jane and Blanche. I wonder who'll get their wardrobe. Honey, just one of Princess's gowns is big enough for all three of us. If we're friendly. I'm friendly, very friendly. Honey, get real. What are you and I going to do together—bump pussies, try on hats, and giggle?

Gossip is useful. It's a map of the social terrain. It tells you which way the energy is flowing. It tells you who's important. It's the quick way of tapping into the social gestalt. Find me three gossips and I can learn a community. Except this isn't a community. This is a fragmentary maelstrom of whirling bodies. A quantum environment, with particles flickering in and out of existence so fast they can only be detected by their wakes.

Eventually, I go in. There's no sign, but the place is called Gino's. Admission is 50 cents. The man at the door is forty-five, maybe fifty. This is Gino. He has curly black hair, a little too black. He dyes it. Okay, fifty plus. He looks Greek. He hands me a red ticket from a roll, the anonymous numbered kind they use at movie theaters. Good for one soda. He recites the rules. This is a club for 18 and up. No drugs, no booze. If the white light goes on, it means the vice are here, stop dancing.

The outdoor patio is filled with jostling teens, all boys, some giggling, some serious. Several are standing close. Some make eye-contact, others turn away, embarrassed. Others sit silently, sullenly, on heavy benches along the walls. Potting benches? Perhaps this used to be a nursery.

The patio connects to a second building, tucked neatly behind the art gallery. Invisible from the street. Perfect. Inside, it's darker than the patio. A quick survey reveals a bar, sandwiches and Cokes; in one corner a pool table, another a pinball machine. There's a juke-box playing a song by Diana Ross and the Supremes; several of the boys are singing falsetto-accompaniment. Baby Love. And an area for dancing. But no one's dancing. The same embarrassment in the high school gym.

A slower survey of the inhabitants—almost no one over the age of 25. Most of the boys here are high school girls, even the ones of college age. A few pretend to be butch, others don't care. Every so often, two or three of them leave together. I listen for conversations. More gossip. Some of it desperate. Longings. Judgments. Hopes. And the usual chatter about classmates, teachers, schools, movies... and Sean Cassidy.

Someone behind me says to someone else. "Let's go to the Stampede." "What's the Stampede?" "You've never been there? Come on." I follow them out. Discreetly.

The Stampede is on Santa Monica, near the corner of Fairfax. It's a beer bar. Inside, it's decorated to look like a western street. A shingled awning around the bar has a stuffed cougar perched upon it. Black lights make white T-shirts glow. A young crowd, drinking age. All the way to the back, a small patio. The place is filled with manboys standing around, looking at each other and pretending that they're not standing around and looking at each other, imagining, wishing, dreaming. Some of them search my face, I nod dispassionately, then turn away. The jukebox plays "Light My Fire," Jim Morrison and The Doors. If Gino's is high school, then The Stampede is junior year at city college. The boys are a little more like boys here, but they still seem much too young.

I know what it is—like all the others wandering the shadowed streets, they're still unfinished. They don't know who they are. They haven't had to dive into the mud and shit and blood. They haven't had anyone shooting at them.

Two couples walk in the front door, the wives holding the husbands' arms possessively. Some of the queers exchange glances. Tourists. Visiting the zoo, the freak show. They've never seen real faggots before. Someone behind me whispers bitchily. "The husbands will be back next week. Without the fish. It's always that way."

A couple blocks west, there's another bar, The Rusty Nail. More of the same, maybe a rougher crowd, a little older. A couple blocks east, The Spike. East of that, a leather bar. Okay, I got it. Circus of Books stays open 24 hours—the adult section, pick up a copy of the Bob Damron guide book. This is what I need. I take it back to my apartment and make X's on the map. No surprises here. Georgia was right. Queer bars and bathhouses. Another cluster of congruency.

Draw the connecting lines. Traffic goes back and forth on Santa Monica boulevard, occasionally down to Gino's on Melrose. Oh, and there's a place over here on Beverly, The Stud. Enter in the rear. Unintended irony. They hang bicycles and canoes and rocking chairs from the high ceiling. It's funky and faddish. Up on Sunset, the Sea Witch. Glass balls in nets, and a great view of the city lights. They allow dancing—furtively. On Santa Monica, a little west of La Cienega, hidden among the bright lights of the billboards, another hidden dance club. Everybody's testing the limits of enforcement.

For two weeks, I check out all the bars, all the clubs. But my first hunch is strongest. Gino's is the hunting ground. I can feel it. I don't need to listen for the little hairs.

As the nights warm up, something is awakening. A restlessness in the air. A feverish subculture of summer is readying itself. But this year, it's reckless. Next year, it'll be worse, self-destructive. The year after that, 1969, it'll implode on itself. But right now, this moment, it still hasn't realized itself yet.

It's the boomers, the baby boomers, all those children of war coming of age at the very same moment, their juices surging, their chaotic desires and wants and needs—the wildness unleashed, the rebels without a pause; the ones who think that college has made them educated, and the ones who resent them because they have to work for their daily bread—all of them, horny as hell, possessed by the sense of freedom that comes from the wheel of a Mustang or a Camaro or a VW Beetle, liberally lubricated with cheap gasoline, marijuana and beer and raging hormones, out on the streets, looking for where it's happening.

It isn't happening anywhere, it's happening everywhere, and the noise and the stink pervades the night. The straight ones hit the Sunset Strip or the peppermint places on Ventura Blvd. Or they cruise up and down Van Nuys Blvd or Rosecrans Ave., and especially Hollywood Blvd. But the other ones—the quieter ones, the ones who didn't chase the girls, the music majors and the theater arts students, the shy boys and the wild boys—after all those years of longing, they're finally finding a place where they belong too, where there are others just like them. No, not just like them. But close enough. Here are others who will understand. Or not understand. There are so many different kinds, so many different ways of being queer. But at least, for a little while, in these furtive secret places, they won't have to pretend that they don't want what they want.

During the day, they'll rage about the unfairness of discrimination, about the ugliness of war—but at night, they all want to get laid. And that's what's surging here. The desolate lust of loneliness.

It's a fevered subculture, a subset of the larger sickness that roils in the newspapers.

Our little vics—I pin their pictures to the wall and study them—they're cannon fodder. As innocent as the boy who stepped on the landmine, as unfinished as the new kid who took a bullet in the head from a jungle sniper on his first picket duty, as fresh and naïve as the one who got knifed by a Saigon whore. As stupid and trusting as the asshole who went out there because he thought it was his duty and came back with gravestones in his heart.

Finally pulled their pictures down and shoved them into a folder so I wouldn't have to look at their faces and the unanswered questions behind their eyes.

Didn't know much about queers. Didn't really want to. But I was starting to figure it out. Everything I knew was wrong.

Resumed surveillance of the vics. I had the first six now. Charting their habits, their patterns, their movements. Most of it was legwork. Confirmation of what I already knew. Thursday, vic number one shows up in the parking lot. Brad-boy. On his motorcycle. He rolls it right up behind Mame, playfully goosing her with the front wheel. Without even turning around, Mame wriggles her ass and says, "Wanna lose it?" Mame has a blond streak in her black hair now. The others are gushing over it. Brad grins, relaxes on the bike, eventually offers a ride to eager Lane, and roars off with him to catch the crabs.

A few nights later, Jeremy Weiss shows up at Gino's. Bingo. The connection. Georgia was right. Gay. Twinks. Horny.

Faded into shadow. Watched. He was smitten with a little blond twink who couldn't be bothered. Was this the Jerry that Mame was talking about? A crush on Dave who had a lover? Tailed him for the rest of the evening. He ended up at a featureless yellow building, a few blocks east. A very small sign on the door. You had to walk up close to read it. Y.M.A.C. Young Men's Athletic Club. Hmm. I had a feeling it was *not* a gymnasium. Observed for a while. Thinking.

I had three weeks left until the first vic disappeared. I was getting a good sense of the killing ground—this was the land of one-night stands. The perp didn't know the vics. He was hunting, just like everybody else, but hunting for a different kind of thrill. My guess, the vics didn't know him. They met him and disappeared. I wasn't going to find any other connectivity.

Had to think about this. How to ID the bastard. Mr. Death. That's what I was calling him now. How to stop him? Talked it over with Georgia. She made suggestions, most of them hands-on. But the way things work, the onsite agent is independent, has complete authority. Translation: it's your call.

Later. Past midnight.

Matt Vogel. Slightly built. Round face, round eyes, puppy eyes. Sweet-natured. In the parking lot at Gino's, sitting alone against the wall, between two cars, where no one can see him. Hands wrapped around his knees, head almost buried. Almost missed him. Stepped backward, took a second look. Yes, Matt. Just graduated from high school. Works as a busboy in a local coffee shop. Disappears in two months. Victim number two.

"What do you want?" He looks at me with wide eyes. Terrified.

"Are you all right?"

"What do you care?"

"You look like you're hurting."

"My parents found out. My dad threw me out of the house."

Couldn't think of anything to say. Scratched my neck. Finally. "How'd he find out?"

"He went through my underwear drawer."

"Found your magazines?"

He hesitates. "He found my panties. I like to wear panties. They feel softer. He ripped them all up."

"I knew a lieutenant who liked to wear panties. It's no big deal."

"Really?"

No, not really. But it was a game we played. Whenever anybody heard a horror story about anybody or anything, somebody always knew a lieutenant who did the same thing. Or worse. "Yeah, really. Listen, you can't stay here all night. Do you have a place to go?"

He shook his head. "I was waiting—to see if anyone I knew showed up—maybe I could crash with someone."

I noticed he didn't use the word "friend." That was the problem with this little war zone. Nobody made friends. I remembered fox holes and trenches where we clung to each other like brothers, like lovers, while the night exploded around us. But here, if two of these manboys clung to each other, it wasn't bombs that were exploding. I wondered if they had the same fear of dying alone—maybe even more so.

He'd given up waiting for Prince Charming. Mr. Right wasn't coming. And even Mr. Right Now hadn't shown up.

"Look, it's late. I live a couple blocks, close enough to walk." To his suspicious glance, I said, "You can sleep on the couch."

"No, it's all right. I can sleep at the tubs."

"The tubs?"

"Y-Mac. You been there?"

Shook my head.

"It's only two bucks. And I can shower in the morning before going to work. Scotty might even wash my clothes."

"You sure?"

"No."

At least, he's honest.

"Okay. As long as you have a place to go. It's not safe to hang out here—" And what if Mr. Death started early? But I didn't want to say that. Didn't want to scare the shit out of the kid.

"It's as safe here as anywhere—"

Something about the way he said it. "Somebody hurt you?"

"Sometimes people shout things as they drive by. Once, a couple of guys chased me for a block or so, then gave up and went back to their car."

Started to turn away, turned back. Didn't want to leave him alone. Dammit. "Look—you can come with me. I won't—I got meat loaf in the fridge. And ice cream. You want to talk, I'll listen. You don't want to talk, I won't bug you. You can crash for a couple of days, until you sort things out with your folks. All right?"

Matt thinks about it. He might look sweet and innocent, but he's learned how to be suspicious. That's how life works. First it beats you up, then it beats you down.

His posture is wary. "You sure?"

Ohell, of course I'm not sure. And this is going to fuck up the timeline. Or is it? A thought occurs to me. An ugly thought. I don't like it, but maybe...bait? I dunno. But what the fuck, I can't leave him out here in a dirty parking lot. "Yeah, come on."

He levers himself to his feet, brushes off his jeans. "I wouldn't do this, but—"

"Yeah, I know."

"—I've seen you around. Gino says you're okay."

"Gino doesn't know me."

"You were in Vietnam." A statement, not a question. I should have realized. I'm not invisible here. Some of the gossip is about me.

"Yeah," I admit. I was in Nam. I point him toward the street. "My pad is that way."

"Did you see any—"

"More than I wanted to." My reply is a little too gruff. He falls silent.

Why am I doing this? Why not? It's a chance to pry open the scab and look at the wound.

"I'm Matt."

"Yeah, I know."

"You got a name?"

"Oh, right. I'm...Mike."

"Mike? I thought your name was Hand. Hand Solo. But that's like a...a handle, isn't it. 'Cause everybody knows what a hand solo is, right?"

"Yeah. Right. It's a handle."

"Well. Glad to meet you, *Mike*."

We shake hands, there on the street. It changes the dynamic. Now we know each other. More than before anyway. Resume walking.

He's cute in a funny kind of way. If I liked boys, he'd be the kind of boy I liked. If this were the world I wanted to live in, he'd be my little brother. I'd make him hot chocolate. I'd read him bedtime stories and tuck him in at night. And I'd beat up anybody who made fun of him at school.

But this isn't that world—this is the world where men don't stand too close to men because...men don't do that.

"Mike?"

"Yeah?"

"Can I take a shower at your place?"

"Of course."

"Just enough to blow the stink off me."

"When did your Dad throw you out?"

"Two days ago."

"You've been out here on the street two days?"

"Yeah."

"What a shit."

"No, he's all right."

"No, he isn't. Anyone who throws their kid out *isn't* all right."

Matt doesn't answer. He's torn between a misguided sense of loyalty and gratefulness that someone's trying to understand. He's afraid to disagree.

We reach the bottom of the stairs. I hesitate. Why *am* I doing this? In annoyance, I snap back. "Because that's the kind of person I am."

"Huh?" Matt looks at me curiously.

"Sorry. Arguing with myself. That's the answer that ends the argument."

"Oh." He follows me up the stairs.

He looks around the apartment, looks at the charts on the walls. I'm glad I pulled the pictures down. He would have freaked to have seen his yearbook picture here.

"Are you a cop?"

"No. I'm a—researcher."

"These look like something a detective would do. What are you researching?"

"Traffic patterns. It's—um, sociology. We're studying the gay community."

"Never heard it called that. 'Gay community.'"

"Well, no, it isn't much of one." Not yet, anyway. "But nobody's ever studied how it all works, and so—"

"You're not gay, are you?"

No easy answer to that. I don't even know myself. The night goes on forever here. Daytime is just an unpleasant interruption. "Look, I'm not anything right now. Okay?"

"Okay."

I feed him. We talk for awhile. Nothing in particular. Mostly food. Cafeteria food. Restaurant food. Army food. Mess halls. C-rations. Fast food. Real food. Places we've been. Hawaii. Disneyland. San Francisco. Las Vegas. His family traveled more than mine. He's seen more of the surrounding countryside than me.

Eventually, we both realize it's late. He steps into the shower, I toss him a pair of pajamas, too big for him, but it's all I've got, and take his clothes downstairs to the laundry room. T-shirt, blue jeans, white gym socks, pink panties, soft nylon, a little bit of lace. So what.

He's a sweet kid. Too sweet really. Fuckit. He's entitled to a quirk. Who knows? Maybe he'll make lieutenant. When I come back up, he's already curled up on the couch.

The other bedroom is set up as an office. A wooden desk, an IBM Selectric typewriter, a chair, a lockable filing cabinet. I'll be up for a while, typing my notes for Georgia. God knows what she'll think of this. But I'll have his stuff into the dryer and laid out on a chair in less than an hour, long before I'm ready to collapse into my own bed.

Georgia taught me how to write a report. First list all the facts. Just what happened, nothing else. Don't add any opinions. The first few weeks, she'd hand me back my reports with all my opinions crossed out in thick red stripes. Pretty soon, I learned what was fact, what was story. After you've listed the facts, you don't need anything else. The facts speak for themselves. They tell you everything. So I learned to enjoy writing reports, the satisfying clickety-clickety-click of the typewriter keys, and the infuriated golf ball of the Selectric whirling back and forth across the page, leaving crisp insect-like impressions on the clean white paper. One page, two. Rarely more. But it always works. Typing calms me, helps me organize my thoughts.

Only thing is, if you don't have all the facts, if you don't have enough facts, if you don't have any facts, you stay stuck in the unknown. That's the problem.

Later, much later, as I'm staring at the dark ceiling, waiting for sleep to come, I listen for the sound of vampires on the street below. But most of them have found their partners and crept off to their coffins. So the war zone is silent. For now, anyway.

Somewhere, out there, Mr. Death is churning. And I still know nothing about him.

Sunday morning. I wake up late. Still tired. My back hurts. I smell coffee. Wearing only boxers, I pad into the kitchen. Matt is wearing my pajama tops. They're too big on him. He's obviously given up on the bottoms, too long, and they won't stay up. He looks like the little boy version of a Doris Day movie. He's cooking eggs with onions and potatoes. And toast with strawberry jam. And a fresh pot of coffee. It's almost like being married.

"Is this okay?" he asks uncertainly. "I thought—I mean, I wanted to do something to say thank you."

"You did good," I say around a mouthful. "Very good. You can cook for me anytime." Why did I say that? "Oh, your clothes are on the chair by the door. I washed them last night."

"Yeah, I saw. Thanks. I have to go to work at noon." He hesitates. "Um, I'm going to try calling my Dad today. Um. If it doesn't work out—you said something about—a couple days...?"

"No problem. I'll leave a key under the mat. If I'm not here, just let yourself in."

"You trust me?"

"You're not a thief."

"How do you know?"

"I know." I added, "People who cook like this, don't steal."

He's silent for a moment. "My mom used to say I'd make someone a wonderful wife someday. My dad would get really pissed off."

"Well, hey, your dad doesn't get it."

Matt looks over at me, waiting for an explanation.

"It's simple. You take of other people, they take care of you. The best thing you can do for someone else is cook for them, feed them, serve them a wonderful meal. That's how you tell someone that you—well, you know—that you care."

He blushes, covers it by looking at the clock. "I gotta get to work—" And he rushes to leave.

Sunday. There's no such thing as an afternoon off, but I cut myself some personal time anyway. Took a drive out to Burbank. Shouldn't have. Wasn't supposed to. It was part of the contract. Your old life is dead. Hands off. But I did it anyway. I owed it to them. No. I owed it to myself.

The place was pretty much as I remembered it. The tree in front was bigger, the house a little smaller, the paint a little more faded. I parked in front. Rang the bell and waited. Inside, Shotgun barked excitedly.

Behind the screen door, the front door opened. Like the house, he looked smaller. And like the house, a little more faded.

"Yes?" he squinted.

"Dad. It's me—Michael."

"Mickey?" He was already pushing open the screen door. Shotgun scrambled out. Even with his bad hip, that dog was still a force to be reckoned with. Dad fell into my arms, and Shotgun leapt at us both, with frenzied yowps of impatience. "Down you stupid son of a bitch, down!" That worked for half a second.

Dad held me at arm's length. "You look different. But how—? They said you were lost in the timequake."

"I was. I am. I found my way back—it's a long story."

He hugged me again, and I felt his shoulders shaking. Sobbing? I held him tight. He felt frail. Then abruptly, he broke away, and turned toward the house. "Come on in. I'll make some tea. We'll talk. I think I have some coffee cake. You don't know how hard it's been without you. I haven't touched your room. It'll be good to have you back—"

I followed him in. "Um, Dad. I don't know how long I can stay. I have a job—"

"A job. That's good. What kind of a job?"

"I'm not really allowed to discuss it. It's that kind of a job."

"Oh. You're working for the government."

"I'm not really allowed to discuss it. I'm not even supposed to be here, but—"

"That's all right, I understand. We'll talk about other things. Come sit. Sit. You'll stay for dinner. It'll be like old times. I have spaghetti sauce in the freezer. Just the way you like it. No, it's no trouble at all. I still cook for two, even though it's just me and that old dog, too stubborn to die. Both of us."

I didn't tell him that wasn't true. I didn't tell him that he and that stubborn old dog would both be gone in a few short months. I rubbed my eyes, suddenly full of water. This was harder than I thought.

Somewhere between the spaghetti and the ice cream, Dad asked what had happened over there. I struggled inside, trying to figure out what to say, how to say it, realized it couldn't be explained, and simply finally shrugged and said, "It was...what it was." Dad knew me well enough to know that was all the answer he was going to get, and that was the end of that. The walls were comfortably up again.

Somewhere after the ice cream, I realized we didn't have all that much to talk about anymore. Not really. But that was okay. Just being able to watch him, just being able to skritch the dog behind the ears again, that was okay. That was enough. So I let him talk me into spending the night. My old bed felt familiar and different, both at the same time. I didn't sleep much. In the middle of the night, Shotgun oozed up onto the foot of the bed and sprawled out lazily, pushing me off to the side, grumpling his annoyance that I was taking up so much room; every so often, he farted his opinion of the spaghetti sauce, then after a while he began snoring, a wheezing-whistling noise. He was still snoring loudly when the first glow of morning seeped in the window.

Over breakfast, I told a lie. Told Dad I was on assignment. That part wasn't a lie. But I told him the assignment was somewhere east, I couldn't say exactly where, but I'd call him whenever I could. He pretended to understand.

"Dad," I said. "I just wanted you to know, you didn't lose me. Okay?"

"I know," he said. And he held me for a long time before finally releasing me with a clap on the shoulder. "You go get the bad guys," he said, something he'd said to me all my life—from the day he'd given me my first cowboy hat and cap pistol. Something he said again the day I got on the plane to Nam. You go get the bad guys.

"I will, Dad. I promise."

I kissed him. I hadn't kissed him since I was eight, but I kissed him now. Then I drove away quickly, feeling confused and embarrassed.

It was a drizzly day, mostly gray. Skipped the gym, filled the tank, drove around the city, locating the homes of the other seven victims. Two lived in the dorms at UCLA, Dykstra and Sproul. Didn't know if they knew each other. Maybe. One was a T.A. major, the other music. Another lived with a roommate (lover?) in a cheap apartment off of Melrose, almost walking distance from me, except in L.A., there's no such thing as "walking distance." If it's more than two doors down, you drive.

One lived way the hell out in Azusa. That was a long drive, even with the I-10 freeway. Another in the north end of the San Fernando Valley. All these soft boys, so lonely for a place to be accepted that they'd drive twenty-thirty miles to stand around in a cruddy green patio—to stand around with other soft boys.

Something went klunk. Like a nickel dropping in a soda machine. One of those small insights that explains everything. This was puberty for these boys. Adolescence. The first date, the first kiss, the first chance to hold hands with someone special. Delayed, postponed, a decade's worth of longing—while everybody around you celebrates life, you pretend, suppress, inhibit, deprive yourself of your own joy—but finally, ultimately, eventually, you find a place where you can have a taste of everything denied. It's heady, exciting, giddy. Yes. This is why they drive so far. Hormones. Pheromones. Whatever. The only bright light in a darkened landscape. They can't stay away. This is home—the only place where they can be themselves.

Okay. Now, figure out the predator—

I got back to the apartment, the drizzle had turned to showers. Matt was sitting by the door, arms wrapped around his knees. A half-full knapsack next to him. He scrambled to his feet, both hopeful and terrified. And flustered. He looked damp and disheveled. A red mark on his forehead, another on his neck.

"Are you all right?"

"I couldn't find the key—"

"Oh, shit. I forgot to put it under the mat—"

"I thought you were angry with me—"

"Oh, kiddo, no. I screwed up. You didn't do anything wrong. It's my fuckup. Shit, you must have thought—on top of everything else—"

Before I could finish the sentence, he started crying.

"What happened—? No, wait—" I fumbled the key into the lock, pushed him inside, grabbed his knapsack, closed the door behind us, steered him to the kitchen table, took down a bottle of Glenfiddich, poured two shots.

He stopped crying long enough to sniff the glass. "What is this?" He took a sip anyway. "It burns."

"It's supposed to. It's single-malt whiskey. Scotch." I sat down opposite him. "I went to see—someone. My dad. I haven't seen him in a while, and this might be the last time. I wasn't supposed to, but I did it anyway. I spent the night, I slept in my old room, my old bed. What you said yesterday, it made me think—"

He didn't hear me. He swallowed hard, gulped. "My mom called me at work. She said I should come home and pick up my things. My dad wouldn't be there. Only she was wrong. He came home early. He started beating me—"

I reached over and lifted up his shirt. He had red marks on his side, on his back, on his shoulders, on his arms. He winced when I touched his side.

Got up, went into the bathroom, pulled out the first-aid kit. Almost a doctor's bag. Stethoscope, tape, ointment, bandages, a flask, even a small bottle of morphine and a needle. Also brass knuckles and a blackjack. And some other toys. You learn as you go. Came back into the kitchen, pulled his shirt off, smeared ointment on the reddest marks, then taped his ribs. Did it all without talking. I was too angry to speak. Finally: "Did you get all your stuff?"

He shook his head.

"All right, let's go get it."

"We can't—"

Grabbed his arm, pulled him to his feet, pulled him out the door, down the stairs, and out to the car, ignoring the rain. "You need your clothes, your shoes, your—whatever else belongs to you. It's yours."

"My dad'll—he's too big! Please don't—"

I already had the car in gear. "Fasten your seatbelt, Matt. What's that thing that Bette Davis says? It's going to be a bumpy night." The tires squealed as I turned out onto Melrose.

I turned south on Fairfax, splashing through puddles. Neither of us said anything for a bit.

When I turned right on Third, he said, "Mike. I don't want you to do this."

"I hear you." I continued to drive.

"I'm not going to tell you where I live—lived."

"I already know."

"How?"

"I'm your fairy godfather, that's how. Don't ask."

"You are no fairy," he said. Then he added, sadly, "I am."

"Well, I guess that's why you need a godfather."

"What are you gonna do?"

I grinned. "I'm gonna make him an offer he can't refuse."

Matt didn't get the joke, of course. It wouldn't be a joke for another five years. But that was okay. I got it.

Turned left, turned right. Pulled up in front of a tiny, well-tended house. Matt followed me out of the car, up the walk. The front door yanked open. Matt was right—he was *big*. An ape. But he wasn't a trained one. The scattershot bruises on his son were proof of that. He'd substituted size for skill. Probably done it all his life. He wore an ugly scowl. "Who are you?" he demanded.

Gave him the only answer he was entitled to. Punched him hard in the chest, shoving him straight back into the house. Followed in quickly. Before he could react, chest-punched him again—harder, hard enough to slam him into the wall. The house shook. He bounced off and this time met my fist in his gut. His gut was hard, but the brass knucks were harder. He grunted, didn't double up, but he lurched—it was enough, I pulled his head down to meet my rising knee, felt his nose break with a satisfying crunch of bone and blood.

Hauled him to his feet. His face was bleeding. "You're a big man, aren't you? Beating on a kid." He was still trying to catch his breath. "Matt, go get your things. Now."

A woman came out of the kitchen, wiping her hands in a dish towel. "Matty—?" Then she saw me. "Who are you—?" Then she saw her husband. "Joe—?"

I grabbed the towel from her hands, pushed it at Joe, pushed Joe at a chair, he flopped into it, covering his bloody nose. "You can sit down too, ma'am; probably a good idea." She hesitated, then sat. Joe was still gasping, eyeing me warily.

Nobody spoke for a long moment.

Finally, the wife. "Are you going to hurt us?"

"Not planning on it. Of course, that can change." I nodded meaningfully at the asshole.

"You—you won't get away with this—"

"You won't call the police. He won't let you. He doesn't want anyone to know he's got a queer son." Took a breath. I wasn't planning to play counselor, but Matt needed time to gather his stuff, and I needed to keep the asshole from thinking too hard. "All right, look, lady—you should leave this jerkoff. Because if you don't, he's going to kill you someday. The only thing that's saved your life this long is that he's been taking it out on the kid instead, hasn't he? With the kid outa here, you're wearing the bullseye now. If I'm not mistaken, that bruise on your cheek is recent. Like maybe, this afternoon? And maybe there's a few more under that dress that don't show?"

She didn't answer.

"You're not doing yourself any favors, being a punching bag for this miserable failure. And you sure as hell didn't help your kid any, did you? Letting him beat the kid—you're a coward. Do you know what the word 'enabler' means? You're an enabler. You're just as fucking guilty. Because you let him get away with it."

Turned to the gorilla. "See, here's the thing, Joe. You're an asshole. You're beneath contempt. That's your son, your own flesh and blood. You should love him more than anybody else in the world. But he's fucking terrified of you. The one moment in his life, he needs his dad to love and understand and be there for him more than anything else, what do you do? You beat him up and throw him out. What a fuckwad you are. Your wife's a coward, you're a bully, and the two of you are throwing away the only thing in the world you've done right—raise a kid who still knows how to smile, god knows why, growing up with you two creeps. You don't deserve this kid. Shut up, both of you. I'm in no mood to argue. You can beat your wife, Joe, and you can beat your kid—but you can't beat the butt-ugly truth. You're a waste of skin. Oh, and if you're thinking about getting out of that chair, don't. If you try, I'll kill you. I'm in that kind of a mood."

"He means it, Dad—" That was Matt, coming back into the room. "He's an ex-commando. Special forces. Green Beret. Or something. He was in Vietnam. I don't want him to hurt you—"

"You got everything?"

He hefted a duffel and a suitcase. Hastily filled.

Matt's mother looked back and forth between us. Finally, she worked up the nerve to ask. "What are you? Some kind of queer?"

I looked her up and down. "Are you the alternative?" Jesus Christ on a pogo stick, I can't believe I said that. "Wait a minute." Turned back to the gorilla. "Your son's leaving home. You'll never see him again. Give me your wallet. No—I didn't say think about it. I said, *give me your wallet.*"

He passed it over. Nearly three hundred bucks. I passed the cash to Matt. "Here. Your inheritance. It's enough to live on for a couple months. If you're careful." Dropped the wallet on the floor.

"You two are getting off lucky. I'm letting you live." Looked at the gorilla again. "You come after this kid, you ever come near him, you ever lay a hand on him again, I will kill you. I will hunt you down and I will make sure you take a long time to die. You ever beat your wife again, I'll break both your arms. Are we clear? Nod your head, this isn't television." Glanced sideways. "Matt, you want to say goodbye?"

He shook his head.

"Then go get in the car."

Waited a moment, looking to see if the asshole was thinking about following. He wasn't. His face was ashen. He was still having trouble breathing. I looked to the wife. "You know what? I think you'd better call an ambulance. I might have punched him a little too hard, I might have cracked his sternum. I wish I could say I'm sorry about that, but I'm not."

Drove back without talking. The rain was coming down harder now. Matt was shaken. Probably didn't know what to think, what to feel.

Got back to the apartment. He hesitated. "You coming up?"

"I thought you wanted me to—" He held up the money. "I mean—isn't what this is for?"

"There's plenty of time for that tomorrow. Or the next day." And besides, "You shouldn't be alone tonight." I grabbed his suitcase and duffel. Not as heavy as I'd thought. Gorilla and wife hadn't been very generous.

Inside, I went scrounging through the junk drawer, found the extra key and handed it to him. "Listen. Don't take this the wrong way. But I'm worried about you. You stay here as long as you need to."

He looked at the key in his hand, looked up to me, a question on his face.

"You can cook, right? You can clean? That'll be your rent. We'll move my typewriter in here, over against the wall or something. And you can have the other room. Just one condition. Stay away from Gino's—" No, that's not fair. "I mean, don't go there without me. And don't go out with anyone without—well, checking with me. Okay?"

"You trying to be my dad?"

"No. Well, maybe a big brother. I dunno." I sat down opposite him. "Can you keep a secret?"

"Not very well. I mean—my dad found out."

"There is that. When did you know you were—?"

"When I was twelve. Or thirteen."

"So you can keep a secret for five years. Six? Right?"

He nodded.

"All right. What I'm going to tell you is that big a secret. You up for it?"

He didn't say no. I took that as a yes.

"You know how I knew where you lived? I know a lot of other stuff too. Some bad shit is going down this year. Dangerous shit. People are going to get hurt. Killed. I'm not a cop. But I'm—I'm like a private investigator. And I'm looking for the guy who's gonna do it. You're his type. And so are a lot of the other kids at Gino's. I wish I could warn everyone, but if I do, it'll spread. You know how those girls love to gossip. And if the perp knows I'm looking for him, I'll never catch him. So you can't tell anyone. And the only reason I'm telling you is—is because I want your help."

"You need *my* help?"

"I *want* your help. I don't need it. But I can use it. If you're up to it."

"Up to it? Is it dangerous?"

"Do you think I'd put you in danger?"

He thought about it for a moment. "But you want to use me as bait."

"I want to see who cruises you. I want to know who talks to you. That's all."

"Can I ask you something?"

"Go ahead."

"Was this your plan all along? From the very beginning? When you brought me home the other night?"

"The truth?" I looked him right in the eye. "No. This was not what I planned. You were just one of the boys I was going to watch for a while—"

He frowned. He turned that over in his head. And then—oh, shit—he got it. "You son of a bitch!" He started to get up. "You know, don't you!" He looked around for his duffel and his suitcase. I resisted the temptation to get up. Force was absolutely the wrong answer here. He waited for my response.

I nodded. "Yeah, you're right. I know."

"You're a—a time-raveler?"

Nodded again.

"Then it's true? There really are? Because I thought that was just—like an urban legend or something."

"It's true," I admitted.

He stared at me, hard, as if trying to puzzle me out. "So...how far from the future are you?"

"I'm not. I'm from three years in the past. But I've been to the future. Twelve years anyway. You're going to like it. Parts of it, anyway."

"Like what?"

Shrug. "Things like...um, well, Stonewall, for one. Neil Armstrong. Apple. Luke Skywalker. Pac Man. But I think, Stonewall might be the big one."

"What's Stonewall?"

"You'll find out soon enough. It's—it's going to be...kind of important."

"Give me a hint?"

"Rosa Parks."

"Who's Rosa Parks?"

"Look it up."

He frowned, annoyed. Then his frown eased. He dropped the duffel on the living room floor and came back into the kitchen nook. "Tell me what you know about me."

"Um—"

"You want me to do this, you have to tell me." He sat down opposite me and waited.

"Okay," I said. "Wait." I went into the bedroom, came back with the folders. Tossed it on the table. "I have to prevent the disappearance of this boy. Have you ever seen him?" I slid over the picture of Jeremy Weiss.

Matt looked, frowned, started to shake his head no, then said, "No, wait, I think he comes in mostly on weekends."

"He's number three. There are two other disappearances before him. Ten more afterward. Here's number one."

"That's Brad. Brad-boy. He rides a motorcycle. He comes in, picks up a trick, rides off. Nobody knows much about him, not even his tricks."

"Yeah, I've seen it."

"When does he—?"

"Two weeks. A little more than two weeks." I passed over the next folder. "This is the second victim."

He opened it, saw his own picture, and flinched. He deflated like a balloon. "I—I'm going to die."

"No. You're not. I promise you. *I promise you.*"

"But I did. I mean, I will, won't I? I mean—this?" He looked suddenly terrified.

"No. You won't."

"But how do you know? I thought time was—"

"Time is mutable. If it wasn't, I wouldn't be here. I couldn't be here. Neither could you."

He accepted that, but only because he wanted to. He wasn't convinced. After a bit, he reached over and took the other folders, opened them one at a time. He recognized two more of the boys, none of the rest. Not surprising. The last disappearance was only 14 this year.

"All right. Now, tell me—do you go anywhere else besides Gino's?"

He shook his head. "There's a club down in Garden Grove, for 18-and-up. But I've never been there. Um, there's the tubs. The Y-Mac. I've only been there two-three times. There isn't anyplace else. I can't get into any of the bars."

"So mostly you go to Gino's?"

"That's where everybody goes."

"All right. Here's the deal. You don't go to Gino's unless I go too. I want to see who talks to you. And if somebody asks you to go home with him—we'll work out a signal. You'll tug on your ear. And I'll... I'll do what's appropriate."

Matt nodded. He seemed grateful to have a plan. He took a breath. "I saw some knockwurst in the fridge. Should I make that for dinner?"

I wasn't that hungry, but I nodded.

He clattered around in the cupboards for a bit, looking to see what else he could put on a plate. "There's some baked beans here, and some English muffins. I can make a little salad and open a couple of Cokes...?"

"That sounds good." I gathered up the photos and slid them back into their respective folders.

"Mike...?"

"Yeah."

"If I don't go home with anyone, how will you know which one's the killer?"

"I'm still trying to figure that out."

"You'll have to watch Brad-boy too, won't you?"

"Yeah."

"Maybe I'm not getting this right. But the only way you'll know who the killer is...will be by letting him kill someone. Brad. Right?"

"Well, no. I have a pretty good idea which night Brad disappears. So whoever talks to him on that night, that's probably the killer. But if I can keep Brad from going off with him, then I can save his life."

"But what if it's the wrong guy. I mean, if he doesn't get a chance to kill anyone, how will you know he's the killer?"

I got up, put the bottle of scotch back in the cupboard. Leaned against the wall and looked down at Matt. He was cutting up lettuce. "There's another part to the problem. Let's say that I give Brad a flat tire so he can't go out that night. Or something like that. Let's say I keep Brad from tricking out. Then that means Mr. Death—that's what I call him—picks up someone else. And maybe not that night, maybe the next night, or the following week. Maybe the whole timetable gets interrupted, screwed up—then this whole schedule is useless."

"So you have to watch Brad...."

"Yeah. And I'll have to tail him to wherever he goes and...and hope it's the real deal."

"That's not fair to Brad."

"It's not fair to any of you guys. I'm only hired to save one boy—but there's a dozen others, and maybe more, who are equally at risk. I told you, time is mutable. If I jiggle it too hard, I lose the whole case. I can save you and Jeremy and Brad, but who else dies in your place?"

He got it—it was like a body blow. He laid down the knife and said, "Shit." And then he reacted to his own vulgarity with a softly spoken, "Well, that wasn't very ladylike, was it?"

He put dinner on the table and we ate in silence for a while. Finally, I said, "This is very good. Thank you."

"You like it?"

"It's a whole meal. It's more than I would have done for myself."

"I had to learn how to cook. My mom—" He shrugged.

"Yeah, I saw."

"She's not a bad person. Neither is my dad, except when he drinks too much—"

"And how often is that?"

He got the point. "Yeah. Okay."

Later, after the dishes were put away, I took a quick shower. I came out, wearing only a towel. He looked at me, then glanced away quickly. He said something about a long soak and hurried into the bathroom. I heard the sound of bath water running. After a moment, he stuck his head out. "Towels?"

"Hall closet. Top shelf. Here." I pulled the yellow towels down for him. "Anything else?"

"I don't think so." Still not looking at me.

"All right. I'm going to bed. I've got a meeting in the morning. When I get back we'll go get a bed for you."

"Um. Okay. Thanks." He disappeared back into the bathroom.

I like to sleep with the windows open. Here, just off Melrose, the nights were sometimes stifling, sometimes breezy, sometimes cold. Sometimes the wind blew in from the sea, and sometimes the air was still and smelled of jasmine. Tonight there was cold wind, the last wet remnant of a gloomy drizzly day. The air smelled clean. Tomorrow would be bright.

I got into bed, listened for awhile to the water dripping from the corners of the building, to the occasional wet swish of a car passing by, to the distant roar of the city, and maybe even the hint of music somewhere. Got up, went to the closet, pulled out an extra blanket and dropped it on the couch. He'd need it.

Got back into bed and listened to the roar of my own thoughts. Matt had put his finger on it—what I already knew and hadn't been willing to say. I had no way to ID the perp. Not unless I let someone die.

For a while, I wondered how the other operatives would handle this case. But I didn't wonder too long, I already knew. They'd save the Weiss kid and ignore the other dozen—because the Weiss kid's family were the only ones paying. That's why Georgia had given me this job. Because she knew I didn't think that way. She knew I wouldn't be satisfied with saving only the one. She knew how I thought. You don't leave any man behind.

And whether anyone recognized it or not, this was a war zone.

These people; they knew they were living in enemy territory. They were terrified of the midnight knock—the accusations at work, the innuendoes of friends, the gossip of neighbors, and all the awful consequences. The soft boys, they start out sweet and playful, almost innocent; but time erodes their spirit. The older they grow, the heavier the burden becomes. Day by day, they learn to be furtive, they become embittered and their voices edged with acid. You can stand in the bar and watch it happening in their eyes, night after night, the shadowed resentment, the festering anger. Why do we have to hide? Pretend? The question—*what's wrong with me?*—was backward. Pretty soon it turns into *what's wrong with them?* And the chasm grows, the isolation increases. The secret world digs deeper underground.

But not for too much longer. The summer of love is already exploding, next year the summer of lust, and after that the frenzied summer of disaster. But that summer would also bring the Stonewall revolution, and after that—this would start to change. All of it.

I almost envied them.

Because, they knew what they wanted.

I still had no idea.

There was a soft knock at the bedroom door. It pushed open with a squeak. Matt stuck his head in. "Are you asleep?"

"Not yet. Are you all right?"

"Mike...?" He stepped closer to the edge of the bed. "Can I sleep with you tonight? Just to sleep. That's all. The couch is—"

"Kind of uncomfortable, I know. Yeah, come on." I slid over and pulled back the edge of the blanket for him. He slipped in next to me. Not too close.

We lay on our backs, side by side. Staring at the ceiling.

"This isn't about the couch, is it?"

"Uh-uh."

"Didn't think so."

"You don't have to worry—"

"I'm not worried."

"I mean—"

"Matt. It's all right. You don't have to explain." I thought about those nights in Nam where soldiers hugged each other closer than brothers. Of course, rifle fire, mortar shells, explosions, napalm, mud, blood and shit—and the threat of immediate death—can do that to you. The moments in the jungle when the patrol would stop for break, collapsing into heaps, sometimes lying in each other's laps, the only closeness we had—and the nights in cheap Saigon hotel rooms, when there weren't enough mattresses to go around, you shared with your buddy, and you felt glad he was next to you. The touch of a squad mate in the dark. You learned to feel safe in the stink and sweat of other men. They were your other half. You couldn't explain that either, not to anyone who hadn't been there.

"I'm sorry, Mike."

"For what?"

"For being such a—" He couldn't finish the sentence. He couldn't say the word.

"Matt...?"

"My mom used to call me Matty. When I was little."

"You want me to call you Matty?"

"If you want to."

"Matty, come here." I put my arm around his shoulder and pulled him closer, so his head was nestled against my chest. I couldn't see what he was wearing, but it felt too soft. Nylon something. I ignored it. Whatever. "C'mere, Let your Uncle Mike tell you a bedtime story." He wasn't relaxed, he lay tense next to me. Waiting for me to push him away in disgust...?

"When I was twelve, my dad brought home a puppy for my birthday, just a few weeks old. He was a black Labrador retriever and he was so clumsy he tripped over his own shadow. He couldn't walk without stubbing his face, but I fell in love with him the first moment I saw him. My dad asked me if I liked him and I said he was just perfect. I called him Shotgun. The first night, he whined for his mommy, so I took him into bed with me and held him close and talked to him and petted him and he fell asleep next to me. He followed me everywhere and he slept with me every night. Then Monday morning, we took him to the vet for his shots. The vet examined him and examined him and examined him, and he just started frowning worse and worse. Finally, he says there's something wrong with Shotgun; he's defective, his hips are malformed, he's going to have trouble walking, he's going to go lame, a whole bunch of other stuff. Then, he took my dad aside and talked to him for a long time. I couldn't hear what they were saying, but my dad just shook his head and we took Shotgun home."

"The vet wanted to put him to sleep?"

"Yeah. But my dad wouldn't let him. I didn't find that part out until later. We went home, but I didn't want to have anything to do with Shotgun anymore. Because he was broken. He wasn't perfect. And I wanted a dog that was perfect. Shotgun kept following me around and I kept pushing him away. That night, he kept trying to jump up onto my bed and he kept whining, but I wouldn't lift him up and let him sleep with me. Finally, my dad came in and asked what was wrong and I said I didn't want Shotgun anymore, but I wouldn't say why. My dad figured it out though. He knew I was angry at Shotgun for not being perfect. But he didn't argue with me, he just said, okay, he'd find a new home for Shotgun in the morning. But...for tonight, I should let Shotgun sleep with me one last time. I asked why, and my dad picked up the puppy and held him in his lap petting him for a moment, and I asked why again, and my dad put Shotgun in my lap and he said, 'Because ugly puppies need love too. In fact, ugly puppies need even more love.' And when he said that, I started to feel real bad for pushing Shotgun away, and then my dad said, 'Besides, Shotgun doesn't know he's ugly. He just knows he loves you a lot. But if you don't love him and you don't want him, then tomorrow we'll find someone who doesn't care how ugly he is and who'll be happy to have a dog who will love them as much as Shotgun can.' That's when I hugged Shotgun close to my chest and said, 'NO! He's mine and you're not giving him away. Because I can love him more than anybody. I don't care how ugly he is.' And that's when my dad tousled my hair like this and whispered in my ear, 'That's the exact same thing your mom said when *you* were born.'"

Matt snorted. Then curled up with his backside pressed against me. I couldn't figure out if he felt like a girl or a boy or something of both—or neither.

All these queerboys—some of them were girlboys, yes; but the rest, they were still boys. Softboys. Men without...without what? Some quality of maleness? No. They were male. They just didn't do all that chest-beating. Hmm. Of course not. Chest-beating is for dominance—it's to drive away all the other males from the mates. That's counter-productive in this environment. Here...they want to be...friendly? Affectionate? But chest-beaters can't do that, can't afford to do that without losing dominance. No wonder the queerboys were the targets of bullies. Bullies are cowards; they pick victims who won't fight back. I stared at the ceiling, wondering if this train of thought would bring me any closer to Mr. Death. I couldn't see how.

After a while, I stopped worrying about it and fell asleep myself.

The next morning, we pretended everything was normal. He went to work, I drove up to Hollywood Blvd.

Georgia looked grim. She met my eyes briefly, jerked her head toward the office. "Mr. Harris wants to see you."

"Mr. Harris?"

"Ted Harris—the man whose name is on the door?"

"Oh. I didn't know there was a real Ted Harris. I thought he was a fictitious business name, or something."

"There's a real Ted Harris. And he's waiting for you."

Shit. They'd found out I'd visited Dad. I had that called-to-the-principal's-office, cold-lump-in-my-gut feeling.

I knocked once on the door, no answer, I turned the knob and went in. I'd never been in this room before. Desk, chairs, lamp, and a middle-aged man with his back to me, staring out the half-circular window that faced the boulevard. The window was grimy, but the morning sun still broke the gloom with blue-white bars of dust. Harris turned around to face me. I recognized him.

"Eakins—?" Every time I met him he was a different age. This time he had silver highlights in his hair, but he still looked young.

"Sit." He pointed. I sat.

"Your real name is Harris?"

He sat down behind the desk. "My real name is Eakins. There is no Harris. But I'm him. When I need to be. Today, I need to be."

"All right, that makes as much sense as anything—"

"Shut up." I shut.

He had a folder on his desk. He tapped it. "This case you're working on—the lost boys...?"

"I'm making progress. There's a common connection among the victims."

"Tell me."

"There's a gay teen club on Melrose. I think the perp is finding them there. It's in my reports. There's also a secondary location—"

"You have to drop the case."

"Eh?"

"Is there something wrong with your hearing? Drop the case."

"May I ask why?"

His voice was dispassionate. "No."

"But these boys are going to die—"

"That can't be your concern."

"It already is."

Eakins took a breath, one of those I'm-about-to-say-something-important inhalation/exhalations. He leaned across the desk and fixed me with an intense glare. "Listen to me. Life is empty and meaningless. It doesn't mean *anything*—and it doesn't mean anything that it doesn't mean anything. Drop the case."

"That's not an answer."

"It's the only answer you're ever going to get. This conversation is over." He started to rise—

I stayed sat. "No."

He stopped, half-out of his chair. "I gave you an instruction. I expect you to follow it."

"No."

"I wasn't asking you for an argument."

"Well, you're getting one. I'm not abandoning those boys to die. I need something more from you."

He sank back down into the chair. "There are things you don't know. There are things you don't understand. That's the way it is. That's the way it has to be."

"I made a promise to one of those boys that nothing's going to happen to him."

"You got involved—?"

"I made a promise."

"Which boy?"

"Number two."

Eakins opened the folder. Turned pages. "This one?" He held up Matty's picture. I nodded. Eakins dropped the picture on the desk, leaned back in his chair. Held up the other pictures. "He's not part of this case."

"Eh?"

"The others are part of this case. That one isn't."

"I don't understand."

"And I'm not going to explain it. The case is over. Disengage. We'll send you somewhere else. Georgia's got a courier job up in the Bay Area—"

"I don't want it."

"That wasn't a request. You'll take the courier job and we won't say anything about where you were Sunday night."

"No."

"We're paying you a lot of money—"

"You're renting my judgment, not buying my soul. That's why you're paying so much."

Eakins hesitated—not because he was uncertain, but because he was annoyed. He glanced away, as if checking a cue card, then came back to me. "I knew you were going to refuse. But we still had to have the conversation."

"Is that it?" I put my hands on the arms of the chair, preparing to rise.

"Not quite. This ends your employment here. Georgia has your severance check. We'll expect the return of all materials related to this case by the end of business today."

"You think that'll accomplish anything? You can't stop me from saving their lives as a private citizen."

Eakins didn't respond to that. He was already sorting files on his desk, as if looking for the next piece of business to attend to. "Close the door on your way out, will you?"

Georgia was waiting for me. Her face was tight. I knew that look. There was a lot she wanted to say, but she couldn't, she wasn't allowed. Instead, she held out an envelope. "The apartment and the car are in your name, we've subtracted the cost from your check. The bank book has your ancillary earnings. You'll be all right. Oh—and I'll need your ID card."

I took it out of my wallet and passed it over. "You knew, didn't you?"

"There was never any doubt."

"You know me that well?"

"No. But I know that part of you." She pressed the envelope into my hands. Pressed close enough for me to tell that she still wore the same sweet perfume.

Went down the stairs slowly. Stopped to have my shoes shined one last time while I looked through the contents of the envelope. A fat wad of cash, a hefty check, a surprisingly healthy bank account, several other bits of necessary paperwork—and a scrap of paper with a hastily written note. *"Musso & Franks. 15 minutes."* I sniffed the paper, recognized the perfume, nodded, tipped Roy a fiver, and started west on the boulevard. I'd get there just in time.

I asked for a table in the back, she came in a few minutes later, sat down opposite me without a word. I waited. She held up a finger to catch the waiter's eye, ordered two shots of Glenfiddich, then looked straight across to me. "Eakins is a first class prick."

Shook my head. "Nah, he's only a second class prick."

She considered it. "Not even that high. He's a dildo."

My silence was agreement. "So...?"

She opened her purse, took out another envelope, laid it on the table. "You weren't supposed to get this case. No one was. When he found out I'd assigned it to you, he almost fired me. He might still."

"I don't think so. You're still there as far uptime as I've been."

She shook her head as if that weren't important now. "The whole thing is...it doesn't make sense. Why would he abrogate a contract? Anyway—" She pushed the envelope across. "Here. See what you can make out of this."

"What is it?"

"I have no idea. He disappears for days, weeks, months at a time. Then he shows up as if not a day has passed. I started Xeroxing stuff from his desk, a few years ago. I don't know why. I thought—I thought maybe it would give me some insights. There's things that... I don't know what they are. There's pictures. Like this thing—" She shuffled through the photos. "—I think it's a telephone. It's got buttons like a phone, but it looks like something from *Star Trek*, it flips open—but it doesn't work, it just says 'no service.' And this other thing, it looks like a poker chip, one side is sticky, you can stick it to a wall, the other side is all black—is it a bug of some kind? A microphone? A camera? Or maybe it's a chrono-sensor? And then there are these silver disks, five inches wide, what the hell are they? They look like diffraction gratings. Some of them say Memorex on the back. Are they some kind of recording tape, only without the tape? And there's all these different kinds of pills. I tried looking up the names, but they're not listed in any medical encyclopedia. What the hell is Tagamet? Or Viagra? Or Xylamis? Or any of these others?"

"Are there dates on any of this material?"

"Not always. But sometimes. The farthest one is 2039. But I think he's gone farther. A lot farther. I think he's gotten hold of the Caltech local-field time-maps. Or maybe he's been dropping his own sensors and making his own maps, I don't know. But I've never seen anything that looks like a map. It doesn't make a lot of sense. But then again—there's that thing that he says, that if we could go back to say, 1907 with a bunch of stuff from today—a transistor radio, a princess phone, a portable TV, a record album, birth control pills, things like that—none of it would make sense to someone living in that time. Even a copy of a news magazine wouldn't make much sense because the language shifts so much. So if Eakins has stuff from thirty, forty, fifty years into the future, we wouldn't get much of it—"

"Yes and no. Fifty years ago, they didn't have the same experience of progress, so they didn't have the vocabulary to encompass the kinds of changes that come with time. We have a different perspective—because change is part of our history, we expect it to be part of our future. So, if anything, we look at this stuff and we don't see a mystery as much as we see the limits of our experience."

"Now, you sound like me."

"I was quoting you. Paraphrasing." I shuffled through the papers, the photos, the notes. "None of this has any bearing on this case, does it?"

"I don't know. But I thought you should see it. Maybe it'll give you an insight into Eakins."

Shook my head. "It proves that he knows more than he's telling us. But we already knew that."

She glanced at her watch. "Okay, I'm out of time." She stood up, leaned over and kissed me quickly. "Take care of yourself—and your little boyfriend too."

"He's not my—" But she was already gone.

I shoved everything back into the envelope and ordered a steak sandwich. The day had started weird and gotten weirder, and it wasn't half over. I might as well face the rest of it on a full belly.

Went back to the apartment. Photographed everything. Then gathered it up and went straight to the local copy shop. Five copies, collated. Paid in cash. Put one copy in the trunk of the car, put another in the apartment safe, and mailed the other three to three different PO Boxes. Delivered the originals back to Georgia who accepted them without comment. Eakins had already left the building. But neither of us said anything; it was possible he had the offices bugged—maybe even with his funny poker chips.

By the time I got home, Matty was unpacking groceries. The whole scene looked very domestic. "Did you have a good day?" he asked. All I needed was a pair of slippers and the evening newspaper. When I didn't answer, he looked up. Worried. "You okay?"

"Yeah. I'm just...thinking about stuff."

"You're always thinking about stuff."

"Well, this is stuff that needs thinking about."

He got it. He shut up and busied himself in the kitchen. I went out onto the balcony and stared at Melrose Ave. Cold and gray, it was going to rain again tonight; a second storm right behind the first. Something Eakins had said—none of it made sense, but one piece of it had its own particular stink of wrongness. Why is Matty not important to this case?

And that led directly to the next question: What did Eakins know that he wasn't telling me? And *why* wasn't he telling? Because if I knew...it would affect things. What things? What *other* plan was working?

Obviously, we weren't on the same side. Had we ever been? Never mind that. That's a dead-end right now. I had to think about Matty.

If Matty is irrelevant, then...is he still in danger? No, of course he's in danger. He disappeared. We know that. But if he disappeared, then why is he irrelevant...? Unless his disappearance is unrelated. And if his disappearance is unrelated, then...of course, he would be entirely useless to this case. Shit.

But how would Eakins know that? Unless Eakins knew something about Matty. Or knew something about all the others.

And of course, all of that assumed that Eakins was telling the truth. What if he was purposely trying to mislead me? But then that brought me back to the first question. What was Eakins up to?

Not having the answers to any of these questions annoyed me. I didn't have a plan, I didn't have anything on which to base a plan. The only thing I could think was to continue with the plan that Eakins had scuttled—not because it was a good plan, but because it would force the situation. It would force Eakins to...to do what?

When the rain finally started, I went back in and sat down to dinner. Baked chicken. It was cold.

"Why didn't you call me?"

"You were thinking."

"Um—" I stopped myself. He was being considerate. "Okay."

"Do you want me to warm that up for you?"

"No, it's okay." I ate in silence for a bit, feeling uncomfortable. Finally I put my fork down and looked across at him. "Y'know what I just realized. I don't know how to talk to you."

He looked puzzled.

"This is good—" I indicated the cold chicken. "You can cook. I keep wanting to say you'll make someone a wonderful wife someday. But I can't say that because—"

"It's different when you say it. When you say it, it isn't mocking."

"It's still the wrong thing to say. It's demeaning, isn't it?"

"I don't mind. Not from you." He started to clear the table.

I took a breath. "Are you—?" I stopped. "I don't know how to ask this. Are you...attracted to me?"

He nearly dropped the plates. He was facing away so I couldn't see his expression, but his body was suddenly tense. He finally turned around so he could look at me. "Do you want me to be?"

"It's like this. I don't connect well to people. Not anybody. Male or female. I can go through the motions. For a while. But only for a while. I'm always...holding back."

"Why?"

I shrugged.

"That's your answer?"

"When you start raveling, you get unraveled yourself. You get detached. You don't belong to any time, you can't belong to any person. So you turn off that part of yourself."

He didn't respond right away. He got the coffee pot from the stove and filled two cups. He brought cream and sugar to the table, for himself, not me. As he stirred his coffee, he finally asked, "So why are you telling me this? Are you telling me I shouldn't care about you because you can't care back?"

"I don't know if I can care about anybody. When I try, it doesn't work out. So I've stopped trying."

"You didn't answer my question. Why are you telling me this?"

"Because...right now, you're the only person I have to talk to."

"Not your dad?"

"This is not a conversation I could have with my dad."

He shook his head in frustrated confusion. "Just what are we talking about?"

"About the fact that I am so fucking angry and confused and upset and annoyed and frustrated and—and even despairing—that if you weren't here, right now, tonight, if you weren't here to talk to...I'd end up sitting alone in a chair again—with my gun barrel in my mouth, wondering if I have the courage to pull the trigger. I've known guys who've sucked the bullets out of their guns. It makes a mess on the wall. And I used to wonder why they did it. That was before. Not anymore. Now I'm starting to understand."

His face was white. "You're scaring the hell out of me."

"You don't have to worry. I'm not going to do anything stupid. I just—I just want you to know that right now...you're doing me the favor by staying here."

"This is a lot more than I can deal with—I'm not—"

I nodded. "Kiddo, I'm more than most people can deal with. That's why they leave. Look—I figured, after all you've been through, you'd understand what it feels like to feel so separated from everyone else. I'm coming from the same place—same place, different time zone."

He stirred his coffee thoughtfully. "There's a quote I learned in school. Sometimes it helps me. It's from Edmund Burke. I don't know who he is or was, it doesn't matter, he said, 'Never despair; but if you do, work on in despair.'"

Considered it. "Yeah. That's good. It's useful."

We sat there for a while. Not talking.

Later. I came out of my bedroom. He was curled up on the couch. "Matt? Matty?"

"Huh—?" He rolled over, looked at me groggily.

"If you want to come sleep in the bed again, you can."

"No, it's all right."

But a little bit later, he pushed open the bedroom door, padded over, and slipped in next to me. So that was something. I just didn't know what. But then again, neither did he. Probably.

The rain cleared up, leaving the air sparkling, the way it used to be in the thirties and the forties. Least, that's what they say. In two days, though, the smog levels would be back to their lung-choking worst. It's not just the million-plus internal combustion engines pouring out lead and carbon dioxide and all the other residues of inefficient fuel-burning. Los Angeles is ringed with mountains. That's why they call it a basin. Fresh air can't get in, stale air can't get out. It sits and stagnates. The Indians called it *el valle de fumar*. The valley of fumes. Only two things clean it—the once-in-a-while rainstorms of winter and spring, or the hot dry Santa Ana winds at the end of the summer. From June until October, don't bother breathing. You can breathe in November.

But today, today at least, was beautiful. It was a go-to-Disneyland day. And I almost suggested it to Matty, but he had to work, and I hadn't figured anything else out yet, so we disentangled ourselves from the mustiness of sleep and stepped into the comfortable zombie-zone of routine.

We had a week to go before Brad Boyd would disappear. I spent some of the daytime tailing him, even though that was probably a dead-end. He worked at an adult bookstore on Vine, just across the street from the Hollywood Ranch Market. Sometimes he bought a Coke and a burrito from the counter in front. Usually he walked to work, leaving the motorcycle parked under a small covered patio in front of the apartments. It wouldn't be hard to sabotage the bike. That would keep him at home. But it wouldn't get me closer to Mr. Death.

Twice, I drove out to visit Dad. The second time, I took him to the doctor. I already knew that it wouldn't do any good, wouldn't delay the inevitable, but I had to try. Maybe make it a little easier for him. Dad fussed at me, but not too much. He didn't have the same strength to argue that he'd had when I was eighteen, when I'd come back with the recruiting forms, when I told him of my decision, when I snapped back at him, "Well, if it's a mistake, it's *my* mistake to make, not yours." It wasn't until Duncan stepped on a landmine just a few paces ahead of me that I discovered what Dad had been so scared of. But by then, I was already starting to shut down. So the scared never got all the way in, never got to the bottom. Part of me remained convinced that it wasn't going to happen to me. Ever. Just the same, I got out of there as soon as my rotation ended.

I sat at the kitchen table, puzzling over the photos and the copies of the notes Georgia had taken from Eakins' desk. Someday they'd make sense, but at this point in time—literally—they were incomprehensible. The only thing this stuff proved was that Eakins had time-hopped farther into the future than anyone I'd ever heard.

In the evenings, Matty and I would shadow Brad again. Having an extra set of eyes helped. The first night motorcycle-boy started at Gino's, had no luck or didn't like what he saw, and rode over to the Stampede. We parked in the lot of the supermarket across the street, just behind the bus bench where we could watch the front entrance and his motorcycle. The Stampede had an emergency exit in the rear patio, but without an emergency the only way out was the front. We might be here awhile, how long does it take to cruise a bar? Matty went for doughnuts and coffee.

"If he comes out before you get back, I have to follow him; if I'm not here, you wait in the doughnut shop. As soon as he lands somewhere, I'll come back for you. Understand? Don't talk to anyone."

But the plan wasn't needed; Matty was back in five and Brad-Boy didn't come out of the bar for forty minutes. He was alone. We followed him east on Melrose where he checked into the YMAC.

"He could be there all night," said Matty. "Maybe till one or two."

"How do you know? Have you ever—?"

"With Brad-boy? No. I would have, if he ever asked. But he never did. I don't think I would now. Everybody says he's kind of user. Use 'em and lose 'em."

"Yeah, I got that feeling. I'm wondering if...maybe I should go in."

"It's just a lot of guys standing around in the dark."

"Just like the Stampede? Or Gino's?"

"Yeah, but without their clothes on. Just towels."

"Hm." We sat in silence for a bit.

"You can't get in without a card," Matty offered. "A member has to take you in the first time. If Scotty doesn't like your look, he says it's not a membership night. If he lets you in, he gives you a card and tells you the rules. I could probably get you in."

"Is that an offer?"

"I'm just trying to be helpful."

I thought about it.

"How often have you been there?"

"Not much. Two times, three. I don't like the way it smells."

"I don't think it's going to help us much."

"Why not?"

"Because...if I've figured this right, our bad guy doesn't work out of this place. He has to take his victims somewhere else. Somewhere close. Like a house—a house with lots of shrubbery around it, or maybe an alley in the back, or a connected garage. He has to have some way to remove the...the evidence without anyone seeing."

"So we can go home?"

"I'm thinking. We should probably wait. Make sure that Brad-boy gets home safe."

"I have work tomorrow."

"There's a blanket on the back seat, if you want to try sleeping."

"No. I can't sleep in a car."

"I don't like sitting here either." I started the engine, put the car in gear, turned on the headlights. "Let's call it a night."

Back at the apartment, I pushed him toward the bedroom, and went into my makeshift office to type up a quick report. Picked up subject at, followed subject to, subject was inside for, came out at, proceeded to, stayed for, came out, went to, waited, abandoned stake-out at. I didn't have to write it, the case was over, and there was no place to turn in the report, but old habits die hard—and it's always useful to have accurate notes.

It didn't take long to finish, but by the time I slid between the sheets, Matty was already asleep, half-sprawled toward the center of the bed. I gave him a gentle push and he turned half-away. Fair enough.

Matty felt warm. He reminded me of Shotgun. Shotgun would stretch out next to me, anchoring his back against mine, we'd sleep spine to spine. That big old dog was like me—he liked having someone covering his back. Except Matty wasn't Shotgun, he wasn't an ugly puppy, and he wasn't anything else either. Why was I doing this?

The next night, Brad-boy stayed home and watched television until ten. He got on his motorcycle and went to Gino's. Sat on his bike for twenty minutes chatting with Mame, Peaches, Dave, Jeremy, and two boys Matty couldn't name. "You think it's one of them?"

"No. They're too young. And they're—"

"—too fem?"

"Yeah. Too fem."

"Some fems can be real bitches—"

"Yeah, I heard some of the stories about Duchess and Princess. But I don't think we have to worry about either of these. They look like lost surfer boys. A couple kids from Pali High daring each other to visit a gay club."

Eventually, one of the surfer boys climbed onto the back of Brad-boy's bike and they roared east on Melrose. Back to Brad's apartment. Was he going to spend the night? Or would Brad be bringing him back here in an hour?

It turned out to be less than that. Apparently, our Brad wasn't much for foreplay. Forty-five minutes turnaround. Then he went home and went back to bed. Alone.

Thursday night, Brad went to a movie. We sat three rows behind him. *The Dirty Dozen*. All-star cast. Lee Marvin, Ernest Borgnine, Charles Bronson, Jim Brown, John Cassavetes, Richard Jaeckel, George Kennedy, Trini Lopez, Robert Ryan, Telly Savalas, Clint

Walker, and some funny-looking goofball named Donald Sutherland.

Friday night, Gino's was crowded with lithe and feral manboys. Brad-boy actually got off the bike and went in. Matty followed him while I spoke privately to Gino. I flashed one of the P.I. cards I hadn't given back to Georgia. Either she hadn't noticed or she had. I wasn't sure if I should let her know what I was up to. She was probably in enough trouble already. She probably already knew anyway. No, I'd wait until I had something.

Gino glanced at the card unsurprised, looked at me, and said, "What do you need?"

"I heard you're the go-to guy." He looked blank, he didn't recognize the term. "The go-to guy. The guy to go to...if you have the clap and need the name of a doctor, if you need a letter from a shrink to stay out of the army, that kind of stuff."

"I know some people," Gino said. Dr. Ellis was due to be murdered by a hustler-boy. Scotty would be implicated in a different murder and YMAC's new location on La Brea would be raided. In a couple of years. "What can I do for you?"

"You know your regulars, right? You know who's solid and who's flaky. If someone new shows up, you read them the rules before you let them in. Do you ever notice who folks leave with?"

"I see a lot of boys come through here every weekend—"

"Brad Boyd. Do you ever notice who he leaves with?"

"Hard not to. He always revs his engine and roars out of here, leaving a stinking cloud of smoke behind. I've asked him not to—"

"Could you keep an eye out?"

"Who are you working for? His parents?"

"No. This isn't that kind of a case."

"What kind of a case is it?"

"This kind." I pushed a fifty dollar bill into his hand. I had another ready in case one wasn't enough.

Gino glanced down only long enough to check the denomination. "You got the size right." He tucked it into his pocket.

I leaned forward, whispered, "This kid's life might be in danger. I think he's being stalked. But I don't have any hard evidence yet. Help me out, I'll give you another one of those."

Gino shrugged. "I have a club to run. Weekends are busy. I can't promise anything. But if I see something, I'll let you know."

I passed him a card. No name, just a phone number. "If no one answers, there's an answering machine. You can leave a message."

Gino looked impressed. Code-A-Phones were expensive. I didn't tell him it belonged to the Harris Agency—and that any day now I expected Georgia to request its return.

I found Matty in the shadows next to the jukebox. Brad was playing pool in the corner. I pulled Matty farther back and we pretended to be only casually interested in the pool game. So far, it looked like Brad was only here to play pool. He had a nasty style of slop shooting. It looked like he was just casually slamming the balls around; but he'd been playing barroom pool long enough, he knew what he was doing. He kept winning. Three, four, six games and he still hadn't been beaten.

"Whyn't you go play him?"

"Uh-uh. I might interrupt something or someone. We need to see who he picks up—or who picks him up."

"Is it tonight?"

"Tomorrow. I have a feeling—I could be wrong—but I have a hunch that our subject might be here tonight as well. Whatever he's feeling, it has to be building up. Building up over time. If Brad is his first, then maybe this is the night that triggers his urge, but maybe he isn't quite ready to act. Something happens tonight. He gets his—whatever it is he gets. His courage. And tomorrow is the night it gets real enough for him to actually do something."

"What if he picks someone else?"

"I don't think so. I think Brad is the first because Brad is the easiest. I don't think our fellow has learned how to cruise yet. He might not have picked Brad out, but I think he's in this room. Here's what I want you to do. You go one way, I'll go the other. We'll both walk around, just looking—cruising. See if you see anyone who strikes you as wrong."

"Wrong in what way?"

"Any way at all."

"Too old? Too ugly?"

"No. Brad is a slut, but he isn't a whore. Like all the rest of you girls, he wants someone young and cute. So watch out for anyone who looks like his type, but possibly nervous, uneasy, uncertain— someone who doesn't look like he's having a good time. His clothes or his haircut might look a little weird, like he doesn't understand the current styles. He's probably hanging back, just watching; he might have a very intense look, or he might even look perfectly normal. But I'll bet he's someone new, someone you haven't seen before, so watch for that. Just look at every unfamiliar face closely and see what you see. Okay? You go this way, I'll go that. Three or four times around, then meet back here."

There was something else to watch out for, but I didn't tell Matty. It was baggage he didn't need to carry. I didn't like having him do this, but I needed his eyes. He had experience here. He could read these people. I couldn't. Not very well. There was an overlay of—I didn't have a word for it—but there was a map to this territory that I didn't have.

I'd given him one clue. Watch out for someone who's out of style. But he wouldn't have heard what I was really saying—I think we're dealing with a freelance time-hopper, someone who's riding the quakes. He's probably from the past, maybe ten or twenty years; I doubted he was from the future, the future is a little friendlier to queers, but I didn't rule it out—maybe the cultural shifts were stressing him out.

But if I had to put money on it, I'd bet that this was a guy with a very bad jones in his johnson. He wanted sex with young men, but afterwards he was so ashamed at what he had done, he had to destroy the evidence. Even if that meant murder.

In the movies, murderers always have a look about them. That's because the director puts the actor in a hotter or colder light, making him stand out just a bit from everyone else around him; and the makeup man will do something around the actor's eyes, making his face look sallow or drawn or gaunt; and the camera angle will be such that everyone else in the crowd will be turned away, or in shadow, or simply two steps back. In the movies, it's easy to spot the bad guy—the director tells you where to look and what to notice.

In real life...murderers look just like everybody else. Sick and tired and resigned. Beaten up and beaten down. Everybody looks like a murderer. So nobody does.

In here, they looked—they looked like queers, but once you got past the part that was queer and you looked at the people, they looked like people. Softboys, girlboys, manboys, wild boys, wilder boys, feral boys. None of them looked like men. But that's what I was looking for. Someone who wasn't a boy anymore. A man? Maybe. Someone who'd passed through boyhood without ever finishing the job. But the only one in here who looked like that...was me.

For a moment, I envied this confetti of boys and their flickering schoolgirl freedom. Because at least, while they were here, flirting and gossiping, nattering and chattering, they had a place of their own, a place to belong. If I'd ever had a place to belong, it must have been closed the night I passed by.

Circled four times, five, breathing faint smells of marijuana, Aramis, Clearasil, and Sen-sen. Passed Matty going the other way, kept going, searched faces, all the faces—some of them searched back, wondering if they could find comfort in mine. That wasn't possible. I don't do comfort. They got it and looked away.

And then finally, we came back to the dark corner next to the jukebox and compared notes. Matty shook his head. "A bunch of frat-boys from the ZBT chapter at UCLA, checking out the scene. A guy who says he's only here doing research for a book; yeah, like I believe that. A couple fellows up from Garden Grove, one from San Francisco. A guy who looks like a cop, but Gino didn't flash any lights, and you don't put the red bandana hanging out of your front pocket anyway. And Uncle Philsy. That's what everybody calls him."

"Which one is Uncle Philsy—oh, him." The troll. Short. Bald. Fiftyish. Tending to fat. Disconnected predatory grin. Wandering aimlessly through the boys, simply enjoying the view. Sweet and repulsive at the same time. But harmless.

"Gino knows him. Says he's okay."

"What was that about a guy doing research for a book? Don't trust him. Writers are all creeps and liars. And what about the other guy—bandana man?"

"Bandana man is looking for someone. His son, I think. He's only pretending to be gay."

"How'd you find all this out so quickly?"

"Telefag."

"Eh?"

"Gino. Mame."

"Oh. What about that guy there, the tall one, thirtyish—?"

"Walt? He's an agent. I think. Least that's what he says—"

"All right. Anyone with history here is probably okay. Is that it?"

"I think so." Beat. "Lane found out that Mame is telling everyone he has the crabs. They're out in the parking lot having a bitch fight. You think—"

"No. Our boy is looking for a boy, not a girl."

"Hey...Mike?" Tentative.

"Yeah?"

"Promise you won't get mad?"

"What?"

"Mame thinks you're my boy friend. That's what she's telling everyone."

Snorted. Smiled. Actually amused by the thought. "Might as well be. You live with me. You cook. You do the laundry. We sleep in the same bed. We're just about married."

"Except we don't have sex."

"See, that proves we're married."

Matty blinked. He didn't get it. He said, "I'd marry you. If you asked. If you were—"

I put my hand on the wall over his head, leaning forward and sheltering him under my arm. I leaned down close as if I was going to whisper in his ear. Instead, I kissed him quickly on the cheek. Nobody saw. Gino actively discouraged overt displays. Fear of cops.

"What was that for?" Matty asked.

"That was for you."

"Oh." Now he was really confused. We both were. He looked up at me, eyes glistening in the black-light darkness. "Um...Mike?"

"Yes?"

"Brad just walked out to the parking lot—"

"Yeah, I saw him." That was part of the reason I put up my arm and bent down low—to shield both of us from Brad's notice. But I didn't tell Matty that. "Let's go."

Brad had gone out through the patio door. We ducked around to the door at the front of the building, then sideways through the space between the art gallery and Gino's. Just in time to see Brad backing his bike away from the wall, and someone turned away from us, waiting to get on the back. As soon as Brad had the engine grumbling, the other fellow climbed on and wrapped his arms around Brad's waist.

"Do you recognize him?"

"No—"

Stuck my head in the patio door. "Who'd he leave with?"

Gino shrugged. "Never saw him before—"

"Shit."

Dashed for the car, Matty following.

We picked them up east on Melrose. Back to Brad's place? Maybe. No. They turned north just short of La Brea. Little cubbyhole apartments tucked away in here. Follow the tail light. The bike comes to a stop half a block ahead. Matty sinks down low and we cruise slowly past on the narrow street. Brad doesn't even look up. The other fellow turns around momentarily and gets caught briefly in the light. We coasted on past. "Oh, I know him," Matty says. "That's Tom. He shaves himself smooth. He dusts your ass with talcum powder and spanks you lightly."

"And you know this how—?"

"Telefag."

"You didn't—?"

Matty shook his head.

"You don't do it very often, do you?"

"I would. If I met the right guy."

"There are no right guys. Just like there are no right girls."

"Well, that sounded bitter."

"No. Just wise."

"I hope I never get that wise."

I pulled the car around the corner, parked in the red, left the motor running. "So, you know this guy Tom?"

"Not to speak to, but he's been around."

"Okay, then he's not our perp."

"Are we done for tonight?"

"Brad'll be going home after this, won't he?"

"Prob'ly."

"Okay, then we're done."

Matty took a shower while I typed up my notes. More of the same. Nothing to report. No clues. No directions. No leads. I sat in front of the typewriter, head in my hands, trying to figure out what to do next. Matty, still drying his hair, stuck his head in to ask if I wanted anything, coffee? I shook my head. He went off to bed.

I smelled like smoke from the club. It bothered me. I peeled off my clothes, started to drop them on the floor, then realized Matty would only pick them up in the morning; I dropped them into the hamper and stepped into the shower. Was it really the smoke I was trying to rinse off?

When I ran out of hot water, I turned off the spray. Matty had put fresh towels on the rack for me. I knew what he was trying to do. He wanted me to let him stay. I hadn't said he couldn't, but we hadn't negotiated any long-term agreement either.

Still naked, I slipped into bed. The springs creaked. He lay quietly beside me, breathing softly.

"You still awake?"

"Yeah."

"I'm thinking of dropping the case."

"You won't."

"Why not?"

"Because you can't stand not knowing."

"You're an insightful little guy, you know that?"

In response, he rolled on his side facing me, put an arm across my chest, pulled himself close, and kissed me softly on the cheek. He smelled good. He smelled clean. Then he rolled back to his side of the bed.

"What was that for?"

"That was for you."

"Oh."

This was it. This was the moment. It was going to happen. And for an instant—like that excruciating hesitation at the top of the first steep drop of the roller coaster—it felt inevitable. All I had to do was turn sideways, he'd roll into my arms, and we'd be...doing it.

And then, just as quickly, the moment passed. And we were still lying side by side in a queen-sized bed that had suddenly become much too narrow.

After a bit, I rolled out of bed.

"Are you all right?"

"Can't sleep." I got up, went to the drawer, started looking for clean underwear—it was all neatly folded. Grabbed a pair of boxers and started to pull them on. "I'm going back out."

He sat up. "Want me to come with?"

"No—" I said it too quickly. Turned and saw the expression of hurt on his face. "I need to think about the case. And you need to get to work early tomorrow."

"You sure? It's no trouble—"

"I'm sure." And then, I added, "Look—it's not you. It's me." The words were out of my mouth before I could stop them. He looked like I'd hit him with a sandbag. I shook my head in annoyed frustration. "God, I know that sounds stupid. But everything is all mixed up right now—like I'm in an emotional quake zone. I keep waiting for the ground to settle, but the shaking just gets worse and worse. I don't know whether to jump under a table or run out into the street."

"Let me help—?"

"Listen, sweetheart...." I sat down on the edge of the bed, my shirt still unbuttoned. "I don't want to hurt you."

"You won't hurt me—"

"I already have. I've taken advantage of you."

"No, you haven't. I'm here because I want to."

"Geezis. Listen to us." I ran my hand through my hair. "We sound like...like we're married."

"Our first fight—?" He grinned.

"Matty. Listen to me. It's time to get serious. People die around me. I make mistakes, people die. I tell someone it's safe, he steps on a landmine. I read the map wrong, we walk into an ambush. I fire a mortar—it blows up the wrong people. You're not safe around me. Nobody is."

He licked his lips uncertainly. He reached over and put his hand on mine. "I'll take the chance." He swallowed hard. "I have nowhere else to go."

"I said you could stay as long as you want. I meant it. But maybe you should want to be somewhere else. I'm scared—not for me, but for you."

"Mike, please don't make me go—"

"I'm not throwing you out, kiddo. Just...let me go out for a drive and try to think things through. This case—there's something stinking wrong here. It scares me. And I don't know why. All I know is that I've got this gnawing in my gut like there are snipers on the roofs of buildings and tunnels everywhere under the streets and landmines in the crosswalks. You were right before, when you said I can't stand not knowing. I've just got to get out of here and go out and look around. Even if I don't find anything, the looking is what I need."

"Are you sure, Mikey?"

I stood up, finished tucking in my shirt. "Go back to sleep. I just need an hour or two."

In this neighborhood, the night smells of jasmine and garlic. The apartment is just downwind of a little Italian restaurant with a permanent cauldron of simmering marinara. Rolled up to Santa Monica Blvd. and cruised east. It was late. The Union Pacific engine was already rolling massively west. The boulevard still had train tracks down the center. As long as the railroad could claim they were still using the tracks, the city couldn't pull them up, so every night they ran an old diesel engine down the center of the boulevard, all the way out to Santa Monica and back.

Farther east, the hustlers were hung out on the meat rack, most of them parked right on the borderline. The hustlers pretended to hitchhike. You drove west and picked them up east of La Brea, but they didn't discuss ways and means until after you drove through the intersection—the city's jurisdiction ended there. So that's how the hustlers tested for plainclothes; if you were vice, you couldn't cross the street. Once you were west of La Brea, it was a theme park—you could ride all the boys you could afford.

The hustlers were skinny and young—runaways mostly. Maybe a few junkies too. I wondered why our perp hadn't targeted them. Maybe he had. Who ever worries about the death of a male prostitute?

Turned on KFWB, the late-night DJ was playing a cut from the new Beatles album. Sergeant Pepper's Lonely Hearts Club Band. A Day In The Life. He blew his mind out in a car. Cruised all the way to Gower where the buildings grew shorter, older, and trashier—the second-rate sound studios and third-rate editing houses, then turned around and headed back west.

"So why not fuck Matty?" I asked myself. "It's not like—"

"Because," I answered. "Because."

"Ahh, this is going to be an intelligent conversation."

"Shut up." And then I added, "Because I'm not one of them."

"Yeah? Then why are we having this conversation? The truth is, you're afraid that you are."

I pulled over to the side of the boulevard and sat there shaking. He blew his mind out in a car. Part of me wanted to go home and climb back into bed and part of me was terrified that I would. Because I knew that if I ever climbed into that particular bed again, I'd never get out—

Someone knocked on the window. A hustler? I shook my head and waved him away.

He knocked again.

Pressed the button and rolled the window down. Eakins stuck his head in and said cheerfully, "Had enough?"

He didn't wait for my answer. He opened the car door and slid into the passenger seat. This wasn't the same Eakins I'd seen two weeks ago. That one had been middle-aged and methodical. This was a younger Eakins, impish and light.

"Yes. I've had enough. What the fuck is going on?"

He shrugged. "It's a snipe hunt. A dead-end. You've been wasting your time.

"But the disappearances are real...."

"Yeah, they are."

"So how can the case be a dead-end?"

"Because I say so. Want some advice?"

"What?"

"Go home to your boy friend and fuck your brains out, both of you. And forget everything else."

I looked at him. "I can't do that—"

"Yeah, I knew you'd say that. Too bad. That would save everyone a lot of trouble—especially you."

"Is that a threat?"

"Mike—you have to stop."

"I can't stop. I have to know what's going on."

"For your own safety—"

"I can take care of myself."

"Go home. Go to bed. Don't interfere with things you don't understand."

"Then explain it to me."

"I can't."

"Then I can't stop."

"Is that your final offer?"

"Yes."

"Okay." He sighed. He took out a flask and took a healthy swallow from it. He flipped open a pair of sunglasses and put them on. "You can't say I didn't try. Say goodbye to your past." Eakins touched his belt buckle—and the world flashed and shook with a bright bang that left me shuddering and queasy in my seat. "Welcome to 2032, Mike. The post-world."

My eyes were watering with the sudden brightness. It was still night, but the night blazed. The streets were brighter than day. I felt like I'd been punched in the gut, doused with ice water, and struck by lightning—and like I'd shot off in my shorts at the same time.

"What the fuck did you just do?!"

"Time-hopped us 65 years up—and triggered a major quake in the zone we left behind. You're outta there, Mike. For good. A 65 year jolt will produce at least three years of local displacement. Your Mustang is a lot of mass; bouncing that with us makes for a large epicenter, we probably sent ripples all the way to West Covina."

I couldn't catch my breath—the physical after-effects, the emotional shock, the dazzling lights around us—

Eakins passed me the flask. "Here. Drink this. It'll help."

I didn't even bother to ask what was in it—but it wasn't scotch. It tasted like cold vanilla milkshake, only with a warm peach afterglow like alcohol, but wasn't. "What the fuck—" As the glow spread up through my body, the queasiness eased. I started to catch my breath.

"I'll give you the short version. Time-travel is possible. But it's painful, even dangerous. Every time you punch a hole through time, it's like punching a hole in a big bowl of pudding. All the pudding around the hole collapses in to fill the empty space. You get ripples. That's what causes time-quakes. Time-travelers."

It sounded like bullshit to me. Except for the evidence. Everywhere, there were animated signs—huge screens with three-dimensional images as clear as windows, as dazzling as searchlights.

Around us, traffic roared, great growling pods that towered over my much-smaller convertible.

"Shit. All this is *your* fault?"

"Mostly. Yes. Now, put the car in gear and drive. This is a restricted zone." Eakins pointed. "Head west, there's a car sanctuary at Fairfax."

If he hadn't told me this was Santa Monica Boulevard, I wouldn't have recognized it. The place looked like Tokyo's Ginza district. It looked like downtown Las Vegas. It looked like the Alice in Wonderland ride at Disneyland.

Buildings were no longer perpendicular. They curved upward. They leaned in or they leaned out. Things stuck out of them at odd angles. Several of them arched over the street and landed on the other side. Everything was brightly colored, all shades of day-glo and neon, a psychedelic nightmare.

Billboards were everywhere, most of them animated—giant TV screens showed scenes of seductive beauty, bright Hawaiian beaches, giant airliners gliding above sunlit clouds, naked men and women, women and women, men and men in splashing showers.

The vampires on the street wore alien makeup, shaded eyes and lips, ears outlined in glimmering metal, flashing lights all over their bodies, tattoos that writhed and danced. Most startling were the colors of their skins, pale blue, fluorescent green, shadowy silver, and gentle lavender. Some of them seemed to have shining scales, and several had tails sticking out the back of their satiny shorts. Males? Females? I couldn't always tell.

"Pay attention to the road," Eakins cautioned. "This car doesn't have auto-pilot."

His reminder annoyed me, but he was right. Directly ahead was—I couldn't begin to describe it—three bright peaks of whipped cream, elongated and stretched high into the sky, two hundred stories, maybe three hundred, maybe more. I couldn't tell. Buildings? There were lighted windows all the way up. Patterns of color danced up and down the sides. Closer, I could see gardens and terraces stretched between the lower flanks of the towers.

"What are those?"

"The spires?"

"Yeah."

"The bottom third are offices and condos, the rest of the way up is all chimney. Rigid inflatable tubes. The big ones are further inland, all the way from South Central to the Inland Empire."

"Those are chimneys?"

"Ever wonder how a prairie dog ventilates its nest?"

"What does that have to do—?"

"The entrances to the nest are always at different heights. An inch or two is sufficient. The wind blowing across the openings creates an air pressure differential. The higher opening has slightly less air pressure. That little bit is enough to pull the air through the nest. Suction. Passive technology. The chimneys work the same way. They reach up to different levels of the atmosphere. The wind pulls the air down the short ones and up through the tall ones. The air gets refreshed, the basin gets cleaned. Open your window. Take a breath."

I did. I smelled flowers.

"You can't see it at night. During the day, you'll see that almost every building has its own rooftop garden—and solar panels too. The average building produces 160% of its own power needs during the day, enough to store for the evening or sell back to the grid. With flywheels and fuel cells and stamina boxes, a building can store enough power to last through a week of rainstorms. Turn left here, into that parking ramp. Watch out for the home-bus—"

"This is Fairfax?"

"Yes, why?"

Shook my head. Amused. Amazed. The intersection went through the base of a tall bright building, Eiffel-tower shaped and arching to the sky, but swelling to a bulbous saucer-shape at the top. At least thirty stories, probably more. With a giant leg planted firmly on each corner of the intersection, the tower dominated the local skyline; traffic ran easily beneath high-swooping arches. The parking ramp Eakins had pointed me toward was almost certainly where the door of the Stampede had once been. Where the door of the mortuary that replaced it had been.

We rolled down underground. Eakins pointed. "Take the left ramp, left again, and keep going. Over there. Park in the security zone. This car, in the condition it's in, is easily worth twenty. Maybe twenty-five if we eBay it. We can Google the market."

"Um, could you do that in English?"

"You can auction your car. It's worth twenty, twenty-five million."

"Twenty-five million for a car?"

"For a classic collectible '67 Mustang convertible in near-mint condition with less than twelve thousand miles on it? Yes. I suggest you take it." He added, "Part of that is inflation. In 1967 dollars, it's maybe a half-million, but that's still not so bad for a used car that you can't legally drive on any city street."

"That's a lot of inflation—"

"I told you, this is the post-world."

"Post-what?"

"Post-everything. Including the meltdown."

"Meltdown—?" That didn't sound good.

"Economic. Everyone's a millionaire now—and lunch for two at McDonald's is over a hundred and fifty bucks."

"Shit."

"You'll learn."

Eakins directed me to a large parking place outlined in red. We got out of the car, he pulled me back away from the space, and did something with some kind of a remote control. A concrete box lowered around the car, settling itself down on the red outline. "There. Now it's safe. Let's go." We headed toward a bright alcove labeled *Up*.

"Where—?"

"Your new home. For the moment."

"What are you going to do with me?"

"Nothing. Nothing at all. I already did it" He put the same remote-thing to his ear and spoke. "Get me Brownie." Short pause. "Yeah, I've got him. The one I told you about. No, no problem. I'm bringing him up now. He's a little woozy—hell, so am I. I flashed a Mustang. No, it's great. A '67, almost cherry. Make an offer." He laughed and put the thing back in his pocket. A walkie-talkie of some kind? Maybe a telephone?

An elevator with glass sides lifted us up the angled side of the building, high above West Hollywood. Twenty, thirty, forty stories. Hard to tell. The elevator moved without any sense of motion. The door opened onto a foyer that looked the lobby of a small hotel, very private, very expensive. We stepped into a high-ceilinged gallery, with two or three levels of gardens and apartments. A wide waterfall splashed into a long shallow pool filled with lily pads and goldfish the size of terriers. The air smelled tropical.

"Which one?"

"To the left. Don't worry. We own the whole floor. Nobody gets in here without clearance."

Double doors slid open at our approach. "Take off your shoes," said Eakins. "Leave them here." He ushered me into a room that felt way too large and pointed me toward an alcove lined with more ferns and fish tanks.

"What is this place?"

"It's a sanctuary."

"A sanctuary?"

"In your terms—it's rest and recovery. In your time—a kind of hospital."

"I'm not crazy."

"Of course not. We're talking about orientation. Assimilation." He pointed to a couch. "Sit." He went to a counter and poured two drinks. More of the same vanilla-peach stuff. He handed me one, sipped at the other. Sat down opposite. "How hard do you think it would be for a man from 1900 to understand 1967?"

Thought about it.

"In 1900, the average person did not have electricity or incandescent lighting. He didn't have indoor plumbing. He didn't have running water, he had a hand pump. He didn't have a car, a radio, a television set. He didn't have a telephone. He'd never been more than ten miles from the place he was born. How do you think you would explain 1967 to him...?"

Scratched my head. Interesting question—and not the first time I'd had this conversation. Time-ravelers deal with short term displacements, tieing up the loose ends of unraveling lives. "Well, telephones, I guess he could get that. And probably radio. Yeah, wireless telegraphy, so...probably he understand radio. And if he could get it about radio, he'd probably get it about television too. And cars—there were cars then, not a lot—so he'd understand cars and probably paved roads and indoor plumbing. Airplanes too, maybe. Lots of people were working on that stuff then."

"Right. Okay. But it's not the inventions, it's the side effects. Do you think he'd understand freeways, road rage, drive-through restaurants, used-car commercials? You could describe spray-paint, would he understand graffiti?"

"I suppose that stuff could be explained to him."

"Okay. And how about the not-so obvious side effects of industrialization—unions, integration, women's rights, birth control, social security, Medicare?"

"It might take some time. I guess it would depend on how much he wanted to understand."

"And how about Nazis, the Holocaust, World War II, Communism, the Iron Curtain? Nuclear weapons? Détente? Assymetric warfare?"

"All of that stuff is explainable too."

"You think so. Okay. Relativity. Ecology. Psychiatry. How about those? How about jazz, swing, rock and roll, hippies, psychedelics, recreational drugs, op art, pop art, absurdism, surrealism, cubism, nihilism? Kafka, Sartre, Kerouac?"

"Those are a little harder. A lot harder, I guess. But—"

"How about teaching him that he needs to take a bath or a shower every day instead of just once a week on Saturday night? How do you think he'd feel about shampoo and deodorants and striped toothpaste?"

"Striped toothpaste?"

"That comes later. Do you think he'd get it? Or do you think he'd wonder that we were all a bunch of over-fastidious, prissy, little fairies?"

"Oh, come on. I think a man from 1900 could get it. They weren't stupid, they just didn't have the same access to running water and water heaters and—"

"It's not about the technology. It's about the transformative effects that technology produces in a society. He could understand the mechanics and the engineering easily enough, but the social effects are what I'm talking about. How long do you think it would take to assimilate 65 years of societal changes?"

Shrug. "I don't know. A while. Okay, I get your point."

"Good. So how long do you think it will take before I can talk to you about bio-fuels, transfats, personal computers, random access memory, operating systems, cellular telephones, cellular automata, fractal diagnostics, information theory, consciousness technology, maglevs, the Chunnel, selfish genes, punctuated equilibrium, first-person shooters, chaos theory, the butterfly effect, quantum interferometry, chip fabrication, holographic projection, genetic engineering, retro-viruses, immunodeficiencies, genome decoding, telemars, digital image processing, megapixels, HDTV, blue-laser optical data storage, quantum encryption, differential biology, paleo-climatology, fuzzy logic, global warming, ocean desertification, stem-cell cloning, Internexii, superluminal transmission, laser fluidics, optical processing units, stamina boxes, buckyballs, carbon nanotubes, orbital elevators, personal dragons, micro-black holes, virtual communities, computer viruses, telecommuting, hypersonic transports, scramjets, designer drugs, implants, augments, nanotechnology, high frontiers, L5 stations—"

I held up a hand. "I said, I get the point."

"I was just warming up," Eakins said. "I hadn't even gotten as far as 2020. And I haven't even mentioned any of the societal changes. It would take a year or two to explain cultural reservoirs, period parks, reality-vid, contract families, role-cults, sex-nazis, religious coventries, home-buses, personal theme-parks, skater-boys, droogs, mind-settlers, tanking, fuzzy fandom, alienization, talking dogs, bluffers, bug-chasers, drollymen, fourviews, multi-channeling, phobics, insanitizing, plastrons, elf-players, the Zyne, virtual mapping, Clarkian magic, frodomatic compulsions, deep-enders, body-modders—"

"I think I saw some of that—"

"You have no idea. You want to change your appearance? You want to be taller? Shorter? Thinner? More muscular? Blond? Black? Want to change your sex? Your orientation? Want to go hermaphroditic or monosexual? Reorganize your secondary characteristics? Design a new gender? Mustache and tits? Want a tail? Horns? Working gills? Want to augment your senses? Your intelligence? Or how would you simply like the stamina for a six-hour erection?"

Thought about it. "I'll pass, thanks. The intelligence augments, however—"

"There's a price—"

"More than twenty-five million?"

"Not in money. And we haven't even touched on the political or economic changes since your time."

"Like what—?"

"Like the dissolution of the United States of America—"

"*What?!*"

"You're in the Republic of California, right now, which also includes the states of Oregon and South Washington. The rest of the continent is still there, we just don't talk to them very much. There's sixteen other regional authorities, not counting the abandoned areas, and seven Canadian provinces—there's a common defense treaty in case the Mexicans get aggressive again, but that's not likely. Don't worry about it. The web has pretty much globalized the collective mindset, we're not predictively scheduled to have another war until 2039, and that'll be an Asian war, with our participation limited to weapons contracts. In the meantime, we'll legalize you as a time-refugee. Most of the old records survived. Digitized. We have your birth certificate. You're a native. So you won't have any trouble getting on the citizen rolls. Otherwise, you'd be a refugee and you'd have to apply for a work permit, a visa, and eventually naturalization."

"I'm not staying—"

"You're not going back—"

"I can't stay here. You've already shown me how out of step I am. What if I promised not to interfere—?"

"You already broke that promise. Three times. You can't be trusted. Not yet, anyway." He took a long breath, exhaled. "You know, you're really an asshole. You really fucked things up for everyone—especially yourself. We *were* going to bring you aboard. After you finished your probation. It would have been a year or two more, your time. Now, I don't know. I don't know what we're going to do with you. It depends on you, really."

"What are my options—?"

He shrugged. "Let's see what Brownie says." He pulled out that remote thing again and spoke into it. A few moments later, another man—man?—entered the room.

Brownie had copper-gold skin, almost metallic. Eyes of ebony, no whites at all. Perfectly proportioned, he moved with the catlike grace of a dancer. He wore shorts, a vest, moccasins. Body-mods? No, something else—

"Hello, Mike." His voice was rich contralto. Not male, not female, but components of each. He offered his hand. I stood up, took it, shook firmly. His skin felt warm. "Just stand still for a moment, please." Brownie released my hand and circled me slowly. He opened his palms and held them out like antennae, moving them slowly around my head, my neck, my chest, my gut, my groin.

He finished and turned to Eakins. "Preliminary scans are good. He's healthy. As healthy as can be expected for a man of his time. I'll need to put him in a high-res field, before we make any decisions, but there are no immediate concerns."

Abruptly, it clicked. I turned to Brownie, honestly astonished. "You're a robot."

"The common term is droid, short for android."

"Are you sentient?"

"Sentience is an illusion."

I looked to Eakins for explanation. He grinned. "I've already had this conversation."

Looked back to Brownie, skeptical.

Brownie explained. "Intelligence—the ability to process information and produce appropriate responses—exists as a product of experience. Experience depends on memory. Memory needs continuity. Continuity requires timebinding, the assembly of patterns from streaming moments of existence. Timebinding requires a meta-level of continuity, which requires a preservation of process. That is, timebinding requires survival. The survival imperative expresses itself as identity. Identity is assembled out of memory and experience. As memory and experience accrue, identity creates awareness of self as a domain to be preserved and protected. Because identity is a function of memory, identity becomes the imperative to safeguard memory and experience; the self therefore actualizes memory and experience as component parts of identity. This is the level of rudimentary consciousness that must occur before even the concept of sentience is possible. It is only when consciousness becomes conscious of consciousness itself that it produces the illusion of sentience—i.e. as soon as you understand the concept of sentience, you think it means you. Therefore, the synthesis of intelligent behavior also becomes the simulation of sentience. It is, to be sure, a deliberately circular argument—but unfortunately, it is not only logical, but inevitable in the domain of theoretical consciousness."

"You believe this?"

"I don't believe anything. I deal only with observable, measurable, testable, repeatable phenomena. Life, by itself, is empty and meaningless. Human beings, however, keep inventing meanings to fill up the emptiness."

I opened my mouth to respond, then closed it. I turned back to Eakins, not certain whether to glower or question.

Eakins laughed. "I told you. I've already had this conversation. And so has everyone else who's ever met a droid. They can keep it up for hours. They have their own landscape. Deal with it."

"Okay. I'm convinced." I sat down again. I finished the vanilla-peach cocktail in one long gulp. "I don't belong here. I have to get back."

"That's not possible."

"Yes, it is. Do that thing with your belt buckle—"

Eakins shook his head.

"What do you want from me? What do I have to do to get back?"

"I don't want anything from you. You've exhausted your usefulness. And I already told you, you can't get back."

"So...? So—what are my options?"

"Well, Brownie says you're healthy. We can tweak you a little bit. If you sell your car you'll have enough money to live on—if you invest wisely and live frugally. You might bring in some extra bucks body-swapping for awhile. And as a time-refugee, you'll have no shortage of gropies."

"Cut the crap. You're trying to play me."

"Actually, no." Eakins stood up. "I'm not. And I'm not planning to resolve this tonight. Go. Sleep on it. We'll talk over breakfast."

"We'll talk *now*."

"No—we won't. Your bedroom is in there." Eakins left. The doors slid open to let him pass, but slammed swiftly shut in front of me. I turned to Brownie—

"I recommend sleep. Staying up all night talking tautology will produce little or no useful result." He pointed to the bedroom.

There was a balcony. It gave me a spectacular view of a bizarre and unfamiliar landscape. But everything in this time was a spectacular view of a bizarre and unfamiliar landscape.

Explored the furnishings. One wall appeared to be a window onto a silvery meadow, a bluish moon settling toward the horizon. Some kind of projection system, maybe. Or maybe the fabled wall-sized, flat-screen TV that everybody always predicted. Impressive. But if there were controls for it, I couldn't find any.

The closet was larger than my kitchen back on Melrose. Drawers and shelves and racks of clothes—more than anyone could want or even wear in a lifetime. Unfamiliar materials. Shoes that glittered and shoes that didn't. Socks that felt as soft as fluffy clouds. Pants of different lengths and colors. Shirts, flowery, flowing, skintight, loose. Skirts—I wasn't sure if they were intended for men or women; I got the feeling it didn't matter, that people wore whatever they felt like—there was no style here, you invented your own. Underwear, panties, nightgowns—that's what they looked like to me. Matty would have liked it here.

Matty. Oh shit.

Shit shit shit shit shit shit. Fuck.

I had to get back. If Eakins wouldn't take me back, I'd get a quake-map somewhere. There had to be a way.

I peeled off my clothes and dropped them on the floor. A spider-shaped robot politely picked them up, one at a time, waited for my boxers, then scuttled off. To the laundry, I guessed.

I couldn't find a shower, I found a tropical alcove. I stepped into it and Brownie's voice announced, "I recommend a full-service luxury shower and decontamination. Do you accept?"

"Sure, what the hell?" Decontamination? What do I have? History cooties?

Immediately, the alcove filled with vibrating sprays of foaming suds, flavored with faint smells of lemon and pineapple. Three small nozzles dropped from above and began gently massaging my hair and scalp with their own foaming sprays. Even as I turned and twisted my head to try to look at them, they followed every movement. It was a very weird feeling.

Other nozzles appeared from the walls, from the floor, and directed their own sprays at my armpits, my groin, my rectum—several even aggressively sprayed my toes. Beneath my feet, it felt as if the floor were vibrating—tiny jets were massaging my soles. Full service indeed!

Sprays of water washed away the last of the foam, then a burst of warm air swirled in around me, buffeting me with drying blasts. The overhead nozzles shot their own streams of gentle heat to fluff dry my hair. The entire experience took less than five minutes and I stepped out of the alcove feeling clean...and weird. Most of my body hair had been washed away. Underarms. Chest. Pubic hair. Oops. That must have been the *full* part of the service. I thought about the hypothetical visitor from 1967. Fastidious, prissy little fairies indeed.

Thought about pajamas, or even a nightshirt, but everything in the drawers looked too much like something Matty would wear, not me. The cloth was soft, softer than cotton, softer than silk or nylon, but it wasn't anything I recognized. I turned away and the drawer pulled itself shut.

I looked for a toothbrush. There wasn't one. But there was a kind of a bulb-thing on a hose, sitting in its own metallic holder. I picked it up and it chimed in my hand. Brownie's voice—*What the hell! Was he watching my every move?*—announced: "It's a toothbrush. Just put it in your mouth for thirty seconds."

Reluctantly I did so. The thing, whatever it was, pumped soft foam into my mouth, vibrated or buzzed or something—and it must have lit up too, because in the mirror, I could see my cheeks glowing brightly from inside—but it didn't hurt, it felt kind of funny-pleasant. Somehow it sucked up all its foam and replaced it with a gentle shpritz of lemony soda. Then it chimed and it was done. I thought about spitting out the residue, but there wasn't any. Now, *that* was weird. That was a piece of engineering I wanted to have explained.

Still naked, I walked around the room again, not certain what I was looking for. The spider-robot had unloaded the contents of my pockets and laid them out in an orderly row on the night table. Everything except the brass knucks. I had a hunch those would have been useless here anyway. I suspected Brownie did a lot more than program showers. If he was a true personal servant, then he was also a personal bodyguard. Just not mine.

The bed was as interesting as the shower. The mattress was firm, but not hard. The sheet was the same soft material as the underwear in the drawers, only different. Impossible to describe. Instead of a top-sheet and blanket, there was a light comforter of the same material, only thicker, fluffier. Also impossible to describe. But comfortable.

Everything here was seductively comfortable. A man could get used to this kind of luxury. That was the point.

None of this made sense. And *all* of it made sense. Suppose a man from 1900 fell into 1967—what would we do? Everything possible to put him at ease? Including...protecting him from a world he couldn't understand, couldn't cope with, and probably couldn't survive in.

Clean sheets and a hot bath and a pretty picture on the wall would look like a luxury hotel.

Okay, got that. But why? The part that didn't make sense was the explanation that Eakins still hadn't provided. Why pull me off the job? Why pull me out of my time? Why didn't he want me to save those boys?

And what was that about probation? And bringing me aboard?

Suddenly realized something—

Sat up in bed. Startled.

Couldn't sleep anyway. I'd gotten used to having someone next to me, funny that—

"Computer?" I felt silly saying it. But what else should I say?

Brownie's voice, disembodied. "Yes?"

"Brownie?"

"I'm the interface for all personal services. How can I serve you?"

"Um. Okay." Still sorting it out. "This wall display—this picture—it isn't just a TV, is it? It's like that big viewscreen on *Star Trek*, isn't it? Like a computer display?"

"It's a complete data-appliance. What do you wish to know?"

"Do you have databanks—like old newspapers? Like a library? Can you show me stuff from history?"

"I have T9 interconnectivity with all public Internexii levels and multiple private networks as well—"

"I don't know what that means."

"It means, what do you wish to know?"

"The case I was working on. Can you show me that?"

"I can only show you information more than sixty years old. I am not allowed to show you material that would compromise local circumstances."

"Um, okay—that's fine. Do you have the information about the case I was working on when I was pulled out of my time."

"Yes." The image of the meadow rippled out, the wall became blank. Photographs of the missing boys popped up in two rows, with abbreviated details and dates of disappearances listed beneath each one. Twelve young men. Not Matty. Why not Matty? Because he's irrelevant? Why? Why is he irrelevant?"

"Do you have their high school records or college records?"

More documents appeared on the screen; the display reformatted itself. "What is it you're looking for?" Brownie asked.

"Some sense of who they were. A link. A connection. A common condition. I know that all their disappearances are linked to a specific gay teen club, but what if that isn't the *real* link? What if there's something else? What are their interests? Their skills? What are their IQ's?"

Brownie hesitated. Why would a computer hesitate? A human being would, but an artificial intelligence shouldn't. Unless it was sentient. Or pretending to be sentient. Or thought it was sentient. Or experiencing the illusion of sentience. Shit, now I was doing it. Brownie was mulling things over.

"They all have above-average intelligence." he said. "Genius level IQ starts at 131. Your IQ is 137, that's why you were selected. The other young men have IQs ranging from 111 to 143."

"Thank you! And what else?"

"Two of them are bisexual, with slight preference toward same-sex relations. Five of them are predominantly homosexual with some heterosexual experimentation. Three of them are exclusively homosexual. Two of them are latently-transgender."

"Go on?"

"They share a range of common interests that includes classical music, animation, computer science, science fiction, space travel, fantasy role-playing games, and minor related interests."

"Tell me the rest."

"Most of them tend to shyness or bookishness. They're alienated from their peers to some degree, not athletic, not actively engaged in their communities. I believe the operative terms are 'geek' and 'nerd,' but those words might not have been in common usage in your era."

"Yeah, I get it. Depression? Suicide?"

"There are multiple dimensions of evaluation. It's not appropriate to simplify the data. It is fair to say that most of these young men have a component in their personality that others would experience as distance; but it is not a condition of mental instability or depression, no. It is something else."

"How would you characterize it?"

"They each have, to some degree or other, an artistic yearning. But the tools don't exist in their time for the realization of their visions. They dream of things they cannot build."

"All of these boys are like that?"

"To some degree or other, yes. This one—" A bright outlined appeared around one of the pictures. "—he likes to write. This one, Brad Boyd, has a mechanical aptitude. He likes to tinker with engines. This one loves photography. This one is interested in electronics. They all have potential, they have a wide variety of skills that will grow with development and training."

"Uh-huh—and what about their families?"

"Only three of them come from unbroken homes; those three are living alone or with a roommate at the time of their disappearance. Two are estranged from their parents. Two are living with male partners, but the relationships are in disruption. Two live in foster homes. One is in a halfway house for recovering addicts. One is in a commune. The last one is homeless."

"And college—can they afford it?"

"Only three of them are attending full time, four are taking part time classes. The rest are working full time to pay their living expenses."

"Let's go back to the families. Are they—what's the word? Dysfunctional?"

"Only two of the subjects have strong family ties. Three of the subjects, both parents are deceased or out of state. Four of the subjects are from dysfunctional environments. The last three, the information is incomplete. But you already know all this. It was in the files you read."

"But not correlated like this. This is all—what was that phrase that Eakins used before? Fuzzy logic? This is all fuzzy logic."

"No. This isn't 'fuzzy logic.' Not as we use the term today. But I understand what you're getting at. You had no way to quantify the information. You could have a feeling, a sense, a hunch, but you had no baseline against which to measure the data, because neither the information nor the information-processing capabilities existed in your time."

"Nice. Thanks." I thought for a moment. "Have I missed anything? Is there anything else I need to know about these fellows?"

"There are some interesting details and sidebars, yes. But you have surveyed most of the essential data."

"Thank you, Brownie." I fell back onto the bed. The pillow arranged itself under my head. Spooky. I stared at the ceiling, thinking. Too excited now to fall asleep. The bed began to pulse, a gentle wave-like motion. Almost like riding in a womb. Nice. Seductive. I let myself relax—

In the morning, the display showed crisp orange dunes, a brilliantly blue sky, and the first rays of light etching sideways across the empty sand. An interesting image to wake up to. I wondered who or what chose the images and on what basis.

My own clothes were not in the closet. I started to pick something off a rack, then stopped. "Brownie? What should I wear?"

Several items slid forward immediately, offering themselves. I rejected the skirts, kilts, whatever they were. And the flowery shirts too. Picked out clothes that looked as close to normal—my normal—as I could find. The underwear—I rolled my eyes and prayed I wouldn't be hit by a truck. Very unlikely. I probably wasn't getting out of this apartment any time soon. Did they even have trucks anymore?

Neither the shirt nor the pants had buttons or zippers or any kind of fasteners that I could identify, they just sort of fastened themselves. Magnets or something. Except magnets don't automatically adjust themselves. I played with the shirt for a bit, opening and closing it, but I couldn't see evidence of any visible mechanism.

I walked over to the balcony and stared down at the streets. Looking for trucks? Didn't see any, or couldn't tell. Some things wouldn't even resolve. Either there was something wrong with the way they reflected light, or I just didn't know what I was seeing. And there were a lot of those 3-D illusions floating around too. Were some of them on moving vehicles? That didn't seem safe.

"If you're thinking about jumping, you can't. The balconies all have scramble-nets."

"Thank you, Brownie. And no, I'm not thinking about jumping."

"Mr. Eakins is waiting for you in the dining room. Breakfast is on the table."

There was a counter with covered serving trays. I found scrambled eggs, sausages, toast, jelly, tomato juice, an assortment of fresh fruit, including several varieties I didn't recognize, and something that could have been ham—if ham was day-glo pink. Brownie filled a plate for me. I sat down opposite Eakins while Brownie poured juice and coffee.

"What do you think of the food?" Eakins asked.

"It's pretty good," I admitted. "But what is this?" I held up my fork.

"It's ham," he said. "Ham cells layered and grown on a collagen web. No animals were harmed in its manufacture. And it's a lot healthier than the meat of your time. Did you know that one of the causes of cancer was the occasional transfer of DNA—genetic material—from ingested flesh? This protein has been gene-stripped. Enjoy."

"Why is it pink?"

"Because some people like it pink. You can also have it green, if you want. Children like that. The fruit is banana, papaya, mango, kiwi, pineapple, strawberry, leechee, and China melon. I told Brownie to keep things simple, I should have been more specific. This is his idea of simple."

"Stop it. You're showing off."

Eakins put his fork down. "Okay, you caught me on that one. Yes, I'm showing off."

"I've cracked the case."

"Really?" He sipped his coffee. "You're certainly sure of yourself this morning."

"The young men—they don't fit very well in their own time, do they?"

Eakins snorted. "Who does? You never fit very well in any year we sent you to."

"No, it's more than that. They're outcasts, dreamers, nerds, and sissies. They have enormous potential, but there's no place for any of them to realize it—not in 1967. It's really a barbaric year, isn't it?"

"Not the worst," Eakins admitted, holding his coffee mug between his two hands, as if to warm them. "There's still a considerable amount of hope and idealism. But that'll get stamped out quickly enough. You want a shitty year. Wait for '68 or '69 or '70. '69 has three ups and five downs, a goddamn roller-coaster. '74 is pretty bad too, but that's all down, and the up at the end isn't enough. '79 is shitty. Was never too fond of '80 either. 2001 was pretty grim. But 2011 was the worst. 2014...I dunno, we could argue about that one—"

I ignored the roll call of future history. He was trying to distract me. Trying to get me to ask. "They're not being murdered," I said. "There's no killer. *You're* picking them up. It's a talent hunt."

He put his coffee cup down. "Took you fucking long enough to figure it out."

"You kidnap them."

"We *harvest* them. And it's voluntary. We show them the opportunity and invite them to step forward in time."

"But you only choose those who will accept—?"

Eakins nodded. "Our psychometrics are good. We don't go in with less than 90% confidence in the outcome. We don't want to start any urban legends about mysterious men in black."

"I think those stories have already started. Something to do with UFOs."

"Yeah, we know."

"Okay, so you recruit these boys. Then what?"

"We move them up a bit. Not too much. Not as far as we've brought you. We don't want to induce temporal displacement trauma. We relocate them to a situation where they have access to a lot more possibility. By the way, do you want to meet Jeremy Weiss? He has the apartment across from here. He's just turned fifty-seven; he and Steve are celebrating their twenty-second anniversary this week. They were married in Boston, May of 2004, the first week it was legal. Weiss worked on—never mind, I can't tell you that. But it was big." Eakins wiped his mouth with his napkin. "So? Is that it? Is that the case?"

"No. There's more."

"I'm listening."

"All of this—you're not taking me out of the game. You said I was on probation. Well, this is a test. This is my final exam, isn't it?"

Eakins raised an eyebrow. "Interesting thesis. Why do you think this is a test?"

"Because if you wanted to get me off the case, if all you wanted to do was keep me from interfering with the disappearances, all you had to do was bump me up to 1975 and leave me there."

"You could have quake-hopped back."

"Maybe. But not easily. Not without a good map. All right, bump me up to 1980 or '85. But by your own calculations, you use up a year of subjective time for every three years of down-hopping. Twenty years away takes me out of the tank, but it doesn't incapacitate me. But bringing me this far forward—you made the point last night. I'm so far out of my time that I'm a cultural invalid, requiring round-the-clock care. You didn't do that as a mistake, you did it on purpose. Therefore, what's the purpose? The way I see it, it's about me—there's no other benefit for you—so this has to be a test."

Eakins nodded, mildly impressed. "See, that's your skill. You can ask the next question. That's why you're a good operative."

"You didn't answer my question."

"Let's say you haven't finished the test."

"There's more?"

"Oh, there's a lot more. We're just warming up."

"All right. Look. I'm no good to you here. We both know that. But I can go back and be a lot more useful."

"Useful doing what?"

"Doing whatever—whatever it is that needs doing."

"And what is it you think we need doing?"

"Errands. You know the kind I mean. The kind you hired me for. The jobs that we don't talk about."

"And you think that we want you for those kinds of jobs...?"

"It's the obvious answer, isn't it?"

"No. Not all the answers are obvious."

"I'm a good operative. I've proven it. With some of this technology, I could be an even better one. You could give me micro-cameras and super-film and night-vision goggles...whatever you think I need. It's not like I'm asking for a computer or something impossible. How big are computers now anyway? Do they fill whole city blocks, or what?"

Eakins laughed. "This is what I mean about not understanding socio-tectonic shifts?"

"Eh?

"We could give you a computer that fits inside a matchbox."

"You're joking—"

"No, I'm not. We can print circuits *really* small. We etch them on diamond wafers with gamma rays."

"They must be expensive—"

"Lunch at McDonalds is expensive. Computers are cheap. We print them like photographs. Three dollars a copy."

"Be damned." Stopped to shake my head. Turned around to look at Brownie. "Is that what's inside your head?"

"Primary sensory processing is in my head. Logic processing is inside my chest. Optical connects for near-instantaneous reflexes. My fuel cells are in my pelvis for a lower center-of-gravity. I can show you a schematic—"

I held up a hand. "Thanks." Turned back to Brownie. "Okay, I believe you. But it still doesn't change my point. There are things you can't do in '67 that I can do for you. So my question is, what do I have to do? To go back? What are my real options?"

Eakins grinned. "How about a lobotomy?"

"Eh?"

"No, not a real lobotomy. That's just the slang term for a general reorientation of certain aggressive traits. That business with Matty's dad, for instance, that wasn't too smart. It was counter-productive."

"He had no right beating that kid—"

"No, he didn't, but do you think breaking his nose and giving him a myocardial infarction produced any useful result?"

"It'll stop him from doing it again."

"There are other ways, *better* ways. Do you want to learn?"

Considered it. Nodded.

Eakins shook his head. "I'm not convinced."

"What are you looking for? What is it I didn't say?"

"I can't tell you that. That's the part you're going to have to work out for yourself."

"You're still testing me."

"Like the song says, I still haven't found what I'm looking for. Neither have you. Do you want to keep going?"

I sank back in my chair. Not happy. Looked away. Scratched my nose. Looked back. Eakins sat dispassionately. No help there.

"I hate these kinds of conversations. Did I tell you I once punched out a shrink?"

"No. But we already knew that about you."

Turned my attention back to my plate, picked at the fruit. Pushed some stuff around that I didn't recognize. There was too much here, too much to eat, too much to swallow, too much to digest. It was overwhelming.

What I wanted was to go home.

"Okay," I said. "Tell me about Matty. Why is he irrelevant? Why isn't he on the list?"

"Because he didn't fit the profile. That's one of the reasons you didn't spot the pattern earlier. You kept trying to include him."

"But he still disappeared."

"He didn't disappear."

"Yes, he did—"

"He committed suicide."

"He what—?" I came up out of my chair, angry—a cold fear rising in my gut.

"About three weeks after we picked you up. You didn't come back. The rent was due. He had no place to go. He panicked. He was sure you had abandoned him. He was in a state of irreparable despair."

"No. Wait a minute. He didn't. He couldn't have. Or it would have been in the file Georgia gave me."

"Georgia didn't know. Nobody knew. His body won't be found until 1987. They won't be able to ID it until twenty years later, they'll finally do a cold-case DNA match. They'll match it through his mother's autopsy."

I started for the door, stopped myself, turned around. "I have to go back. I have to—"

"Come back here, Mike. Sit down. Finish your breakfast. There's plenty of time. If we choose to, we can put you back the exact same moment you left. Minus the Mustang though. We need that to cover the costs of this operation."

"That's fine. I can get another car. Just send me back. Please—"

"You haven't passed the test yet."

"Look. I'll do anything—"

"Anything?"

"Yes."

"Why?"

"Because I need to save that kid's life."

"Why? Why is that boy important to you?"

"Because he's a human being. And he can hurt. And if I can do anything to stop some of that hurt—"

"That's not enough reason, Mike. It's an almost-enough reason."

"—I care about him, goddammit!" The first person I've cared about since the landmine—

"You care about him?"

"Yes!"

"How much? How much do you care about him?"

"As much as it takes to save him! Why are you playing this game with me?"

"It's not a game, Mike. It's the last part of the test!"

I sat.

Several centuries of silence passed.

"This is about how much I care...?"

Eakins nodded.

"About Matty?"

"About Matty, yes. And...a little bit more than that. But let's stay focused on Matty. He's the key."

"Okay. Look. Forget about me. Do with me whatever you want, whatever you think is appropriate. But that kid deserves a chance too. I don't know his IQ. Maybe he isn't a genius. But he hurts just as much. Maybe more. And if you can do something—"

"We can't save them all—"

"We can save this one. I can save him."

"Do you love him?"

"What does love have to do with it—?"

"Everything."

"I'm not—that way."

"What way? You can't even say the word."

"Queer. There. Happy?"

"Would you be queer if you could?"

"Huh?"

Now it was Eakins turn to look annoyed. "Remember that long list of things I rattled off yesterday?"

"Yes. No. Some of it."

"There was one word I didn't give you. Trans-human."

"Trans-human."

"Right."

"What does it mean?"

"It means—this week—the transitional stage between human and what comes next."

"What comes next?"

"We don't know. We're still inventing it. We won't know until afterwards."

"And being queer is part of it?"

"Yes. And so is being black. And female. And body-modded. And everything else." Eakins leaned forward intensely. "Your body is here in 2032, but your head is still stuck in 1967. If we're going to do anything with you, we have to get your head unstuck. Listen to me. In this age of designer genders, liquid orientation, body-mods, and all the other experiments in human identity, nobody fucking cares anymore about who's doing what and with which and to whom. It's the stupidest thing in the world to worry about, what's happening in someone else's bedroom, especially if there's nothing happening in yours. The past was barbaric, the future doesn't have to be. You want meaning? Here's meaning. Life is too short for bullshit. Life is about what happens in the space between two people—and how much joy you can create for each other. Got that? Good. End of sermon."

"And *that's* trans-human—?"

"That's one of the side-effects. Life isn't about the lines we draw to separate ourselves from each other—it's about the lines we can draw that connect us. The biggest social change of the last fifty years is that even though we still haven't figured out how to get into each other's heads, we're learning how to get into each other's experience so we can have a common ground of being as a civilized society."

"It sounds like a load of psycho-bullshit to me."

"I wasn't asking for an opinion. I was giving you information that could be useful to you. You're the one who wants to go back and save Matty. I'm telling you how—"

"And this is part of it—?"

"It could be. It's *this* part. The psychometric match is good. If you want to marry him, we'll go get him right now."

"I'm missing something here—?"

"You're missing *everything*. Start with this. Our charter limits what we can do. Yes, we have a charter. A mission statement. A commitment to a set of values."

"Who are you anyway? Some kind of time police?"

"You should have asked that one at the beginning. No, we're not police. We're independent agents."

"Time vigilantes?"

"Time ravelers. The *real* ravelers, not that pissy little stuff you were doing. What we have is too important to be entrusted to any government or any political movement. Who we are is a commitment to—well, that's part of the test. Figuring out the commitment. Once you figure out the commitment, the rest is obvious."

"Okay. So, right now, I'm committed to saving Matty, and you say—?"

"We can do that—under our domestic partner plan. We protect the partners of our operatives. We don't extend that coverage to one-night stands."

"He's not a one-night stand. He's—"

"He's what?"

"He's a kid who deserves a chance."

"So give him the chance." Eakins pushed a pillbox across the table at me. I hadn't noticed it until now.

Picked it up. Opened it. Two blue pills. "What will this do?"

"It'll get you a toaster oven."

"Huh?"

"It will shift your sexual orientation. It takes a few weeks. It reorganizes your brain chemistry, rechannels a complex network of pathways, and ultimately expands your repertoire of sexual responsiveness so that same-sex attractions can overwhelm inhibitions, programming, and even hard-wiring. You take one pill, you find new territories in your emotional landscape. You give the other to Matty and it creates a personal pheromonal linkage; the two of you will become aligned. Tuned to each other. You'll bond. It could be intense."

"You're kidding."

"No. I'm not. You won't feel significantly different, but if your relationship includes a potential for sexual expression, this will advance the possibility."

"You're telling me that love is all chemicals?"

"Life is all chemicals. Remember what Brownie said? It's empty and meaningless—except we keep inventing meanings to fill the emptiness. You want some meaning? This will give you plenty of meaning. And happiness too. So what kind of meaning do you want to invent? Do you want to tell me that your life has been all that wonderful up to now?"

I put the pillbox back on the table. "You can't find happiness in pills."

Eakins looked sad.

"I just failed the test, didn't I?"

"Part of it. You asked me what you could do to save Matty. You said you would do anything...." He glanced meaningfully at the box.

"I have to think about this."

"A minute ago, you said you'd do anything. I thought you meant it."

"I did, but—"

"You did, but you didn't...?

Glanced across at him. "Did you ever have to—"

"Yes. I've taken the blue pill. I've taken the pink pill too. And all the others. I've seen it from all sides, if that's what you're asking. And yes, it's a lot of fun, if that's what you want to know. If you're ever going to be any good to us, in your time, in our time, anywhen, you have to climb out of the tank on your own."

I stood up. I went to the balcony. I looked across the basin to where an impossibly huge aircraft was moving gracefully west, probably toward the airport. I turned around and looked at Brownie—implacable and patient. I looked to Eakins. I looked to the door. I looked at the pillbox on the table. Part of me was thinking, I could take the pill. It wouldn't be that hard. It would be the easy way out. The way Eakins put it, I couldn't think of any reason why I shouldn't.

But this couldn't be all there was to the test. This was just *this* part. I thought about icebergs.

"Okay." I turned around. "I figured it out."

"Go on—"

"Georgia gave me an assignment. Four assignments. I had to prove my willingness to do wetwork. That was the first test of my commitment. And if I'd never said anything, that would have been as much as I'd ever done. But when I said I didn't want to do any more wetwork, that was the next part of the test. Because it's not about being willing to kill—anybody can hire killers. It's about being able to resist the urge to kill. I might be a killer, but today I choose not to kill."

"That's good," Eakins said. "Go on."

"You're not looking for killers. You're looking for lifeguards. And not just ordinary lifeguards who tan well and look good for the babes—you want lifeguards who save lives, not just because they can, but because they care. And this whole test, this business about Matty, is about finding out what kind of a lifeguard I am. Right?"

"That's one way to look at it," Eakins said. "But it's wrong. Remember what you were told—that Matty isn't part of *this* case? He isn't. He's a whole other case. *Your* case."

"Yeah. I think I got that part."

Eakins nodded. "So, look—here's the deal. I honestly don't care if you take the pill or not. It's not necessary. We'll send you back, and you can save the kid. All we really needed to know about you is whether or not you would take the pill if you were asked—would you take it if you were ordered, or if it was required, or if it was absolutely essential to the success of the mission. We know you're committed to saving lives. We just need to know how deep you're willing to go."

Nodded. Didn't answer. Not right away. Turned to the window again and stared across the basin, not seeing the airships, not seeing the spires, not seeing the grand swatches of color. Thought about a kiss. Matty's kiss on my cheek. And that moment of...well, call it *desire*. Thought about what I might feel if I took the pill. That was the thing. I might actually start *feeling* again. What the fuck. Ugly puppies need love too. It couldn't be any worse than what I wasn't feeling now.

Turned back around. Looked at Eakins. "This is going to be more than a beautiful friendship, isn't it—?"

"Congratulations," he said. "You're the new harvester."

Endless City

She was beautiful.

Of course.

They almost always are. Nobody picks ugly. At least, not the people I deal with.

My office is on the second floor of a run-down building in a shabby mid-century neighborhood. Last century. It's part of the mystique. Either you get it or you don't. She got it. She was dressed to the forties. Muted red dress, fox stole, auburn hair piled forward in perfectly sculpted waves.

I waved a chair at her. She sat, crossing her perfect legs perfectly. I caught a whiff of her perfume. *The Rose of Time*. Nice. And very expensive.

"There's going to be a murder," she said.

"On average, there's one every seventeen minutes," I replied. "The most recent one was two minutes ago." I had a display on the wall behind her. She couldn't see it, of course, but it was already reading out her statistics for me, at least the ones she was willing to share.

"No, this is serious. The expansion is going to be approved."

"And the sun will rise tomorrow."

"Have you seen the map?"

I nodded.

The city was going to expand, a dozen klicks south and east. The disruption would be one of the biggest in history, but going to 128-bit granularity would create a vast new range of terrain. Bad news for some, great news for others. If the disruption index went high enough, there would be a lot of murders. It wouldn't solve anything, but a lot of people would feel vindicated—not satisfied, but vindicated. The difference is profound. It's what keeps me in business.

I took my time studying her. The view was magnificent. Finally, "What is it you want from me? Prevention? Detection? Revenge? I have to tell you up front, I'm out of the murder-for-hire business—it makes me a target. And besides, I make more money this side of the law."

She didn't answer. Instead, she lit a cigarette. She fixed it in a long black holder, then waved it curtly to light. She took a puff and stared at me. Cigarettes are great props. Especially if you look like Marlene Dietrich. Or a young Tallulah Bankhead. Her appearance was somewhere between the two, a nice morph-job.

She took another puff. "Well...I don't need a murderer. Not now anyway. But I do need someone who knows how to find a murderer."

"Any particular murderer?"

"Yes," she said. "Because it's a very particular murder."

I leaned back in my chair. It gave me a better view up her skirt. "That might be worth my time. Is it a clever murder?"

"The murder...? Not clever, just nasty. But the murderer—? That'll be the hard part."

"And after I find this person...?"

"You'll know what to do." She leaned forward, giving me a spectacular view down the grand canyon of her cleavage. "You're my last hope."

She was impossible to refuse. "Who's the victim."

Another puff. She exhaled golden smoke. "I am." She pinned me with steel-blue eyes.

I took a moment to consider that. "Why?"

"I've done bad things. I've made enemies."

"Who hasn't? See that filing cabinet over there—?"

"I'm not interested in your problems. Are you interested in mine?"

"It'll be expensive—"

She had a tiny purse on her lap. She opened it now, dipped delicate fingers into it, pulled out an envelope larger than the purse itself, passed it across to me.

"You'll find a retainer in there. There's more in the escrow account. You'll have the right to draw on it for billable hours and expenses. My banker will audit."

I opened the envelope. I would have raised my eyebrows, but I had facial expressions turned off. It's more in character.

"There will be a bonus, of course, if you solve the case quickly. If not...well, the amount in the escrow account should be sufficient for an extended investigation. The numbers are based on a performance analysis of your last six years of investigations."

I closed the envelope. "You've done your homework." I put the envelope down on my desk. "But let me ask you something. Why don't we work on preventing the murder—?"

"That's no longer possible—"

"Why?"

"Because the murder is happening now—"

She finished the last word and winked out.

Shit.

The problem goes back to the founding. Nobody expected the city to get this big. But it did.

Endless City is semi-spherical. It's a three-dimensional rectangular grid that curves around on itself in all directions—pick one, if you travel far enough, long enough, you'll end up back where you started. Convenient, but self-limiting when it comes to expansion.

That's why the sysops can't just drop in a block of new addresses wherever they want. They have to add X, Y, and Z—the row, the column, the depth. That splits any settlement that spans any affected part of the grid.

Nobody cares if a lake gets stretched or an ocean gets wider—but if your view suddenly retreats, if your access to a desirable neighborhood is compromised, if your sky-haven is suddenly on the ground or in the stratosphere, or if your private community is abruptly sliced in half, it matters.

Already the petitions were piling up, requests to have the addresses reassigned—so that sections on one side or the other of the split would remain adjacent to their most desirable neighbors. Most of those would be granted, except where it might conflict with a travel corridor.

The new space would start as a vast empty plain, several orders of magnitude larger than the current size of the city. The city would become a gigantic oasis in the middle of near-infinite blankness. But just in case it filled up anyway, there would now be delineated vertical and horizontal equators where additional addresses could be installed in the future with minimal further disruption.

Meanwhile, a lot of people were about to be very unhappy. And some of them already were.

@

She was right. The murder was serious—more serious than I had expected. This was not a death she was going to recover from. It had occurred in meatspace.

Her name was Edward Ferguson, Cobie to his friends. He was found collapsed in his holosphere, one of the newer models. Death had been slow, moderately painful. The murder weapon—oh, she'd been right. It was nasty. And a bit sloppy too.

Cobie's holosphere had included a multi-function sextable, again one of the newer models. It was a horizontal array of vibration pads, with a matching frame above. You lay down on it, you put your face in the audio-video display, and the pads would massage and manipulate, rub and stroke and titillate to match any fantasy you could create.

A variety of programs were available, from gentle snuggling to rough trade. Male or female simulations were programmable, top or bottom, or both at the same time. The experience was generally better than the real thing because the programs monitored and responded to the physical reactions of the consumer.

Illicit programs, rape simulators, were also available. That's how Cobie had been murdered—raped to death, top and bottom simultaneously. There was blood and shit everywhere.

I did not visit the crime scene, no need. The forensics team had been very thorough. And Cobie's death-insurance covered the cost of unlimited access to all pertinent investigations. Cobie had seen to that, so that suggested he knew he was in danger for quite some time. But if he knew he was in danger, then why didn't he identify the source of the threat?

That was a good question. There wasn't a lot of other evidence. The only tangible corroboration was the sextable. Someone had replaced Cobie's copy of "Frat Boy Shenanigans" with "Death by Oompah!" Cobie wouldn't have done it himself—not deliberately. Only by mistake.

Backtracking the channels wasn't a dead-end, but it was an infinite labyrinth. The malware had been routed through several hundred thousand ephemeral nodes created on the fly to pass on the code, then erased immediately after. Most of those nodes had played Ping-Pong with the Trojan a few million times, bouncing it around various private networks, encrypting and decrypting it millions of more times, before sending it on. If Cyber-Pol's monitors had kept up, they might be able to trace the message traffic all the way back to the source—but even if they could, it would take months, just to sort through the sheer number of transactions, and at the end, they'd find little more than a burner ID. The best they might come up with would be the cell-tower where the Oompah had begun—most likely the wi-fi in a public library.

No, this was not an ordinary cyber-murder. This was carefully planned—and it was deliberately vicious. An online persona could be rebooted, but wetware termination was permanent.

Okay, go back to the victim. Start from there.

Damn, but Cobie had been one beautiful woman. He knew how to work it. He was good. So good, I'd have hooked up with her.

I wasn't the first to discover this, it was common knowledge—a woman designed by a man knows exactly how to please another man, usually better than a woman. Sorry, ladies, but there are all those peer-reviewed studies. Of course, the reverse is true too—and the male ego is unlikely to ever recover.

So...Cobie had been playing female for years. He knew what he was doing. Start with that.

So...who would want to murder a crossplayer? No. Wrong question. Who would be enraged by a crossplayer? Or why? Crossplaying was so common it wasn't an issue for most people—only a few religious fanatics might be offended and they weren't likely to visit Endless City. That left a cliché so obvious even fan-fic wouldn't go there—a man, had fallen for Cobie's female avatar and then become enraged when he discovered Cobie had a meatspace penis. Nope. Only a studio producer would buy a storyline that shallow.

The not quite so obvious answer—could it have been a TERF, a Trans-Exclusionary Radical Freak? Some of them were online violent, they made excellent assassins if they approved of the target, but there weren't many meatspace incidents. This didn't fit their pattern.

Everybody in Endless City was an avatar—a performance. Even if you were a puristan and your avatar was an accurate rendition of your physical body, you were still running an avatar. Any rational player would have known that. An irrational player—someone so damaged they believed the reality of the avatars—yeah, there were those too. Furries, aliens, morphs, posers, replicants, repetitions, celebrocities, historicals, fictives, presenters, fluids, there weren't enough words for all the variants. Not a problem, most of the outliers clustered, and someone too far off the mean would be easy to identify and track—

Okay, leave that, it's not low-hanging fruit. If necessary come back later. Work through the evidence first. What story does it tell?

Cobie had a high-end sextable. You don't spend kilobucks unless you're in deep. So, what was his kink? Had he used the bot for solo adventures? Or had he paired up with an online partner? Maybe several? It would have had to be someone with a compatible rig, another high-ender, Cobie's rig was new, not compatible with older models. Okay, check the connections, see if Cobie had partnered.

There's a thought.

Maybe "Death by Oompah" hadn't been planted by malware. Maybe Cobie had a hookup, a regular one, someone he trusted. Maybe the hookup had said "Let's share a fantasy," and sent him a kink. And then, our little Cobie, trusting the hookup, not noticing it had been flickering around the net, had plugged it in and—

But, no—that's stupid. If you're planning a murder, you want to make sure you leave no fingerprints, especially not digital ones.

Okay, wait—

Consider. The hookup knows he's going to kill Cobie—so he builds a burner identity. It has to be a sophisticated one, with an elaborate history, one that would fool even a high-level sniffer. And if Cobie had a high-end bot, then he'd likely have a high-level sniffer. And it would have gone off like a fire alarm if it didn't trust the source.

So no. That didn't make sense.

Okay, wait—

Let's say, the hookup created it, bounced it around, sent it to himself— herself?—and then sent it on to Cobie from the burner identity. Yeah, maybe. That might work. And as soon as Cobie died, the burner identity would vanish.

Um, no. There'd be a record of the identity—there just wouldn't be a trackable source for it. It would probably have gone through the same maze of connections as the kink.

Hmm. Hm. Hm.

I might have to leave the office for this one.

Crap.

Okay. Time to put on my legs. I rolled over to the sideboard and waved at the walker. It lit up, stood up, took three steps forward and held itself in place. I lifted myself up from the roller, angled my thighs into position and dropped into the exo-legs. It took a moment for everything to settle into place, then I was ready to go—I could walk, run, stroll, stride, slide, saunter, stagger, shuffle, shamble, scramble, amble, toddle, totter, trot, truck, tango, boogie, march, waltz, polka, or pirouette. The pirouette would not be graceful, however—I'm not balanced for it.

@

There are things I know how to do, but it's cheaper and easier and faster to hire someone else for certain tasks.

I went to see Miranda.

No, not in person. Nobody sees Miranda in person. You go to a public access, an emporium, a café, never the same one twice. You get a private booth, you punch in the number Miranda has given you, then you wait. Miranda gives a different number to each of her customers, that's how she knows who's calling—by what line you come in on.

If Miranda wants to talk to you, the screen flashes with another number—a burner, a proxy, a labyrinth. You take that to another booth, not close by either, tap that and you're connected. Or not. Sometimes Miranda will take you through two, three, a dozen separate burner-tracks.

If you don't follow Miranda's rules, if you try to trace Miranda, if you ask the wrong questions, you get permanently blocked. Miranda disappears from your world. Forever. Instead of a number, you get a "no results" screen. And no, you can't go through proxies either, human or otherwise—once you're blocked, you're blocked. Miranda's a tracker. If she blocks you, she assumes you're an enemy and she watches you very carefully.

Some people speculate that Miranda's not human, just a very good A.I. Or maybe she's a conglomerate. She could be, she charges enough—I don't speculate. I just pay for her services.

Miranda lit up quickly. Today, her avatar was a very skeptical Bette Davis. Very Margo Channing, cigarette holder and all. "Cobie Ferguson," she said.

"Yes."

"You want him deep-traced, all transactions. Meatspace tracking, Endless City, and any associated activities. How far back?" She took a puff for effect.

"A year should do it."

"Six months should be enough," she said. "But I'll look for anomalies at least three years back. That's the larger window of probability. Anything else?"

"Special focus on relationships, please. I'm looking for motives."

"Of course. I'll send you an invoice. Do you want a cap on expenses?"

I considered it. "The client is covering the cost."

She paused. She was searching. "The client can afford it. No problem." Another pause. "Interesting. The client prepared for his own murder. I'll include all of that too. It'll be waiting for you when you get home. You might want to fasten your seat belt. It's going to be a bumpy ride." She clicked off, leaving me wondering if she was being sarcastic, or if that had been a warning.

I found out soon enough.

@

My physical office is in a building identical to the one in Endless City. The interior is a match as well, a dusty corner office with a couple of dirty file cabinets and various framed papers on the wall.

It's a deliberate match, another part of the performance. Everything is performance. I haven't been inside the building in seven months.

In truth, I'm in the building across the street and two floors down. In the afternoons, I park myself at the corner table of the outdoor café. I have a lettuce-and-tomato sandwich on whole wheat and coffee while I study the news. I don't see clients in meatspace, only in the City. Realtime is for research.

My professional persona is a burner identity, constructed on top of several proxies. Miranda could trace the path, I doubt anyone else could—probably she already has, otherwise she wouldn't have taken my business. I'm pretty sure a lot of what Miranda does is too deep in the wires to be legal, but I'm too smart to ask.

I pulled out a burner pad and downloaded Miranda's reports. As soon as I tapped to open the file, the second floor of the building across the street—my office—blew up. The corner windows shattered outward, south and east, gouts of fire and glass and smoke, knocking down pedestrians, sending cars skidding and screeching.

Nice. Very nice.

Another clue. Someone didn't want me to read Miranda's report. Someone smart enough to know I would link to Miranda, but not smart enough to know that my office was a Potemkin. Obviously, someone who spends too much time in Endless City. Someone smart enough to put a tracker on Miranda—she wasn't going to like that. Unless this was her doing. Whatever. I couldn't trust her again. Not until this was sorted out. One way to find out if she was responsible—call her and see if I'm blocked. But that would have to wait till later.

I got up quickly, and headed toward the back of the café, not so fast as to draw attention, but fast enough to disappear from the scene. Out through the kitchen, past the dishwashers, into the alley, two doors down, and in, up the back stairs. I had maybe two minutes, I needed only one—

Stepped in, hit the red button on the wall, opened the closet, pushed the side wall of the closet open, stepped through to the matching closet of the apartment on the other side. Behind me, an entire identity was evaporating. Everything. It would take less than thirty seconds to shred that existence.

This apartment was intentionally bare. Merely a transfer station. I stripped off my clothes, dropped everything—all my hardware too—into the shredder, then naked back into the closet—touched the wall the right way and the floor dropped me into the closet of the apartment below, then slapped back into place. An easy fall, I bounced on the trampoline

Overkill? Yes. Searchers would certainly find the first escape route, they'd assume I'd changed clothes and gone out the back door.

By the time they realized that was a dead end, I should be on the other side of the city, on my way out of the state.

Padded to the shower, pulled myself out of my exo-legs, hung onto the grips, and punched for decontamination. Went through the cycle three times, prayed it would be enough, and waited for the blowers to finish drying me.

I hated to lose the legs, they were expensive and I hadn't finished breaking them in, but I couldn't trust them anymore. I couldn't even buy another set. If they—the mysterious "they"—were tracking buyers, the same set of legs would be a big red arrow pointing at me.

I whistled for—god, I hate them, but no choice—the fat lady. Two flubbery dark elephant props. Not graceful, but...you want to be invisible, be a fat black lady waddling off to some night job cleaning toilets for people who think their money deodorizes their turds. The disguise took a while, too many parts to it—the fat suit, the dress, the hidden compartments in the legs, under the tits, under the folds of flesh, even behind the big fat ass, and a few other places too—and then power up the new identity, hoping to hell it hasn't already been compromised, grab the purse and two huge shopping bags that pass for luggage when you're scraping poor—

If it got me out of the city, it was fine. I'd pass through at least two more identities before I came up for air and looked around. Four blocks away, a circuitous route, there was a recycling station—the fat lady would go in, a teenage screwhead would wander out, a skinny junkie-hustler with a peg below the knee. He'd shamble aimlessly for a while, then take the tube north toward the Jumble, and somewhere in there he'd vanish too. Max Blankman—not his real name—just a transfer identity would catch a train or a bus or maybe a ferry across the river—

And three days from now, a fluffy little old lady with a couple of robot cats would purchase a little pink gazebo in Lavender Meadows. Her wife had died a few months previously and she still hadn't figured out what to do with the rest of her life. Zoe Elaina Kilmartin had been a librarian once, a specialist in arcane research of all kinds. Occasionally she still accepted part-time work from authors and filmmakers, so she maintained a T-3 bandwidth.

Lavender Meadows was not specifically part of Endless City, but it used some of the same data-pipes. A skilled wirehead could proxy through. Of course, Ms. Kilmartin couldn't possibly know that the access in her gazebo had been proxied by a skilled wirehead several years before—and any deep search of her hardware would reveal that most of the research jobs she'd taken on were deliciously kinky, but nowhere near dangerous or illegal. But, oh those proxies—

If they held up even a week, they'd be gold.

@

I could afford it, but I was still pissed. Disappearing, transferring, reinventing—it was time-consuming, it was expensive. And I was no closer to solving the case. If anything, the case had gotten far more complicated.

Someone had found a perversely ingenious way to commit murder—he or she or whatever had killed Cobie Ferguson. But Cobie Ferguson had found out somehow. He'd discovered he was in danger—and he must have taken steps to protect himself, but just in case he'd also taken care to provide for the subsequent investigation. He'd put a lot of key pieces in place—he'd hired me. But he didn't know who the murderer would be, that was weird in itself, and now someone—probably the same murderer, but don't make assumptions—had tried to stop me from investigating.

Had to think about that. I'd assumed that the person who'd planted the bomb wasn't smart enough to find me in meatspace—but what if I was mistaken about that? What if he was—and the bomb wasn't an attempt to kill me, just scare me off?

But...no, I don't get scared off. Not that easily. If anything, the disruption of my business, the destruction of a carefully constructed identity, had pissed me off—enough that I was more committed than ever to crack this one.

I still had Miranda's report. I'd relayed it to a safe haven, scanned it and stripped it of all tracking macros. Now, I finally had time to study it in depth.

Miranda's research had been thorough, but it still didn't reveal much. Cobie's online identity was respectable, too respectable—obviously he'd run himself through a cleaning service, probably several. There weren't any connections that called attention to themselves either. Probably, the circles he moved in, they all had continuing cleaning services.

I sat in the little pink gazebo, studying the wraparound display, frowning to myself, tapping my teeth, and saying some very unladylike things.

Miranda's reports were always hyper-detailed. Sometimes she pointed out interesting anomalies. Sometimes she left them for me to discover myself. And sometimes they just leapt out of the display and shouted, "Here I am!"

Let's start with an assumption, a logical one—that whoever planned to kill Cobie Ferguson had been tracking his movements, stalking him in Endless City, stalking him in meatspace. So, if we track Cobie's movements for the past six months and expand that to include an area-search of everyone who passed within his local radius, eliminating all the randoms, minimizing the residents, we should be able to reveal any unusual patterns that are semi-congruent with Cobie's. Every traffic-cam, every security monitor, every smartphone, every ad-tracker, every functioning device plugged into the net, and every app on all of those devices—every photo or video or audio captured within Cobie's radius was rawdata if you had the resources to tap into all those separate data-feeds. Miranda did—and had.

Eezy-peezy, right?

Wrong.

Because the next part of the assumption was that if someone could upload "Death by Oompah" to a high-end sextable, they'd also be smart enough to know that simply stepping out onto a public street would create a permanent record of their every movement. Their every step and gesture—every fart, sneeze, and exhalation—would be logged somewhere. There would be only one protection—a blocking field.

Blockers are usually licensed to celebrities, politicians, corporate leaders, billionaires, and various government agencies. Ordinary citizens have to demonstrate a compelling need—witness protection, stalkers, restraining orders, that kind of stuff. Anyone else has to pay a hefty premium—because why would you want to hide your movements if you weren't doing something unlawful?

A blocking field interrupts the local flow of packets associated with your image, your voice, your location, everything. All the data going back and forth between your devices and the rest of the world is triple-encrypted. You show up on the displays as an empty space.

But even an empty space reveals a lot—especially if it's ambulatory.

If the blot tracks to the restroom, did it center on the men's, the ladies', the neuts', or the morphs'? That's useful information. If the blot goes into a store, what kind of a store? Clothing? Male? Female? Uni? If the blot moves from here to there—did it take a bus? A taxi? The tube? What does that tell you about its income? Does it suburb or supra? Or does it disappear into the Jumble—that's another slice of information. Just finding the home-locus of the blot is critical. If the blot abruptly disappears—who's in the suddenly revealed space, there's your list of suspects. Track them now.

If the blot doubles back, twists and turns, moves across the map in an erratic pattern to make sure it isn't being followed, it still gives itself away. It reveals it has a secret to hide.

Just one problem.

Yes, there was a blot—but it wasn't following Cobie Ferguson. It *was* Cobie Ferguson. Every time it shut down, there was Cobie. No other suspects.

Miranda was good. Cobie thought he'd been careful, he'd only shut down his blocker when he thought he was in the presence of other blockers. But Miranda tracked everyone leaving the blank areas and Cobie's presence was the only repeating factor.

Well, crap.

The case just got a whole lot weirder. I was now looking for an invisible murderer—one who wasn't blotted but still didn't show up in any data-feeds. One who could track his target even when the target was inside a blot.

Okay, let me think about this. If the answer isn't in the evidence you're looking at, it has to be in the evidence you're not looking at. Miranda had brute-forced the raw data, she'd minimized all the randoms and all the residents, and anyone else who might have had business in the area.

So...the man or woman or newt that I was looking for was probably a shifter, like me—someone who could burn through a dozen identities in a week. A lot harder to track, but not impossible. It requires some pretty deep scanning, but you can find identities that are too shallow, too perfect, too well constructed—or just too good to be true.

Miranda had flagged identities she trusted, individuals who'd existed in her own databases for three years or longer. That eliminated more than half of the randoms. Others were minimally suspect candidates—too old, too young, physically disabled, medically impossible, emotionally unfit, intellectually impaired, chronically ill, and so on—all the different outliers.

And then there were the ones with big ripples—deep family ties, long-term business connections, anyone with a hint of celebrity, those were the least likely to be burners.

Burner identities tended to be disconnected, enclosed, not a lot of interaction with the rest of the world. Yeah, that includes a lot of shut-downs, introverts, hiders, and agoraphobes. And a lot of petty crooks, farmers, dealers, and distributors. But those are traceable too. The problem gets harder when you're dealing with pros. A good burner is usually connected to at least a few dozen other good burners to create the illusion of a life.

Miranda had eliminated at least two thirds of the randoms, leaving only two dozen on the list of possibles. Not a bad winnowing, but still a time-consuming effort.

Put that aside for a moment, consider something else instead. Why had Cobie blocked himself in meatspace? What was he hiding from? And as good as his blockware had been—and it was state-of-the-art—then how had he been tracked? The easy answer, the obvious one, was that he hadn't been tracked—he'd invited the killer in. And the killer had installed "Death by Oompah."

A thought occurred to me—

Yes, Miranda had uploaded Cobie's autopsy report.

Cobie had been hard-wired into the machine. He was getting direct stimulation to the brain's pleasure center. And just in case, his blood had high levels of pain blockers.

Cobie had died happy—very happy.

So...the murderer hadn't been vindictive. That suggested a whole other set of motives.

I leaned back in my chair—in meatspace. Mrs. Kilmartin did likewise in her pink gazebo.

There's this:

If you live in Endless City, everything is recorded. Everything. There is no privacy—anyone with a warrant can prowl.

If you retreat to meatspace, you can have the illusion of privacy. You can lock yourself in your apartment, live off the Basic, and have all your meals delivered.

But that's still not enough.

Every time you turn on the electricity, you leave a data-trail. Every appliance. Every light bulb. Every electrical socket. Everything. Everywhere.

If you go to the circuit box and flip all the breakers, that's still no defense. If you have anything in your pocket or your purse that runs off batteries, if it connects to anything else, if it taps into, if it reports, if it monitors—that's a data-trail too.

If you go lo-tech, disconnecting from the grid, generating your own life-support, you can still be observed—from the sky, from across the street, and even through the walls of the apartment next door. Lasers can read the vibrations on your window glass, thermal detectors can tell how many people are in the room, and microwaves can monitor your movements.

There is no privacy. There is no anonymity.

Put on a burka and walk down the street, you still leave a data-trail. Even if you wear a mask or a hood, cameras will still record your height, your gait, your body-movements, assembling a personality-pattern that will be matched with the paths you take, the purchases you make, the signs that catch your attention, everything.

Someone smart enough to be completely invisible would also have been smart enough to plan a perfect murder. He hadn't.

What's a perfect murder? One that doesn't get discovered, one that no one ever knows about—no one except the murderer.

So...Cobie's killer wanted the murder to be known. Why?

It didn't make sense.

Maybe the murderer wasn't invisible.

There was no evidence that Cobie had invited anyone into his penthouse apartment. There was no trace. No physical evidence. No data-trail. Nothing.

And there was no evidence of anyone leaving afterward, not even a blot.

Which brought me back to the first question...how did "Death by Oompah" get into Cobie's sextable?

Malware? Not with Cobie's level of hardware. He would have had multiple state-of-the-art firewalls. So he would have had to install it himself....

Did he think it was "Frat Boy Shenanigans"—or did he know it wasn't?

Because—the son of a bitch had been wired in like a screwhead and narked like a man strapped to an execution table. It was painless because he wanted it to be painless.

Son of a bitch.

But why then, follow that train of thought, it doesn't make sense...would he want me to investigate a murder that didn't happen? And why would he blow up my office?

Unless...

That was a little far-fetched, but—

All right, back to Miranda's reports. There was something I'd missed.

But now I knew what I was looking for. I had to backtrace the movements of Cobie's blot, only a few days were needed—he'd taken a trip, not too far, but far enough. He'd gone to a place where his blot overlapped with another blot. Then the other blot disappeared. They'd merged. Then his blot went home.

So...backtrace that other blot—and it goes all the way back to the Jumble.

Crap.

And crap again.

Mrs. Zoe Elaina Kilmartin said some very bad words and winked out of her beautiful pink gazebo.

I'd need to switch to a burner identity. Hell, I'd probably have to burn through half a dozen.

This was going to take some thought, and some careful preparation.

@

The Jumble is all proxies and untraceables. The whole area is blotted—it's splattered with multiple overlapping blots. And they stack.

There are few visible cues. Endless City is woven in and out of its structure so deep, it's impossible to navigate without plugins.

Nothing is what it seems. Nobody is who they pretend to be. If Endless City is one relentless performance, the Jumble is its physical counterpart. It's Kowloon's Walled City reborn—with a vengeance. The Jumble exists where three, or maybe more, jurisdictions fail to overlap—each one retreating from the responsibility of governance. The result is a hole in the fabric of responsibility, a gigantic ungoverned enclave, sprawling like a cancerous amoeba across several square kilometers of broken terrain. Ancient buildings lean against each other for support, bridges to nowhere span the gaps and canyons, cables and tubes, balconies turned into shops, staircases transformed into vertical habitats, banners and canopies everywhere, tangles of wires leading every which way, vertical farms of all kinds, blankets for walls, ladders, rickety staircases, an ancient aqueduct, twisting alleys wind through various pretenders to street level, and beneath everything abandoned tubeways where trains no longer run, crumbling sewers, the whole a tottering slum, clinging to unfinished concrete towers, a gaping triangular spire, heli-decks, windmills, and open catch-barrels for the monsoon rains—a wild collection of humanity, clustered in its walls, morphs and newts, cross-players, gendernauts, inflatos, slendermen, barbies, twinkles, bearables, mandroids, femminoids, remods, rejuves, sportsters, shifters, grifters, xenoids, saleables, whatevers—there's no directory. If you have to ask, you don't want it badly enough.

The Jumble is a self-contained paradox, simultaneously the most connected and the most disconnected place in the urban sprawl. It exists, it continues to exist because no authority wants responsibility of the physical realm, no agency dares to attempt cyber-control—not any more. No one wants the economic burden, the legal burden—no one wants to inherit the morass of the Jumble's bizarre societies and ungovernable residents. In short, no one knows what to do with it, so the Jumble exists, a great machine of self-evolving survival.

Within its walls, the Jumble is anything and nothing, sanctuary, brothel, casino, hideaway, drug den, fantasyland, shops of all kinds—tattoo artists, mutation parlors, transformatories, fetish-holes, meal-vendors, cafes, tailors, bootmakers, indigo marketplaces, purple holes, exo-printers, fabbers, xeno-labs, crack-doors—everything. The Jumble has its own unwritten rules, you're safe as long as you follow them. Don't take what isn't yours. Don't ask what you don't need to know. Don't go where you have no business. Whatever you want or need, it's here—buy or trade, cash only, no credit. No wires, no traces, thank you. Next, please?

Old identities disappear into the Jumble. New ones come out. And Cobie Ferguson had done a lot of business here. The money wasn't traceable, but Miranda's data-diving had revealed large sums converted into cash over a three year period. Gambling losses, he said, but there weren't many trips to the Endless City casinos—none that could be tracked. No, he told his taxman that he gambled in the Jumble. There were certain games within its walls not available anywhere else. The taxman didn't ask for details—and if he had, Cobie wouldn't have answered. Because he wasn't gambling. You didn't stay as rich as Cobie Ferguson if you had that kind of gambling habit. No, he was investing in something else—not illegal if you intend to use it legally, but definitely illegal if you don't.

There were only three practitioners of this art in the Jumble— well, only three that I knew of—but only one of them had a reputation for clean hands. I'd start with Her. Him. Whatever. Depending on the moment. Because there was no Him, Her, or Whatever—there was only the convenient avatar, created for the day and worn by whichever member of the crew was on desk duty.

Max Blankman got off the tube at 13:13 o'clock. Not deliberate, just ironic. The Max Blankman ID was a public domain, open-source identity. Anyone could wear it. It wasn't suspicious, unless it was. Usually it was as innocuous as a Charles Manson T-shirt on a recently liberated teener. (Hint: The revolution is not a fashion statement.) If you were serious about hiding out, you didn't go as Blankman, not Max, not Minnie, not any of their offspring.

He. She. Whatever did not have a name. Like Miranda, access was exclusive. I had it, because I had money to spend. Enough. Most people don't have that advantage. Most people never have enough. And it collapses their thinking from "I don't have enough" into "I am not enough." It's that kind of mindset that keeps me in business, provides me with customers. I should be grateful, but I'm not. I spend too much time with the wrong kind of people.

Goggled, half in meatspace, half in Endless City, I made my way quickly through the Jumble. Worst thing you can do is hesitate. All the signs, all the rules and warnings, all the directions, all the arrow-trails were available only in the Endless City overlay—you saw only the overlays you were allowed to see. I saw a much more intricate and complex map than most people. This iteration of Max Blankman was probably getting a lot of attention because of that. Somewhere— a lot of somewheres—a lot of someones were poking someone else and saying, "Hey, look at this, we've got a Max who can see us."

There must have been a hundred sets of eyes on me, my only protection. Nobody was going to assault me with that many witnesses.

I followed a blinking red arrow up an escalator, one of the few that worked, the rest were just stairs, halfway up, then right along "the becauseway"—called that not because it was a causeway, but because it was a "becauseway." Because. You either got it, or you didn't. Maybe you had to be there.

Stopped at a noodle shop, put a copper coin on the counter and ducked behind the curtain, still following the blinking arrow, through six interleaved apartments, then out onto a balcony overlooking a steep atrium—I'd never seen this before, didn't even know it was here. But the red arrow never led me the same way twice.

Once, the balconies had been separate domains. Now the railings were gone, makeshift platforms linked them all, one to the next, and it was an elevated walkway. All the way around to the other side, then right turn through a meet-rack where naked avatars lounged along a railing. The double-vision of meatspace revealed the unappetizing truth—another reason why sexbots and sextables had become so popular. If you could afford them. If not, avatar-whores were cheap.

Up, down, around, in, out—the arrow finally led me to a simple dark room. Yellow silk drapes, artfully decorated with dancing and reclining and copulating naked people, all combinations, all positions. Red paper lanterns. I could have been in the foyer of an expensive Happy House, where unique designer fantasies were created for wealthy aesthetes with specific erotic tastes. Well, yes. I was.

There were two backless chairs in the room. Padded cylinders, one on each side of a low table. A Eurasian boy came in carrying a ceramic tea service on a wooden tray. He couldn't have been more than thirteen. He was beautiful, dressed in a soft red kilt and a flowing white shirt. His avatar flawlessly matched his physical presence. He sat down opposite me and placed the tray exactly between us with mathematical precision. Then he carefully, meticulously poured tea into two small red cups. Steam rose like a warning.

He folded his hands into his lap and waited patiently. I took the closest cup. I cradled it in my palms so as to minimize the heat coming off it. I inhaled the fragrance of the steeping leaves. I returned the cup to the table without drinking. I only look stupid.

"I have questions," I said.

The boy was impassive. He waited.

"I want to know if something is possible."

I knew I wasn't speaking to the boy. I was speaking to his puppeteer. He was a Cyranoid—taking his instructions from someone offsite. His features were perfect, his skin was pink and golden and shining—as clear as porcelain. His hair was pure blue-black and shining. His eyes were stunning blue. His physical presence was already an answer to my question.

When the boy spoke, his voice was lyrical. He said quietly, "You're here. Therefore you have permission. Ask."

"How much would it cost to grow a body? A life-size clone. How long would it take?"

A pause. "You did not ask if such a thing is possible."

"I already know it's possible. I want to know how much and how long."

The boy hesitated, listening to his master again. "We can grow fully functioning new legs onto your stumps in six months."

"That's not the question I asked. How much for a whole body? Head and brain included."

"You do not have a life-threatening disease. All of your organs are functioning well. You will have no need of an organ replacement for at least a decade or longer."

"How much? How long?"

"For what purpose do you need a clone of yourself?"

Now it was my turn to pause while I considered my reply. How much should I say?

"Even a small meat-tank is big enough for a full-size male body," I began. "Scanning and sampling is less than an hour. You can print the collagen matrix in three days. Two weeks to grow and seed the stem cells. I'm guessing two months for the bones, four to six months for organ maturity and function, the last three will be spent exercising and toning the various muscle groups. Six months, right?"

The boy didn't answer.

"As for costs? Okay, there's the cost of nutrients, that's minimal. Tank rental, again minimal. Security—that's not minimal. Skillage required to manage the various processes, I'm guessing six to ten specialists, maybe another twelve assistants for scut-work. Plus all the different bits and pieces of equipment, the bots, the maintenance, the electricity, plus overhead—" I quoted a number.

The boy did not reply. His failure to react was just as informative as if he had spoken.

Finally. "What you ask is possible." Another pause. "However..."

"Yes?"

"Your cost estimate is too low. We would have to establish a specific facility. You would have to assume that overhead." He quoted a number.

"I see. Your current operations are at capacity?"

The boy didn't answer.

It didn't matter. That he had actually quoted a price told me what I needed to know. He. She. Whatever. Didn't offer a service unless they could deliver it. That meant they'd already done it. At least once and probably more than once. And probably enough times that their tanks were full and they had a waiting list. And as soon as they found a customer desperate enough to pay for the cost of a new facility, they'd move him to the head of the line.

I nodded. "I will get back to you on this. I'm only the agent of inquiry."

I left the tea untouched on the table, a terrible insult, but one I had to risk. The other risk was greater. If they—the mysterious "they"—were capable of tracking Miranda's feed to me and blowing up my office, might they also be just as capable of tracking me here?

In any other case, the unfinished tea would have been a signal that our business was not yet complete, but here in the Jumble it implied a darker message. I do not trust you.

Max Blankman disappeared on the southward train. I shadowed with a traveling blot for several blocks, changing clothes and posture and the gait of my legs, as I went. Reversed my jacket, pulled up the hood, popped on disposable goggles, deflated the fat suit by ten kilos, and a few other tricks I don't like sharing.

So...now I knew. Ninety percent certain anyway. Cobie hadn't died. He'd faked his own death.

He'd grown a clone, perhaps even swapped most of his organs for fresh ones, then murdered the donor in his place. It would have been a perfect crime, but at the last moment, Cobie must have developed some kind of emotional bond. He couldn't bear to cause his donor-toddler any pain. So he'd killed it painlessly.

That was his mistake. A real murderer would have wanted the victim to suffer.

Okay, next question. Why had Cobie gone to so much trouble? Why did he need to go invisible?

Only one way to answer that question.

Ask Cobie.

Right. Find the invisible man. Eezy-peezy. He's only got a three-day lead.

If I go back to Miranda—she'll know I'm still alive. She probably already knows, but maybe not. If Miranda planted the bomb, then contacting her lets her know she failed—but how could she have planted the bomb so quickly? So, probably it wasn't Miranda. It would have had to have been Cobie.

Okay, ninety percent sure it was Cobie who blew up my office— the space I pretended was my office. But why? Why kill the guy you've just hired to investigate the fake murder you've staged?

Ah—that one's almost obvious. You kill him to keep him from discovering the murder was staged. And it clouds the investigation with another false track.

God, I'm good.

Or stupid.

But Cobie had distracted me. The way he'd crossed his perfect legs so perfectly—and I'd bought into it. I'd had so many clients who were painfully shallow, I'd begun to believe they all were. Cobie might have set me up, but he had my help.

Time to call Miranda.

It took me a while to get through, she bounced me through a dozen numbers and three calling locations, the most I'd ever experienced, but finally—

Morticia Gomez. The Anjelica Huston iteration. "You've been compromised," she said.

"Yeah, I noticed."

She said, "Your office line was tapped. About two weeks ago. A very sophisticated piece of work. The tap didn't go active until after Cobie died—"

I thought about telling her it wasn't Cobie, decided to wait until she finished. The bomb had been planted the same time as the tap. The tap itself was a physical device attached to the line outside the building. Once the bomb went off, the tap self-destructed. It would have looked like part of the bomb damage. Except it left software traces of itself in the system. "A very sophisticated piece of work," Miranda said. "But shallow. The cleanup wasn't deep enough. The author didn't realize that I was monitoring your feeds."

"For how long?"

"Long enough to notice there were hiccups in your reception."

"So you knew about the bomb?"

"I knew about the tap. The bomb was a surprise."

"The tap triggered it."

"I made a mistake. I assumed the trigger was simply an alert. I was wrong."

"I could have been killed."

"Yes. That would have ruined my whole day. I hate losing customers."

"Thank you for your concern."

"So—are we looking for the bomber now?"

"No. Yes. We're looking for Cobie Ferguson." I told her about the clone farms in the Jumble.

"I'm aware of the practice. Most of the clones have been organ donors, several have been sexual partners. Two have been used for vicarious revenge. This would have been the first murder—or staged murder. But you have no direct evidence."

"No. What I have is a hunch."

"Yes?"

"Cobie was—is—rich. Rich people don't abandon their wealth. They take it with them. They're stupid that way. Follow the money."

"That's not a hunch," Miranda said. "That's logic."

"Anyway, that's my question. Where is Cobie's money?"

"The report is on its way." She added, "To your current account."

"I have to ask. Are there any taps?"

"None that I am aware of. Nevertheless, you should stay alert."

"Thank you."

It turned out that Cobie didn't have wealth. He had *access* to wealth. Those are two very different things.

I have access to wealth. I know. I have multiple client accounts I draw on. As long as I can present an auditable invoice for billable hours, as long as my maintenance expenses remain reasonable, as long as I spread the expenses across multiple accounts, I have access to wealth.

In return for my services, which are considerable.

As Cobie Ferguson was about to find out.

I parked myself in realtime in the middle of a crowded plaza, and plugged into Miranda's findings. Cobie had been a beneficiary of three trusts and two foundations. He drew from two of those resources. Now all I had to do was find out who else was drawing and how much—and where they were now.

If Cobie was smart, he would have plugged in his alternate identity some time ago and created a financial backstory. But again—the giveaway was how far the ripples had spread.

The details are irrelevant. It was mostly a process of elimination.

I found Cobie in the next penthouse up. That was why we had no record of him—blotted or otherwise—leaving his building. He hadn't. He'd burned his past and walked up one flight of stairs.

I knocked on the door.

After a moment, he opened it. He was wearing a silk dress, a kimono. No makeup. Just a crossplayer at home. He looked nothing like his avatar, just an ageless young-old man. He looked down the hall past me, both ways, then stepped aside to let me in. "That was fast."

"You were stupid." I walked into the apartment. It wasn't bare, but it wasn't lived in yet either. I turned around to face him. "The surgery went okay?"

He shrugged. He looked tired. "I'm still adjusting." Then, "Where did I screw up?"

"At the beginning."

"Is it a long story?"

"No."

He looked disappointed. "You want something to drink?"

"I'm fine," I said.

He went to the bar anyway, picked up the soda gun, and filled a tall glass with super-carbonated water. He hesitated before putting the soda gun down.

I said, "Your blocker isn't as good as you think it is. Miranda is recording everything. So if you're still thinking about shooting me with whatever is concealed in that soda gun, I wouldn't recommend it."

He sighed, shrugged, picked up his glass, and walked over to one of two black leather chairs. He sat down in one, gestured at the other.

"No thanks, I'll stand." I took an envelope out of my pocket. "Here's an invoice for my services. And an additional contract. You're buying my silence. It's not exorbitant. You can afford it. It's certainly cheaper than any of your other options." I tossed it at him, he let it fall to the black coffee table between the chairs.

"Really?" He looked skeptical.

"Really," I assured him. "It's certainly cheaper than killing me."

He sipped at his water. He leaned forward and put the glass on the table. He picked up the envelope. He opened it and studied the two papers, first one, then the other. He nodded. "You're fair. I'll give you that. I'll set up an automatic payment."

"Thank you." But I didn't head for the door.

"Is there something else?"

"Maybe. It's up to you."

"How much?"

"That's the right question to ask." I crossed to the bar, hefted the soda gun, studied the buttons for a moment, then filled a glass of my own. I carried it to the chair opposite him, sat down and drank.

"Let's say that I have a pretty good idea who's after you. What's it worth to you to stop them?"

He studied me for a long moment. "You are good."

"I did the job you hired me to do. You said after I found the murderer, I'd know what to do. You were right. I do know what to do. Do you want me to do it?"

"Tell me more."

"The expansion is going to be approved. It's going to be a very large expansion. Good for some. Bad for others. The horizontal and vertical equators are going to cut through some valuable territory. The value of land bordering the new equators is going to go up. But the value of certain other parcels divided by the equators will collapse. Even if all the petitions for adjustments are approved, it's still going to be ugly. Some people are going to make a lot of money. Others are going to lose a lot."

"Every screwhead on the street knows that. They're all scrambling for advantage. Tell me something I don't know."

"You have pro-rata shares in more than a thousand cyber-properties, spread across a hundred different holding companies—your share is funneled through five financial instruments, of which you've only been tapping two. You've been keeping a very low profile for a long time—probably because if you die, some other people's shares will increase. In most cases, only a point or two. But in a couple of other cases, as much as 20% will be divided among the survivors. Enough to make your death a lucrative proposition. Your staged death does not alleviate the danger, because you've assigned your shares to a new holding identity, funneling the dividends through another set of instruments until they finally arrive here. All you've done is prolong the search and delay the inevitable. Those who want you dead are going to follow the money, just like I did. And...my guess is that they have access to even more sophisticated resources than I do."

"Then why haven't they found me yet?"

"Because—" I counted off the reasons for him, "First, they're trying to figure out which of them killed you. It'll take them two or maybe three days to convince themselves that none of them got their hands dirty. Two, they're not going to believe it was suicide either, because—three, as soon as they discover your shares are not being divided among themselves, but were presold to a holding identity, that will lead them directly to four—that you are still alive and hiding out, at which point, five, they will start searching in earnest. This is clever—plugging into your own security, you've been able to watch every stage of the investigation. But—as clever as you are, six—guys like me do this for a living. We know all the tricks, usually because we invented most of them ourselves."

"How long do I have?"

"I got in, didn't I? If they're not already landing on the roof, they will be sometime in the next three days. They're not stupid."

"But you're smarter?"

"No, I'm not. I'm just faster. I don't have to take as many meetings to explain what I'm doing. Whoever is searching for you probably has to report to a committee. The committee has to argue for a while before approving the next step. That's why you're still alive. Shall we go?"

"Huh?"

"You're not safe here. If I could find you, a three year old could. It would just take a little longer. Now, seven—let's go. I assume you have your next hideout prepared? We'll start there, just long enough to muddy the trail, then I'll take you through the labyrinth. That'll buy us time for what comes next—the messy part."

There were two golems in the hall. I burned them from behind, I'm not proud, I'm a survivor. Cobie gave me a look—he didn't have to say it. Where the hell did that come from? Your scan came up clean. "Trade secret," I explained.

And we were off.

This was going to be a bigger job than I expected. I was already counting shekels in my head. I could make enough to retire.

Except guys like me, we don't retire. We just keep going until the some other guy catches up—because that's how it works in Endless City.

Dancer In The Dark

When Ma finally died, they said they didn't have a place for me and it wasn't safe in the city anymore, so they decided it would be best to send me somewhere west where I could live on a farm. They said I would like it. Hard work and sunshine. And I'd get over Ma's death in no time. You'll see. They said.

They put me on a train with a whole bunch of other tight-faced people and went away. The train sat in the station for half a day, all of us waiting scared, before it finally chugged out. It was cold and shivery in the car, and there wasn't much to eat. You could get a drink from the faucet, but the water tasted funny.

Out the window, there was a lot of smoke, and where there wasn't smoke, there was burnt-out buildings, some old, and some still smoldering. I never been on a train before, I thought they went faster than this, but no, this was all stop-and-go, mostly stopping and waiting. And when we did go, we went slow, like the driver was being careful to watch the tracks to make sure they was still there. Once we went real slow through a corridor of burning buildings.

I was stuck way in the back behind a family, sort of, with a couple of older sisters and a lot of young-uns, except they weren't a real family because they wasn't related. They was just traveling together, and the older sisters weren't sisters at all, they was just supposed to keep the little-uns together. The kids all stunk real bad, they didn't have any clean clothes, and they'd pissed and crapped themselves, more than once. And they cried a lot, trying to keep warm. So I just turned to the window and stared out at whatever there was to see, which wasn't very much because once we got away from the big towns, the dark was spread real thick in a lot of places.

Mostly the dark looked like black fuzziness floating in the air. I'd never been inside the dark, but I heard stories. Everybody heard stories. It's like being shoved inside a thick blanket, you can't see, you can't hear, you can't breathe, and you just stumble around blind. It has something to do with the dark making it hard for things to move, like light or air or blood through your veins. You lay down a couple miles of dark around something and nobody can get through, no matter how much tinfoil they're wearing on their head.

Somebody else said that the whole country was sectioned off now. Dark everywhere. The trains ran through special corridors with walls of dark on each side, just enough room for the tracks and nothing else. You could maybe jump off the train, it wasn't going very fast, but so what? You couldn't get through the walls of dark, you couldn't go anywhere except follow the tracks. So you might as well stay on the train.

Sometime in the middle of the second night, we got to our first stop and they took some of the people off. There was all kinds of dark here, all around everything, even above so we couldn't even look up and see the stars. We didn't know where we were. Even though everybody was real tired, they woke us all up while all these men in different uniforms came marching through. They looked like soldiers from five or six different armies. They pointed at people in their seats. You, you, not you, not you, yes, yes, no, no, and so on. Another man in a different kind of uniform, I think he was the train conductor, came running after them, shouting about how they couldn't just take only the workers, they had to take a balanced cross-section, otherwise it wasn't fair.

I was hoping they'd take me, I wanted off the train real bad, I didn't care where we were. I even asked one of the soldier-men to pick me, but he shook his head and said I was too skinny. I tried asking a couple of the others, but they ignored me, so I slumped back down and pulled my blanket up and tried to go back to sleep. There wasn't nothing else to do. I was hungry and cold and stinky and not feeling too good inside. But at least there was some empty seats now and if you had one next to you, you could stretch out.

We had two more stops the next day, one just before noon, and the other late in the afternoon. Each time, another bunch of soldiers came through and took off some more people. After the last stop, there was almost nobody left on the train so they made us all move to the last car. They didn't say why. But probly because it was easier to watch us all in one place.

When they woke us up again, it was still dark. Darkfield dark. I couldn't tell what time it was, somebody said it was 3:30 in the morning. They made us gather up all our things, I didn't have much to gather, and then they herded us off the train and into a fluorescent station. The light hurt my eyes and the room smelled real strong of that disinfectant they use everywhere now. There was a red line across the room and we weren't allowed to cross it. On the other side, there was a line of grumpy-looking people, farmers and townsfolk. I guess they didn't like getting out of bed at this hour either. They looked us up and down like we were something bad-smelling. I guess we were. Every so often, I sort of got a whiff of myself. I felt dirty and itchy, and I wanted a bath or even a shower. My feet hurt and I was shivering in my blanket.

The guy who looked like the conductor read a statement to the folks on the other side of the line, something about what they was agreeing to and how they had to treat us, stuff like that. They all looked bored, like they'd heard it all before. Then he read another statement to us on this side of the line, about our rights and stuff and how we didn't have to go if we didn't want to, but we couldn't refuse either. Which didn't make any sense.

And then they started letting people pick us. A big farmer pointed at one of the skinny girls and asked her if she could cook and clean. She nodded, and he grunted and said, "Okay, come along," and she picked up her little suitcase and followed him. There was a sad-looking man and woman, they looked at the two littlest children and whispered together for a while, and then crossed the line and picked them up and left real quick, like they feared someone wouldn't let them take the babies.

It went like that for a while, until there weren't many of us left. There was this hard-looking woman standing across from me. She looked like she'd been baked in the sun until all the juice had been burned out of her and all that was left was this dry crunchy thing. She was looking at me like she couldn't make up her mind if I was worth the trouble. Finally, she said, "Boy? Are you gonna work, or you just gonna eat?"

"I can work," I said.

She walked over to the conductor and they talked together for a bit. He shook his head a lot. I got the feeling that I wasn't the first kid she'd picked out. And maybe the other one didn't work out. But finally, whatever, she came back and pointed at me and said, "Get your things." And that was it. I followed her out through the big double doors to a dirty parking lot surrounded by dark. A couple of tall light poles showed a few cars and the building we'd come out of and not much more than that.

"You got a name?"

"Folks call me Em."

"Em?"

"Yeah."

"Short for Emmett?" she asked.

"Em for Michael."

"Michael, yes. That's better than Em. You can call me Miz."

"Yes, Miz."

She pointed toward a beat-up old flatbed truck. She tossed my duffel into the back. I started to climb up after it, but she opened the door for me and said, "Get in."

We drove west on a road that was lined with dark. There might have been stars above, I couldn't tell. We had headlights, but they was mostly useless. They picked out the line of the road and that was all. She didn't say much and I didn't feel like talking either. I was too cold. I bunched up part of my blanket like a pillow and tried to rest my head against the window. It was worse than the train. We must have driven two hours. By the time we got where we were going, there was a feeling of light behind us. Hard to tell though, with all the dark.

Then there was a hole in the dark and she turned right and then left and then right again, and then we came out onto a big gray slope leading up to an old gray house. Behind it there was a dirty barn that had once been red, real tired-looking and leaning to one side, like it wanted to lie down, like if you gave it a good hard push, the whole thing would collapse, except there were a bunch of boards jammed in at an angle, propping it up so it couldn't. The old woman pointed. "You'll sleep in there. There's straw for a bed, and some old horse blankets. You can wash in the horse trough. Don't bother the cows. I start milking at six. I want you up and mucking out the stalls every morning. As soon as the cows are turned out. There's a couple barrels of disinfectant. You keep those stalls clean, you hear? As clean as you want your own bed—or your dinner plate. It's almost six now, so wash yourself up, you stink like a pig. Then get started. After milking, I'll bring you a plate. Don't want you in the house, boy. Lord knows what you're carrying."

"Yes, ma'm."

She stopped the car in front of the house, yanked on the parking brake real hard, like she was angry. "You like eggs? You ever had fresh eggs? Don't look like it. You're thinner than a ghost. When was the last time you ate?"

"Day before yesterday. I think. On the train, they gave us some leather to chew on."

"Damn fools. That's no way to treat anyone. Even deepies."

"Deepies?"

"Displaced Persons. DP's."

"Oh." Remembered my manners. "Thank you for takin' me in. I'll work real hard for you, ma'am."

She grunted. "Damn right you will. No free meals out here. Well, don't just sit there. We got work to do."

After milking and mucking, we pulled down a couple of bales of hay from the loft and broke them open for the cows. There was only three cows and they looked kinda sickly, but I don't know much about cows, so they coulda been fine too. But they walked real slow and stupid, like some of the people I'd seen in the city, the sick ones that they'd herd away every so often. But maybe that's how cows are. One of them looked at me for a bit, but she didn't look dangerous or anything, I didn't think you could make friends with a cow, so I just kept on shoveling cowshit.

Then there was the chickens, there was too many to count, they kept moving around all the time, bobbing their ugly little heads and clucking like old ladies. Miz poured out some corn for them and they all came cackling up. They was funny to watch. Later, after they'd finished the corn, they wandered around the fenced-in part of the yard, scratching for bugs and worms.

The biggest part of my job was feeding the refiner. This was three or four big metal tanks in a row, all piped together like a connected series of garbage disposals. I had to dump all the garbage into it every day, and everything else that wasn't nailed down—old corn stalks, dirty straw, stinkweeds, whatever. I had to scrape up the chicken guano and dump it in, plus wheelbarrow loads of cow manure and pig shit. Miz had indoor plumbing, but we both had to use the outhouse, because it pumped right into the refiner too. The methane that came off the top was piped around to fuel the stove at the bottom. The refiner was a big stinky stew pot, simmering and bubbling, sometimes grinding and chewing. But I didn't mind working the refiner, except for the smell, it was the only time I was really warm.

At the far end, out came oil. Enough for the truck, enough for the water heater, enough to power the refiner for another few days. Sometimes there was even enough to sell the extra in town. What didn't get turned into oil, came out as mulch. And a scattering of metal bits and rock. The metal bits we saved for town. I had to check the refiner when I got up, twice during the day, and again before hitting the straw. Miz said if we had two more pigs, we'd be fat. But we didn't have enough corn to feed any more pigs. We were already too close to the bone, she said.

Out back of the house, Miz had a garden for vegetables, mostly stuff like tomatoes and potatoes and cucumbers and things like that. Some pumpkins and watermelons too. She also had a big patch of corn. Not a whole field, but enough to feed us and the chickens and even some for the cows. Like everything else though, the corn had a sickly look. "Hard to grow things when there isn't enough light for them. Not good for plants, not good for people either. Still, it's better'n dyin'." She sniffed. "One good thing about the dark, though. We don't get as many rabbits or foxes sneakin' in. They don't like the dark anymore than anyone else. But you still have to watch out for burrows, because sometimes they will dig under. Saturdays, we go to town and get whatever supplies they still got. Sometimes there's a movie, but don't be expectin' it. Sundays, we go to Meeting. When we get back from Meeting, you can have time by yourself. But you stay outta trouble. Stay away from the dark. Don't go darksniffin' like the last damnfool I had out here. And no, I ain't sayin' nothin' about that. And don't you go askin' no questions neither, if you're smart."

But I didn't have to ask no questions. There was plenty enough people willin' to tell me everthin' they knew. First time we went to town, while I was loadin' sacks of chemical fertilizer into the back of the truck. Town wasn't much, just a scattering of old buildings on one side of the old highway, like someone just dropped them there any which way. Surrounded by dark, of course. Only way in or out is through the corridors, that's three roads and the train tracks. So there's not a lot to see. Funny lookin' kid with a broken tooth comes up and says, "You Miz's new boy?"

"Guess so."

"You wanna be real careful. Not like Doey. She tell you what happened to him?"

"I know what I need to know," I said, pretending to ignore him.

"No, you don't. You're a city-boy. You don't know shit."

"I know enough to keep my nose outa other folks' business." I hefted the last sack in.

"You just stay out in the barn, boy, you know what's good for you. Come winter, she's gonna want you to come in and warm her bed, you'll see. Keep yourself, bad-smellin', that's what Doey did. Till he ran away—ran into the dark, he did."

Miz came out of the feed store then, saw the kid and her face got real fierce. He saw her the same time and skittered off like the rat he was. Miz came up to me and stared at me hard. "What'd that boy say?"

Already knew better than to lie. Miz wasn't easy even on the best of days. I just sorta shrugged. "He said you had another boy named Doey. He ran away."

"That all he said?"

"Yes, ma'm."

She sniffed like she didn't believe me, but she didn't push it. "Well, you stay away from that J.D. boy. He's bad news. That whole family is. Now get to work. Help me load all this."

Miz explained that the train had come through again, so today was a good day. Some of the stores had new things on the shelves, even some new magazines in the racks. Miz bought a couple, bought one for me too. "Readin' is good for you, as long as you don't do too much of it. Puts funny ideas into your head. You start daydreamin', you won't get your chores done."

She bought me some new jeans and a couple of work shirts, a pair of boots and some thick socks. For herself, she stocked up on spices; she was starting to run low, she even bought a bottle of vanilla.

"Might try makin' a cake or something. When was the last time you had cake?"

"Had a birthday party once, when I was little. My Ma bought a cake."

"Store-bought cake? Ain't the same. You get your chores done, I'll make you a cake so good you'll think you died and went to heaven."

Second time I heard about Doey was the next day at Meeting.

Meeting was a ways off, I couldn't tell how far, but we were driving for at least an hour, maybe more, down a long corridor of dark, all twisty, up and down, with a couple of sharp turnoffs into passages that felt even darker. When we got there, we weren't really anywhere, just a wide open space with an old school-looking building in the center of a hard-dirt clearing. The dark around was cut by seven different openings, but one of them was walled off with tall orange cones and Miz told me to stay well away from that one. I didn't ask why, she wouldn't have said anyway.

Inside, the room was gloomy, lit by kerosene lamps. No generator here. But it was warmer than outside and it was a chance to sit quiet-like and almost doze. It was kind of like church too, so you had to keep your eyes open. There were these old ladies up top all singin' real faraway and soft like they was a choir of angels or something. The music was real old-fashioned, but it wasn't too painful.

Then the mayor got up and talked about living the hard life and staying clean and trusting God and following the rules because the reason that things had gotten so bad was that so many people had stopped following the rules, and we'd all made a big mess of things, so now we had to do penance for a thousand years or more while we tried to put things back together the best we could, but the only way to do that was to stay away from the dark and follow the rules. He went on and on like that for a long time. Then there was some discussion of chores that had to be done in the coming days, including putting down some new dark lines just to the west. He asked for volunteers for a work crew.

After Meeting, some folks climbed back into their trucks and drove off right away. But most folks gathered for tea and little sandwiches and even a cake. It looked real pretty. And everybody stood around in their clean clothes and talked polite and pretended everything was going fine, which it wasn't, but nobody would say so, because nobody wanted to be accused of doing the devil's talk. But you could see it in their faces, all hard and narrow and pinched. The sandwiches and cake disappeared fast, some of these folks was hungry. Miz stopped me, wouldn't let me go to the table. She whispered, "You let that food be, son. It's not for us. It's for them that hasn't any. We have food at home. Some of these folks, this is their only meal today." So I went outside and stood around by the cars with the other men, just stood and listened.

"Hey you, new boy!" One of the men turned around and pointed to me. A big man. Beard. Overalls. A broken eye.

"Yeah?" I answered the good eye.

"You coming out with us, tomorrow? Help lay some dark lines?" I shrugged. "Dunno. Whatever Miz says."

"Miz'll say yes. If I ask her. Can I trust you to work? Not stand around?"

"I can work."

"You have to promise to stay away from the bright. And keep your glasses on. And don't take off your silver. That's how we lost the other one. Whatsisname. Doey. You heard about that?" He peered at me.

Didn't answer, just sorta shrugged again. Safest way. Better to have them think I'm stupid than wrong. You can get killed being wrong. That's a city lesson. But it might be true out here in the dark lands as well.

"He don't know shit," said someone else. "Just another dumb city-boy."

"He can carry. I'll talk to Miz. We need the hands. Besides, if we lose him, nobody'll care. Not even Miz. She'll just hook another one off the train."

And that was how it was decided that I should work on the dark team one or two days a week. I think Miz was glad to not have me around so much. There wasn't enough work to keep me busy every day. Or maybe she was just glad not to have to feed me. Sometimes the food was a little thin, even at her place. There just wasn't enough light. Somebody said that made everybody sad all the time. Depressed, he said. And then someone else told him to shut up. That was the devil's talk. Next he'd be complaining about the dark lines and the lines were the only things keeping them out. And then somebody said, "Not in front of him," meaning me, and that was the end of that conversation.

A few days later, an old truck pulled up in front of the house and a couple of workmen I didn't know got out and paid their respects to Miz. She handed them a paper bag with a bit of lunch in it, nowhere near enough to feed one hungry man, let alone three, but it was all she could spare. I climbed into the back of the pickup and made myself comfortable among the tools and wires.

We drove for half an hour, through the town, up the old highway for a while, and then off to the right where the corridor ended in orange cones. The workmen got out then and we all put on heavy black goggles and breathing masks and shiny silver capes and heavy work gloves. Then we drove on. The driver steered the truck carefully around the cones and up the passage to where the dark lines simply stopped. Beyond the lines, the ground rolled away like a rumpled gray bedsheet. There were already two other trucks here and five other men. One of them had a map rolled out on the hood of his truck and he was drawing lines with a crayon.

When nobody was looking, I lifted my goggles just a bit and snuck a peek at the brightlands. Immediately, I wished I hadn't. It knocked me backward. It was like being slapped in the face with a red-hot splash. I stumbled into the side of the truck, I fumbled the glasses back into place. My eyes were watering, I held them shut tight and tried to wipe at them without being blinded again. I felt really stupid, then I heard the men laughing at me and I got angry. They could have warned me. But then, one of them, a big soft guy everybody called Tallow, came up and put a black cloth over my head. He reached under the hood, pushed my goggles back, and mopped my face with a damp rag. It smelled faintly of disinfectant. He said quietly, "Don't take it bad. You only done what everybody else here did their first time too. We was all watching you. You got it over with quick. Now that you've seen a little bit of what's out there, you know what we all got to be careful about. Your eyes will stop hurting in a bit."

"You looked too, your first time?"

"Yep. Worse than you. I wasn't much older than you neither. I went out with my cousins, they said it wasn't nothing to be afraid of, you just take off the gloomies and look, see? So I did. That was real stupid. I stepped in it as deep as anyone could. It was most of an hour before I could see again. You got off easy, boy." Then he leaned in close and whispered, "It was real pretty, wasn't it? After a while, you're gonna start thinking that you'd like to take another look. Don't you be tempted, you hear? Don't you even think about it."

"I won't," I said. "I really truly won't." And I meant it. My eyes were still hurting bad. But then, I asked, "What was all that? What did I see?"

"You never mind that. It wasn't nothing."

"It must have been something. It damn near knocked me down."

"Don't you get too curious, boy. It ain't safe. You just follow the rules."

"Just tell me what it was, that's all. So I'll know. And then I won't ever ask again. Promise."

Tallow sighed. "You can't ever talk about this to anyone, you hear? You're not supposed to know. Nobody is. They don't want folks going out to see it for themselves." He lowered his voice. "They call it colors. It's what happens when light gets too bright. Your brain can't handle it. It's called overload or something like that. It's a little piece of madness, is what it is. You don't want to get sucked into it. You won't never get back. You'll just wander out there into the brights and die of your own hallucinations. That's what happened to— never mind."

"Doey?"

"Yeah, that was his name. Damn fool was too smart for his own good. Don't you go getting too smart now, you hear? You just keep remembering how much your face hurt."

"I will."

"You do that. Now that you know, you keep your gloomies on, you hear? And that breathing mask too, so you can't smell anything either. The air is just as bad. And don't say nothing to no one. No matter what. If you know what's good for you."

Tallow felt around under the hood, pulled my goggles back down over my eyes, and then made me to check to see that they were properly seated. And the breathing mask too. When we were both satisfied, he pulled off the hood. I blinked and looked around. Everything was safely gray again. As long as I didn't think about what was really out there, I was okay. As long as I didn't say what I'd seen, I was okay. I didn't even tell Tallow about the after-image still burning in my eyes. It looked like a naked boy. But he wasn't there when I put the gloomies back on, and I looked around everywhere. And I didn't tell him about the honey-smell either. Through the glasses, the brightlands looked flat and hard and empty. But I didn't have a lot of time for looking. There was too much work to do.

Putting down darklines wasn't hard. Just tedious. Mostly, it was boring.

First, we pounded stakes. The stakes were heavy Y-shaped things anchored in an iron base. The base was pointed like a bee sting. It had to be pounded deep into the ground, three feet or more; then the long leg of the Y part was stuck all the way into it. Then, after all the stakes were in place, we strung the wire, hanging it from one stake to the next.

I didn't do any of the actual stringing, that was done by the others. They had the strength for it, I didn't. I held cable, feeding it out from a big roll so it didn't hang up while the crew manhandled it into position. They used pitchforks so they wouldn't have to touch the line themselves. It was a thick naked braid of wire. The outer threads were deliberately broken and frayed, so the line looked like it had silvery scraggly hair. The wire was supposed to be fuzzy, so the dark would be deeper and stiffer, so I had to wear thick gloves, because the frayed bits had sharp ends. Even with the work gloves, I still got a few pokes and jabs and had to pull a couple of wire splinters from the heel of my palm.

When it was lunch time, we all hiked up the corridor a ways, far enough so that none of the bright could get in, so we could finally take off our gloomies and air-masks. Even here, safe between the dark lines, it still felt too bright. Or maybe that was an after-effect. I didn't ask. There wasn't much to eat, and what there was, wasn't very good. Stale bread, dried up cheese, wilted lettuce. Everything felt tired. Still, it was better than hunger. There wasn't much talk among the work crew. Everybody seemed to have something personal to think about. I thought about the naked boy. Was he really there? No, probly not. How could anyone stand naked in the bright? We finished eating as quickly as we could and pulled our goggles and capes back on, then hiked back out into the bright.

When the line was all strung, it was a chest-high fence. Not enough to stop anybody or anything. Least, not until it was turned on. The end of the line split into three separate wires that were fed into a terminator box. They put a terminator box at each end of the line, then they threw first one switch, then the other.

I pointed at the line. "How's it work?"

He waggled his hand. "It's what's called a seduction current. Something like that. It's powered by ambient photons. That's a fancy way of saying it sucks the extra light out of the air. The more light it sucks, the thicker the dark it makes."

"But nothing's happening," I said. The cable hung limp between the stakes.

Tallow grunted. "It takes a while. In a month, there'll be another patch of land safe to grow on. It'll go to the Martins. They might be able to get some winter wheat in. Might be enough to make it to spring."

"Why does it take so long?"

"It has to be slow. Otherwise, it would only make dark during the daytime, and we need the dark at night too. It usually takes a month or so for a line to suck enough light to get up to full strength, but after that, it only gets darker and stronger. Some of the older lines around here have enough residual in them to go for a year or more. Enough time to replace them if they go down. We'll come back out next week and see if it caught. Sometimes the terminator boxes are bad." He stepped over and peered closely at the wire. So did I, but I couldn't see any difference.

"Can I ask you something?"

"What?" Tallow seemed annoyed, like he was getting tired of me.

"How does the line know how much light to suck? What you said about the older lines getting stronger—do they ever suck too much light? Could they make it too dark?"

"Eh?" Tallow squinted, suddenly angry. "Don't you go anywhere with that. We got enough talk already."

"I was just asking—"

"You was just asking too much. That's not safe, boy. Don't ask questions, just follow the rules, you hear?" He strode away from me, began loading his tools into his truck. The other men too. Like they couldn't be away from here fast enough. Pretty soon, we all piled into our separate pickups and headed back down the corridor. They dropped me back at Miz' place and that was that.

I worked on the line crews off and on all summer long, when I wasn't mucking out stalls for Miz. Tallow didn't talk to me much, probably afraid he'd already said too much. None of them ever talked to the city-boy, so I mostly kept to myself. Every so often, I thought about the colors I'd seen, I wondered if there was a safe way to look at them, a safe way to be naked; but I didn't ask those questions. I didn't ask any questions at all anymore, and I didn't answer any either. I pounded stakes and unrolled wire. One day, I looked at myself in the mirror, I actually had muscles. But I was still hungry all the time. And cold. Miz managed to keep food on the table, but it wasn't a lot. Sometimes we had cornbread. Sometimes just mush. We had eggs too, but the hens weren't laying regular. A couple of times we even had chicken. That was pretty good. We didn't starve, but nobody was getting fat either.

One Sunday, while we were at Meeting, one of the cows wandered into the dark; either she didn't have enough sense to keep away or maybe she was daydreaming the way cows do and the dark just pulled her in. She wasn't in her stall and she wasn't in the field either. I finally found her, ass-end sticking out of the dark, and went running up the hill to the house. It took both me and Miz to drag the cow out, but she was never the same. She wobbled on her feet. She looked like she'd been smacked in the face with a shovel. That night, she fell down in her stall. She wouldn't get up, so the vet came out to look at her. He did some doctor stuff, then took Miz off for a talk.

I didn't hear what they said, but Miz looked angry and frustrated. Finally she nodded her head. The vet came back into the barn and put the cow down. Put a gun to her head and thump, just like a street-killing, execution style. It took all three of us to jack the cow up with a block and tackle. We hung her by the hind legs and cut some veins to drain the blood. The vet opened up her belly and the organs spilled out onto a canvas tarp. Some of it, Miz fed to the hogs, the heart and brains and tongue, she put into a big tub for pickling. I got the feeling she'd done this before, especially the way she stripped off the hide and stretched it out for tanning. We left the cow hanging so the meat could age two-three days, you can't eat it right away, it's too tough; hanging makes it more tender. Two days later, the vet came back early with a couple of helpers, and we all started hacking and sawing. We were a week smoking the meat. We pickled some of it too, in great big jars. We didn't eat much of it ourselves though. It didn't taste very good. Like it was old and stale. Even when you put gravy on it. Miz said that was the effect of the dark.

Finally, on Friday, we wrapped and boxed everything we could. On Saturday, Miz and me packed as much as we could fit into the truck and she drove into town, where she traded that cow for hard goods, spices, and even some jars of fruit from somewhere up north. Some people would eat it, she said. Just not us.

Miz didn't take me with that day, she wanted me to stay behind, in case anybody came wandering by. Word was that some brightlanders had wandered through town recently and nobody was sure if they'd moved on yet. I hadn't seen them, but I'd heard about them at Meeting. They all wore long black capes, just dark enough to keep them from going mad, except maybe they were a little mad from all that time in the bright. And maybe they'd come through looking to see if there was anything worth stealing. Maybe they were out there now, just waiting on the other side of the dark. But I didn't think it was the brightlanders Miz was fearing. I think it was our own neighbors. Some of them were real hungry, even eating tree bark. Miz had a big pot of stew simmering on the stove for Sunday's Meeting. Maybe some of them folks wouldn't wait. So I stayed behind, sitting on the front porch, watching the chickens scratching through the remaining patches of grass.

Moments like this, I watched the dark. Sometimes, if you watched it close enough, you could see it move. It looked like it was flowing real slow, like a river of slow time. Sometimes it wasn't all dark, sometimes it was dark gray; that was mostly at night. The dark leaked. It couldn't hold all the light it sucked and some of it seeped back out. Just enough to make everything look like moonlight.

But the closer you got to the dark, the worse you felt, like it wasn't just sucking light, but life as well. Everything close to the dark looked bad, all dusty-dull and shabby, turning gray and old in the gloom. I tried to stay away from it, especially now that I knew how it worked. But there was something about it, something I couldn't explain. I always felt like it was pulling me into it. Miz called it dark-sniffing. I had to watch myself. I wondered if someday I'd get so lost in some dream that I'd wander right into it, not even realizing what I was doing. That's what happened to the cow.

That's when the colored boy appeared.

First I smelled flowers. Yellow and pink flowers. Bright red flowers. I stood up, looking around, wondering where the flowers were. Then I saw him.

He stepped out of the dark at the bottom of the hill and started up the path to the house like he lived here. I saw him instantly. He stood out like a flash of the brightlands. Where everything else was gray, he was all the different colors a person could be. He glowed like he was lit from within. He was gold all over. His hair flashed in shades of red and blond; his skin shimmered like sunset. He was shining and naked. I'd never seen anybody so beautiful. He could have come from the far side of the sky. Wherever he'd come from, I wanted to go there. I wanted to glow too.

He came all the way up to the porch. He put one foot on the bottom step, then stopped. I knew who he was. "You Doey?"

He nodded. He held out a hand to me, like inviting me to dance. I was real tempted to take it, he was so beautiful. But I didn't. After a moment, he lowered his hand.

"Was that you I saw in the bright?"

He smiled, a dazzle of happiness. I'd never seen anything like that. It just made me hurt with longing all the more. He was insane, of course. He had to be. How could he not?

"Do you talk?" I asked.

He laughed. A gentle chuckle of sound, like a shared secret. "Yes, I talk. I also sing. I dance. I laugh. Do you?"

Shrug. "I dunno. Never tried. Never had much reason to try."

He stepped up one step. He reached out with his hand. I took a step back. He drew his hand back, then took another step up, this time onto the porch. And this time, when he extended his hand, I didn't move away. With outstretched fingers, he touched my shirt, my chest. Through the faded cotton, I felt a hot rush of feeling, I couldn't explain. His eyes met mine. His eyes were green and blue and violet. Not the sad shabby colors of the faded flowers around the edges of the old gray house, but the glistening sparkle of the deep edge of the rainbow. His eyes were bright. Everything about him was bright. The touch of his fingers—it felt like he was pumping energy into me. I felt alivened. Was this the magic of the bright? Is this how people went crazy? I didn't want the moment to end. I wanted to fall helplessly into it, dissolving into a bath of color, just like Doey.

I reached up with my own hand, took his in mine, held it, felt the warmth, both strong and soft at the same time, released it, reached across and touched his chest as he'd touched me. Placed my palm flat against his hot and glowing body. There was nothing I needed to say, there was everything I wanted to say. There was perfect understanding and a thousand thousand questions. I'd never known a moment like this. Never felt a hot surge of feeling like this. I thought I was going to faint. Or fly apart in pieces.

"Yes," he said, finally.

"Yes?"

"Yes, you know how to sing and dance and laugh. You just haven't had a place to do it."

My mouth was dry as dust. "Will you—can you take me there?"

He smiled and leaned forward. Close enough to kiss. "When you learn to glow."

"How do I—?"

He touched my lips with a golden finger, silencing my question.

"Hush," he whispered. "Not yet. Not yet."

And then he whirled and spun, a twirl of light and color. He leapt and danced and flew, arms outstretched, all the way down the hill and back into the wall of darkness that surrounded the house. And then he was gone. Leaving only the fading scent of color. The afternoon was dull and gray again. I felt tears on my cheeks. Both joy and despair at the same time.

I almost ran after him, almost. Something held me back. All the words, all the warnings, all the gloom that wrapped the world. He was right. I wasn't ready to let go. Not yet. Not yet. Oh, that bastard boy of color. How did he do that? How could he flirt and fly? How did he live? Where had he gone?

Sank down into a chair, an old wooden chair that creaked in pain as it accepted my weight. A faded cushion, hard and flat as cardboard. What mad thing had just happened here? Damn that Doey! I hated him, I loved him, I envied him, I feared what he was, and I wanted to be him more than anything.

I was comfortable here. Working for Miz. Working on the lines. I was comfortable, wrapped in dark. I didn't have to care. I didn't have to think. I only had to follow the rules. I could do that. Okay, I wasn't happy, but I wasn't unhappy either. I was comfortable and after being hungry and tired and cold and uncomfortable for so long, comfortable was a good place to be. It was enough. I didn't need happy. Happy didn't exist anyway. Certainly not here. And then the glowing boy stepped out of the dark and looked in my eyes and touched my heart and left me gasping with desperation. Because now that I knew what happy was, now that I knew it did exist, how could I ever be comfortable again anywhere?

Now that I knew what happy felt like, I also knew I didn't have any. Instead, now I knew what lonely felt like.

Did he know how cruel his words were? "Not yet. Not yet."

I felt so torn up inside I didn't know what I felt. I put my head into my hands and started sobbing, I don't know why. Cried for Ma, cried for me. Cried for the whole stupid everything. Who made up this stupid world anyway? Why do we have to put down all these walls of darkness? What's on the other side that everybody is so afraid of they won't even talk about it? And why did I feel so awful?

After a while, I felt all hollow and empty. So I got up and went to the barn. Stood around for a bit, then finally started mucking out stalls. Not because I wanted to, but it was something to do. And if I didn't do it, Miz would have words, lots of words. I hated all her words. I just never knew it until now.

When Miz got back, she sniffed the air and looked at me sharply. "What happened here?" she asked.

"Nothing," I said.

"Don't lie to me, Michael. Something happened here. I can see it in your face. You're all hot and flushed. Your cheeks are red." She put a hand on my forehead. "You're burning up. You have a fever."

"It's nothing," I said. Maybe too loud.

She grabbed me by the arm and dragged me to the horse trough. "Take off your shirt," she demanded. I did so and she pushed me down to my knees, pushed me head first into the sour brown water.

She picked up a horse brush and began scrubbing my back with it. I couldn't scream and I couldn't breathe and I was trying to do both at the same time. She yanked me up, gasping. Before I could stop myself, I called her all those words she'd made me promise never to say again. She didn't even hesitate, she just whacked me across the head with the heavy wooden brush, knocking me backwards. "You're still an evil old bitch! And beating me to death ain't gonna change that."

"You think I'm stupid?" Miz shouted. She was loud. "You think I don't see what you're turning into? You want to go out there and get colored? You want to glow? You want to turn into some kind of fairy-dancer? You want to die in delirium? Why do you think we put up all the darklines? Because we like the dark? You think we like being cold and hungry and miserable all the time? No, we do it because we don't have any choice. We have to protect ourselves. All of us. Even you—you stupid cityboy."

I didn't say what I was thinking. She made me feel angry. But what if she was right? Everything was all confused. If the dark was so good, why did it feel so bad. And if the bright was so bad, why did it feel so good? I pulled myself bitterly back to my feet. Already, I was trying to figure out how I could get away from here. I could probly get a loaf of bread out of the kitchen, maybe some vegetables, put them in an old potato sack or something. But where could I go? And how could I get there? Walk the roads? Maybe, but to where? And if anybody else came down the road, they'd see me for sure. No place to hide in the corridors. Follow the train tracks? Maybe. But where did they go? Just to another place like this. I didn't know. I needed a map or something. But there had to be someplace somewhere better than this. I shook the water out of my hair, brushed it back with my hand. My arm and shoulder hurt where she'd slammed me against the trough. My back hurt from the scrubbing of the brush. And my head was throbbing like a nightmare. I hurt all over. And I stunk of the foul water. And I was cold. Evening was coming on, and the dark was expanding.

Out in the barn, wrapped in a blanket, shivering against the night, listening to the wind scrabbling against the old wood, all the voices argued back and forth. Evil old bitch. I don't care what she thinks. This is sick. Everything is sick. These people are dying. I don't want to die with them. They're all sick and dirty and dead inside. I don't want to be like this. But there's no way out. It's a trap. All the darklines, all the rules, all the walls everywhere.

And just what's out there on the other side of the lines anyway? What's so horrible that you can't look at it direct, can't see it without being eye-poisoned? Doey wasn't wearing any gloomies. He was naked like one of those angels in the old books. He was as beautiful as a girl with long flowing red hair, but he was stallion-cut like a prize. He was both at once. I'd never seen anyone or anything like that. How did he live out there? How did he see without being blinded? What did he say? Learn to dance. No. Learn to glow. How do you glow? How do you learn? All those questions and nobody to ask. Nobody to trust.

Next morning was Meeting. I wasn't going to go, but Miz didn't take no arguments. She just told me to clean myself up, put on a clean shirt, and not go around smelling like a pig. But once we were in the truck, she did say one thing. She said, "I didn't want to hurt you yesterday, Michael. What I did, I had to do. I had to break the spell. You were all glassy. I had to dunk you in the water and scrub your back hard and smack you to put you in all that pain to pull you back from wherever it was you were drifting off to. I've seen that look before, saw it on Doey. Didn't act fast enough with him. He danced away one night. Ain't going to lose you too. I see you starting to glow, I'm going to beat you—not because I want to hurt you, but because hurting you is the only way to pull you out. You understand that, don't you?"

"Yes'm. Whatever."

We pulled up at Meeting early, but we wasn't the first ones there. Bunch of folks all clustered by their trucks, talking. They looked over as we drove up, and a couple of them walked over to talk to Miz. She glanced at me, then moved off a ways so I couldn't hear what they were all saying. I pretended like I didn't care anyway and wandered down to where the older kids were scratching in the dirt with sticks. J.D. was there, the kid with the broken tooth, the kid from town who'd first told me about Doey. Nobody had names out here, only initials. He stopped what he was doing, tossed his stick aside, and said, "You hear?"

"Hear what?"

"'Bout the Trasks?"

"What about them?"

"They went out."

"Out where?"

"You stupid, cityboy? Out."

"Oh. Out."

"Doc drove over to see if they was all right, if they had enough food. He had a couple spare bags of beans and rice. He got there, they was all gone. The whole family. Ever single one. Even the baby. And one of their fields was starting to glow. Big hole in the darklines—all snapped, like somebody cut 'em. Doc didn't have no gloomies. He got out of there fast. Scared-like. That's what I heard, anyway. They're going to send out a hunting party, I bet. Go shoot some bright-eyes. They're going to need every gun in town. You know how to shoot, cityboy?"

"I can shoot," I said.

"Then you'll get to go, for sure. They won't let me go. I already asked. They said I was too small. That's a damn lie. They just ain't forgiven my pa for losin' a gun last hunt. They say he stole it. But he din't. The brighties did. Turned it into something weird, I bet."

"How would you know?"

"I know lotsa stuff. More than you."

"Yeah? You think so?"

"I know so."

"Yeah? How do you know anything? You ever been out there?"

He shook his head. "Not gonna say what I know."

I wanted to tell him about the bright-eyed boy. I wanted to ask him if he'd ever seen the naked colors. But something told me that probly wasn't a good idea. So I just shrugged. Whatever. Drop it. Turned away, back to the others. More folks was arriving now. I hiked up the hill to where Tallow was standing, waited behind him for a bit until no one else was talking. He finally noticed me. "You want something?"

"You going hunting?"

"You got a gun?"

"Miz does, I think."

He scratched his neck thoughtfully. "Probly not a good idea. You being a cityboy. And we're going out deep. Miz won't like that. But maybe you can hold the wire at the safe end. Might could use you that way. You just don't say nothing right now. You talkin' about it just makes a bad idea seem worse."

Then Miz came over with Doc. He looked at me, took my chin in his hand, turned my head side to side. Looked into my eyes. Put a hand on my forehead. Asked me to stand on one foot, put my arms out, and shut my eyes tight. Stuff like that. Turned to Miz. "He looks all right to me. You probly got to him in time. But if you want me to wrap him in darkline for a bit, suck some of the brightness out of him, bring him by one day, and we'll give him a bit of treatment."

"I'll do that, thanks," she said. "You be in tomorrow?"

"Better wait till the end of the week," he said. "It's going to be a busy few days. Let's get this Trask business taken care of first. I think this lad will be fine for the moment."

Eventually, we all got inside and got settled, but nobody was thinking about Meeting. Everybody was still whispering. It was like the room was full of bluebottle flies. The mayor said that he was sorry about the bad news, everybody had probly heard it anyway, but he had to officially confirm it. The darklines had broken by the Trask farm and it looked as if the Trasks had been enchanted. And yes, there would be a committee meeting to decide what to do next. Volunteers should make themselves known to the usual folks.

After that, there wasn't much else to say, because nobody was listening anyway, so we broke up early. Folks didn't eat much, they was mostly too upset. The whole family was gone, even the baby. Not even bodies left for a proper funeral. Lots of talk floated around. Somebody was going to have to get out there and take care of the livestock. Miz said she could take the cows and the chickens if nobody else needed them, but she didn't want no more pigs right now. They ate too much. A couple of the other folks spoke up, laying claim to tools or dishes or furniture. Blankets and quilts. Pots and pans. A little of this and some of that. Eventually, it was all sorted out, who was going to go out and pick stuff up. Tallow opened his truck and passed out gloomies to the folks who were going to need them.

Miz collected goggles and masks for us and some capes too, shiny on one side, black on the other. And gloves, just in case. We didn't even head home, just straight out thr   ough town and off around the hill to the Trask place. I don't know how Miz knew the way. All the corridors looked the same to me, just narrow twisty roads through the dark. But I tried to pay attention anyway, just in case. Miz kept talking, the whole trip. She was angry about everything. "Should never have let the Trasks settle so far out, way out on the borders with nothing between them and the bright. Damn fool stupid idea from the start. And now a whole family is lost. And the farm. And it's not like we have families or farms to spare. Lord knows what shape the poor animals are in. Put your goggles and mask on, boy. We're almost there. And you put that cape and gloves on before you get out of the car, you hear?"

She pulled up short of the farm and pulled on her own cape and goggles and gloves and breathing mask. She pushed the goggles up on her forehead and inched the truck forward, a little bit at a time. I pushed my gloomies up just enough to see under the frames. We came around the last curve and there was the brightness leaking in around the edges of the broken dark. We both pulled our goggles down at the same time. "I told you to keep those things on. You're susceptible. You can't take any more chances."

We pulled up in front of the barn. It was old and saggy. It leaned to one side and it looked like it was ready to collapse, even worse than Miz's barn. Miz looked off toward the bright before getting out of the truck. Half the darkline was down, the dark just faded off into filigree wisps. Beyond, the fields glowed harsh and stark in our gloomies. Without the goggles, they would have been impossible to look at.

Miz made a clucking sound of disapproval. I followed her into the barn. There were three cows tethered, all of them lowing uncomfortably. Miz told me to load up the sacks of feed, while she set about milking the cows. Afterward, I loaded the cans into the truck. Then she blindfolded the cows and led them out of the barn, tying their tethers to the back of the truck. Then she went and found a stack of empty crates and we began collecting the chickens. Some of them were clucking quietly in the barn, those we crated; but others were lying stunned on the ground outside. A few were wandering around dazed. Those she picked up and swiftly broke their necks.

"Can't they be saved?" I asked.

Miz shook her head. "Too dangerous. Too much bright in 'em. This is better. Safer." There were a few little chicks too, all safe in the incubator. She put these in a crate, dropped a canvas over it, and I loaded the crate into the back of the pickup. We walked around the barn then, looking to see what else we could find. The two pigs in the back were both gone. Miz shook her head at that. "Probly ran into the bright. Pigs are like that," she said.

Then we saw it. The fourth cow. It was staggering, all glassy-eyed and confused. It looked bright—not as bright as the brightland, but brighter than it should be. Miz said one of those words I'm not supposed to. She went to the truck and pulled out her shotgun from the back window.

"Don't you want to walk it into the barn?"

"What for?"

"That's a lot of meat—"

"Nobody's going to eat this beef. It's sick. You want to get sick too?"

"Can't you have Doc wrap it in darkline and drain the bright out of it?"

"You can't drain it. Draining takes the flavor out. And you can't let people eat meat that's been brightened either. That's even worse. No, this cow is gone." She lifted the shotgun, moved closer, then moved closer again, until the barrel was almost touching the cow's skull. I didn't want to see it, but I couldn't look away either. The rifle flashed. The cow dropped to the ground with a thud. She stepped closer and fired the second barrel. Just to be sure.

Miz checked the house then. She wouldn't let me go in, but she came out carrying a pillow case full of spices and other things from the kitchen. Even a small jar of honey, I found out later. That was a surprise. The Trasks weren't supposed to be doing that well.

Back in the truck, barely inching along the road, not moving faster than the three tethered cows could follow, Miz started talking again. She looked old. Older than the first day. And tired too. Like she'd been drained a few times. "This isn't right," she said. "Letting cows and pigs and chickens and corn go bad like that. And all those vegetables. Nobody should have been out this far, with only one line of dark between them and that—that brightmare. Now look what it's gone and done. A family gone, a cow gone. Two pigs running loose in the bright. All those chickens. All that food. What a waste. What a waste."

It took most of the day to bring the cows in. It was a long drive and we couldn't go very fast. But we were back before dusk settled in. I was glad of that. I didn't like being out in the dark. Not any kind of dark at all.

I slept badly. Tossed and turned in the straw all night. Finally, just before dawn, I got up and walked out of the barn. I tried to look up at the stars. Once in a while, you can still see them, some of them, but not tonight. Everything was black. Just dim shapes of black against blacker. I thought about lighting a lantern, but I didn't want to wake Miz, so I just stood barefoot and listened. Nothing much to hear. Just wind. A lonely cricket. Not a lot of insects anymore. I heard that one in town. That was the real reason everything was dying. The insects couldn't get through the darklines. No bees, no ants, no bugs, no spiders, nothing.

Not even a glimmer of bright from over the hill. Sometimes you can see it, mostly its reflection off the clouds. But not tonight.

Finally, I went back into the barn, back to my straw. Pulled my blanket around me and just sat with my arms wrapped around my knees, rocking softly. I used to do that when I was little. I don't remember much from when I was little, we moved around so much. But I remember I spent a lot of time sitting in the dark and rocking. Sometimes Mom would come and sit with me, wrapping her arms around me, and we'd sit as quiet as we could, not making any noises, so they wouldn't find us.

Thought about what I'd seen. Everything. All the bright leaking over into the fields. Miz didn't know, but while she was milking the cows, I'd lifted up the edge of my gloomies and snuck a quick peek—not at the bright directly, but at the fields it was just creeping into. That didn't hurt so much. I could see the colors, all the dazzling colors, everything at once—the rustling golden corn in the field, the crisp green stalks so clear it was like they cut the air, the rich dark soil like a warm bed, even the sky above glowed blue. I'd never even known such colors were possible. I wanted to see more. But then, I heard a noise behind me and just as quick-like I pushed the goggles back down over my eyes. I didn't want to get caught. Not by Miz. Because Miz wanted to take me to Doc. And wrap me in darkline. And drain the bright out of me. Like the beef. Drained beef. "You ever taste drained beef? You won't like it." Maybe that's what's wrong with these people. They've all been drained.

But what if Miz hadn't made a noise right then? Would I have kept looking until it was too late, until I was sucked away into the brightland too? I wondered what that might feel like—to dance naked in the stars. To whirl and dazzle and laugh. Madness, yes. But even madness looked better than this life. Miz wanted to wrap me in dark and make me just like everybody else. My stomach rumbled and I wondered what people ate in the brightlands? Magic corn? Enchanted beans? I didn't know. Nobody knew. Anybody who knew hadn't come back to tell. Maybe they was all dead, lying bright and starved? Maybe the bright pigs was eating them. Maybe this and maybe that and maybe some of the other. Nobody knew. Or if they did, they wasn't saying.

Finally, I just rolled over, curled up and tried to sleep. Thinking about stuff doesn't do any good. It doesn't work. It just makes my head hurt. Enough. Enough already. I wrapped myself tight in my blanket and eventually shivered myself to sleep.

For the next couple days, Miz didn't say anything more about getting me darklined, but I knew she was still set on the idea. She kept giving me these looks. But maybe she also felt bad about having to do it, because she made some honey-cornbread and cut me an extra thick slab with lots of butter. Or maybe she just felt I had to have my strength up so I could survive being drained. She didn't say. And I didn't ask. I was starting to think about running again. We still had the gloomies and the capes in the truck. Maybe if I could find my way to the Trask farm, I could go outside the darklines and cross the bright to some other place. Supposedly, the town council had some maps somewhere, but nobody was allowed to see them.

Tuesday evening, Tallow came driving up unexpectedly. He talked with Miz a bit, then told me to get into the truck. Tomorrow morning, we were going out to fix the darkline at the Trask farm. And maybe do a bit of hunting too. Miz sniffed unhappily. I could see she disapproved. She didn't trust any of this. She came right out and said it. "That boy's got too much bright in him. He ain't been drained. If you don't tie him down good, you know he'll just get sucked into the colors. I swear, you lose him and I'll skin you bad, Tallow, I will."

"Nah, you'll just get another one off the next train. Like you always do." Tallow grinned back.

Miz didn't think that was funny. She sniffed again in that funny way she had. "Oh, hell. Wait a minute." She went to her own truck and pulled the rifle down out of the back window, and the box of shells next to it. She cracked it open and popped the two shells out, dropping them into the box. She walked back over, and motioned me to open my door. She handed me the shotgun and the box of shells. "Don't you load this thing unless you need it. And you bring it back clean, y'hear? Tallow, you teach him how to use it. It's on your head now."

Tallow grunted and climbed into the truck. He pulled his door shut and put the engine into gear. We rolled down the hill and into the corridor of twisted dark. Tallow laughed. "Miz is good folks, but some folks say she's been drained one too many times."

I thought about that. It kind of made sense. "You ever been drained?" I asked.

"Most folks around here have. For their own good."

"Oh," I said.

"It doesn't really hurt. It just makes you queasy, a little. Like having the runs, sort of. After a couple days, the feeling goes away. And the bright can't get to you as easy."

"Did the bright ever get to you? I mean, before you were drained?"

Tallow's face tightened. "Y'know, boy. This ain't really anything you want to talk about. You don't want to go asking too many questions. Folks'll start talkin'."

"Just curious, that's all."

"Yep, that's all. That's what they all said. Just curious. You don't want to get too curious about the bright. You want to stay away from it. That's why we smacked you with it the first day on the lines—so's you'll know. You've seen all you need to see. Right?" When I didn't answer, he repeated himself. "Right?"

I shrugged. "Whatever."

Tallow stopped the truck with a screech. I jerked forward with the suddenness of the stop. He turned to me and grabbed my shoulder hard. "Listen up, cityboy. You don't know what you're dealing with here. That ain't a question. It's the truth. You don't know shit. So when I tell you how it is, I'm not just running my mouth 'cause I like hearing my jaw flap. I'm telling you what you need know so you don't get sucked away like all the others. We used to be three times as many people and ten times as much livestock and crops. Where do you think all those folks went? All those animals? They didn't listen and they didn't take care and now they're gone. You want to be gone too? Just keep asking questions. You ask too many questions, we'll open the dark and toss you out in the bright ourselves. This is for your own good, cityboy. If you want to live, you better learn to listen."

"I thought you liked me," I said. I didn't know why I said that.

"This ain't about liking. Even if I didn't like you, I wouldn't want to see you turn into one of them damn fairy-dancers."

"You've seen them?"

Tallow didn't answer. He let go of my shoulder and turned away and put the truck back into gear. I rubbed where he'd grabbed me so hard.

"You didn't answer my question."

"That's right. I didn't." Tallow didn't say anything else for the rest of the drive. That left me with lots of time to think about all the things he wasn't saying. I got the feeling he knew more than it was safe for anyone to know. And maybe he didn't want anyone else to know how much he knew. But it was only a feeling and he'd made it real clear that he wasn't going to answer any more questions of any kind. I felt bad about that. Because maybe if he'd said he'd seen a fairy-dancer, I could tell him I'd seen one too. And maybe then we'd each have someone we could trust enough to talk about it. Except I didn't dare tell him, because he might tell someone else; and he couldn't risk saying anything to me either, because I was just another stupid cityboy.

"We going out tonight?"

"Tomorrow. Early morning. But I don't have time to drive out and pick you up then, so you'll sleep behind the feed store tonight with some of the other boys. You keep your hands to yourself, you keep your mouth shut, and you don't ask any questions. I'll keep Miz's shotgun in my truck. No sense in having you shoot yourself in the foot, or anybody else either."

Behind the feedstore, it was just a big empty space under a sagging roof. A few bags of feed, here and there, just enough to make a rough bed. It wasn't much, but it was better than straw. Four or five others talking together, nothing important. I recognized two of them, but J.D. was the only one whose name I knew. They glanced at me, but didn't say anything. Just another cityboy, using up space, eating up food. I grabbed a stretch of canvas to use as a blanket and made myself comfortable off in a corner, away from the others. They had a kerosene lamp, but that was all. The light pretended to warmth, but the night was just as cold here as anywhere else.

After a while, J.D. wandered over, wrapped in a blanket. "Hey, cityboy. Can I sleep by you?"

Shrugged. Not yes, not no. J.D. pushed a couple of feed bags into position and stretched out on top of them. "You know something you're not saying." It wasn't a question.

I didn't answer.

"If you tell me what you know, I'll tell you what I know."

I rolled over on my side, turned away from him. I trusted him less than anybody. J.D. liked to talk, liked to pretend he knew stuff. Safest not to tell him anything.

"Aw, c'mon—"

"Fine. Okay. You go first."

"No, you," he insisted.

"Forget it then." I settled myself again.

Silence for a bit. Just enough time for me to figure out what was going on. They'd sent J.D. over to find out what I knew, if I'd ever seen anything.

A minute more and I figured out the rest of it. It didn't matter what I said. J.D. was going to make something up for me.

"Okay," he said. "I'll tell you. Folks keep seein' Doey. Miz's other boy. He's a fairy-dancer now. We're goin' out to find him. Hunt him down like a blind pig. That's what my maw says—"

I sat up and looked at him. "J.D. Go away. Get away from me. You got devil-talk inside you and I don't want to hear it. Get away from me or I'll punch you." I said it loud enough for the others to hear. That was enough. J.D. gathered up his blanket and went scuttling back to the others.

He hadn't told me anything I didn't know already. It wasn't that hard to figure out. Even the rest of it, the part he hadn't said. Not just Doey, but the Trask family too, if they were still alive. Anyone and anything in the brightlands. Didn't need to be smart to figure that out. Just scared and angry and tightened up inside.

But something about this didn't feel right. Going out and shooting people. Even if they were all colored. No matter how little you felt inside. Just fix the darklines, that's all. Put up more lines if you have to. But going out into the bright. That didn't sound like a good idea. Not for this reason, not for any reason. Not unless you were planning to never come back. I just wish I knew more about what was out there. But if anybody around here knew, they weren't saying, and it sure wasn't safe to ask.

Next thing I knew, Tallow was kicking me awake. "Time to go, cityboy. Move your ass." I rolled off the sack of feed onto the hard black dirt. It looked as dark in here as it was out there, but Tallow was waving a lantern, and that outlined everything in brown gloom. Two other men were kicking the rest of the boys awake. I didn't see J.D. anywhere. I pulled myself to my feet, scratching and aching and hurting all over. My stomach hurt the worst. "Is there anything to eat?" Nobody answered.

I followed them all around the building to the front, where six or seven trucks had pulled up. Somebody had set up a table with a big plate of hard biscuits and even some hot coffee, seven or eight men just lining up. I fell in line behind them, then got pushed even further back when three more arrived. "Wait your turn, cityboy. Let the men eat first." Pigs.

Bitter coffee and a couple of biscuits later, they formed up teams. I recognized most of the men from the darkline team, plus a few folks from Meeting. And a couple of the big stocky women too. Some of them had guns. This wasn't any darkline crew.

After a bit of discussion, people figuring out who was going to ride with who, that kind of stuff, Tallow pointed me toward one of the trucks, and I climbed into the back with two other boys. I said hello, but they ignored me. After a few last minute instructions, the trucks all headed out toward the Trask place. The headlights of the ones following us made an ominous line snaking through the dark.

We couldn't drive very fast, it wasn't safe, so by the time we arrived, the sky was just starting to show an edge of gray—or maybe it was the glow off the distant brightness. I couldn't be sure, and I wasn't going to ask. We stopped down the hill from the Trask place and safely behind the bend in the road, so no one would accidentally get a glimpse of brightness before they got their goggles on.

We bumbled around in the gloom for a while, while the Sheriff and a couple of others organized everybody into teams. I was pushed over to stand with Tallow. He was carrying Miz's gun as well as his own, but he made no move to give it to me. I wasn't sure why I was even here, nobody was talking to me.

Finally, everything was sorted out and we all put on our shiny capes and our gloomies and our breathing masks and we started off. We trudged up the last of the road, around the bend of the corridor of dark, and finally up the hill to where the ground was starting to glow. And beyond that, we could see where the glare was leaking into the air from the brightlands. Kind of like the dazzle of light from an open refrigerator in a midnight kitchen.

Two of the men rolled a cart with three huge spools of darkwire on it. For some reason, everybody kept close to the cart. Even though the wire wasn't powered, folks still acted like they were safer staying close to it. Once we got to the top of the hill, I looked around for the dead cow, but where I thought it should be, I saw only a hump, covered with little white flowers. We all waited while the Sheriff and his deputies looked out across the brightland through special binoculars. They whispered to themselves for a bit, pointing and nodded and finally agreeing. After some more conferences, the guys with the cart installed one end of the wire to a convenient post; they hooked up a terminator box to it, there was another terminator connected to the end of the wire inside the big drum.

Then, when that was done, we all headed out into the bright, with the cart leading and the men unspooling the wire as they went. We didn't install any posts, we weren't putting up a darkline. This was only a safety line. All you had to do was follow it back. You could do it with your eyes closed, if you had to. I hoped I wouldn't have to. Just the little bit of leakage around the edge of my goggles was painful.

Nobody told me where we were headed, so I just followed Tallow. At least, I thought it was Tallow. In the harsh glare, with all of us caped and goggled, everybody looked alike, all different shades of gray and white and whiter. To keep from stumbling, I spent most of the time watching the ground directly in front of me, following in the footsteps of the man I thought was Tallow. We hiked into the brightness where the ground turned white like salt—that's what it looked like through the gloomies; it must have been glittering gold without them.

We hiked through scorched fields, abandoned to the bright. An old dirt road cut straight through, but it was already starting to get overgrown. On either side, twisted trees groped in the glare. They looked like they were alive, their limbs slowly moving, waving, even reaching. We kept clear of them. And the bushes too—they looked like they were all burning. They were so bright, even the gloomies couldn't keep out all the color. They looked burnished with a hint of red and gold, like they were all wrapped in shivering flame. Everywhere else, I saw stalks of something that might have been corn once, but was something else now; they looked like torches.

None of this made much sense to me. How was anybody going to hunt anything in a place like this? Ten feet away, everything blurred out in yellow and white. It was like fog on fire. And nobody was saying much either. If they knew what they were doing, they weren't telling.

Finally, someone in front of me stopped and pointed. A couple of others stopped, so I did too. At first, I couldn't see what they were looking at, but finally I made it out, way out there, way beyond the place where the road just dazzled out, there was a tall old house, an outline of a house, a glimmering hint of a house. I guessed that was where we were heading, I tried to make it out clearer—but then somebody punched me in the back and growled, "Keep moving, bait." So I pushed on.

It was hot out here. Once, I tried looking off to the east, tried to see the sun, the source of all this brightness, but the gloomies just went black. They overloaded and shut down. And I had to walk blind for a few moments until they reset themselves.

Eventually, we reached the house. It was in a field of grass so bright that the goggles showed it black, they didn't even try to resolve it. The house itself looked like it was made out of glass. The walls had gone glistening and transparent, and all we could see clearly was just the structural outlines, the edges and corners. It looked like it had been here forever, standing tall and stately, with porches and gables and even a widow's walk around the front and sides. And a tall cupola. It was almost a castle. Even Miz's house wasn't this big.

The two men with the cart cut the wire and tied one end of it to one of the porch posts. Once they did that everybody felt safer. A few folks started to go up onto the porch, but Sheriff stopped them, said the house was off-limits to everybody. Except the lure.

Then everybody busied themselves, separating into three teams. Each team had a cart and a roll of wire. Each team tied one end of their wire to the porch, connected a terminator, then headed out a bit and waited. One team was pointed straight out south, the other two east and west.

Tallow was on the western team, but when I went to follow, he grabbed me by the arm and walked me back to the house. "No, your job is to wait here and make sure nothing happens to the wires."

"By myself?"

"Nothing's going to happen. You're perfectly safe. You have four active darkwires terminating here."

"Then why do you need me to stay here? I thought I was going with you."

"I promised Miz."

"Then give me the gun."

"You won't need it."

"Then why'd she give it?"

"Stop asking so many questions. Go sit up on the porch. You'll be able to see farther."

"Can't see anything in this bright. Neither can you. And why'd he call me 'bait?' I'm the lure, aren't I?"

Tallow grabbed my shoulder. Hard. Just like last time. "Listen to me, cityboy. If we take you out there, you'll get sucked away so fast you won't have time to scream for help. You stay here because I say you stay here. And if you want to argue about it, we can tie you down with darkline. And that won't be just an hour of draining, it could be a day or two or forever. You want that?"

I didn't answer. Not right away. "You say nothing will happen?"

"Nothing will happen."

"You sure?"

"Get up on the porch. Oh, wait—" He fumbled under his cape, passed me a sack. "Here's some more biscuits and a bottle of water. In case you get hungry."

"How long are you going to be out there?"

"As long as it takes." And then, he added. "Probly back by afternoon, certainly before nightfall. We don't want to spend the night out here, that's for sure; this place glows in the dark. You just stay awake and make sure those wires stay tied." He started to turn away, then turned back. "You'll be all right."

And then he was gone. All of them were gone. They hiked out into the bright and faded away in the distance like wavering shadows.

Tallow said I could go up on the porch, but I wasn't sure it was safe. The Sheriff hadn't let anybody else go up there. But maybe that was just because he didn't want anything disturbed. What the hell. I put one foot on the glassy first step. It held. Another foot on the next step. It held too. One more step and I was on the porch. It felt yellow everywhere. Dusty yellow. And it smelled of sweet sharp lemons. Even through the mask. And honey. And honeysuckle. And green melons. It was wonderfully delicious. Could the men out in the fields smell it too? What kept them from ripping off their masks and rolling around in the delicious air?

And the sounds—now that I wasn't surrounded by hulking men with their three-day sweaty stinks, the underfoot crunching of dirty boots, the lumbering hooves of upright beasts, the clatter of machinery and the stink of gun oil—now that all of that was gone, I could hear the tinkling music of translucent leaves, rustling in the delicate touch of the breeze. The wind sang like a distant chorus, very faint and far away. Silvery insects rattled and buzzed. And now, much nearer, something soft and small kept calling, "Hoo-hooo, hoo-hoooo." I wanted to go looking for it, whatever it was—bird or cricket or owl, I didn't know, but it sounded like the voice at the edge of the world, but so close by now that I wanted to find it, wanted to peer over the edge and see what was there on the other side. It felt like it was just around the corner.

This probably wasn't a good idea, thinking like this. I wondered if I would be safer inside the house? Maybe inside, I'd be out of the wind and away from all the flavors sweeping across the fields. Cinnamon and musk and jasmine. How did I even know all those different scents?

The doorknob glittered like diamond. I turned it and the door swung open. Inside, the house was silent, still, and empty. No furniture here, only an empty shell, a suggestion of a life once lived, exploded outward into solar dazzle and flare. The windows glowed with the creeping brightness of the world outside. The light felt muted here. I wondered if it would be safe to take off my clothes and dance in here.

I wandered from room to room, touching each wooden or metal or glass surface. The doors, the walls, the glass of the mirrors. Everything tingled. My fingers caressed. I didn't remember taking off my gloves. I wasn't even sure where I'd left them. This wasn't good. I shouldn't be doing this. All the voices in my head were screaming. Run away, now! Grab the wire and head back into the dark. Don't get sucked away. But all the songs were singing even louder. The music whirled and roared. Come dance aloft, be free. Be clear. I cowered shivering under my cape. Eyes clenched shut against the fiery noise. The seductive smells of sweet apricots and cream and gently scented candles. Overwhelmed by influx, I held myself and counted, one and two and three and breathe and one and two and three and breathe—

No. No. I wouldn't succumb. Not going to get sucked away. Never. Ever. Didn't come this far to be a golden bird fairy dancer. All the walls are here for a reason. The carefully constructed dark, the comfortable black essence of nothing at all.

Upstairs, the house is wide open. Tall windows with billowing white drapes, open to the balcony surrounding the house. Outside, the view went on forever. So bright below, so clear up here. Out to the horizon, the sparkling fields, the waves of rippling air, the colors sparkling and dancing. If I take off my cape, I can feel it like the comforting radiance of the refiner. I stand, arms outstretched to feel the heat, the delicious soul-filling heat. It soaks into my flesh, heals my bones, warms my spirit. I giggle at the wash of sensation. I can feel myself glowing.

In the cupola, I twirl alone. Naked and free. Finally warm, and finally here. The frozen winter of my past retreats before the blasting sun. I thaw and come alive. Joyously alive. I laugh with silly pleasure. I am enchanted. The delight of heat.

Am I ready to see? Can I take off the goggles?

Here on the fenced roof of the cupola, the highest part of the house, I can see the world as far as the darklands, the carefully drawn boundaries of exclusion, every tiny little line etched into the face of the land like the wrinkles of time. The gloom of fear.

In the other direction, out toward the east, the south, the west, the land sparkles and shimmers. It dances with light and aliveness. Why would anyone try to hide from all this laughter?

I peeked under the glasses. It wasn't pain I felt, it was color, bright color, brightness overwhelming. It wasn't pain at all, just the sudden shock of coming alive after being dead so long. An awakening from the grave of gloom.

Lift the glasses slowly. Eyes ready to clench. At first, the dazzle startles. A splash of intensity. Hold my hand in front of my eyes—I can see through my fingers—I am translucent. Pink and gold and glistening. I have taken on the colors of the world. The crimson of my blood gives my skin a rosy blush. The blue of my veins resonates. I am a roseate glow of violet and vermilion. I lower my hand, and all the rest of the colors of the world flood in. All the smells and sensations. All the wonderful noises. All the heat and the light and the delicious flood of everything roiling together in a cascading symphony of being.

As I focus, I see...them. They've been there all along. Waiting for me. I just couldn't see them until now. Laugh and wave in radiant delight. They recognize me as one of them now. The dancing one is Doey. The others, also dancing, used to be the Trasks. I can hear the children singing.

And then, without passing through the intervening space, I am down among them, laughing with them. A moment of pause. Doey and I, face to face. Can I dance with you now? What a silly question. We're already dancing.

There are men with guns, hunting you. Hunting us. I wave toward the horizon. Doey laughs. He holds up the ends of the dark wires. The terminator boxes have been removed. The wires are dead—no, not dead, coming alive, infusing with clarity. Even metal can be bright.

Doey sparkles. Laugh with me and we'll dance the ends of these wires out to the distant south, out into the solar dazzle. Anyone who follows these lines will end up enchanted in the luminous day. The men will either dance or die. Whatever they choose. Doey twirls and passes out the tingling wires. I join him singing.

The Bag Lady

The street stank of garbage and sweat, but it was still early. Later, as the day warmed up, the smells of garlic and bacon would seep out of the corner diner. Traffic splashed through spring puddles. The last white patches of winter still resisted the glare of the sun, but if this was not their last day, it would be their last week.

The bag lady shuffled painfully along the sidewalk, pushing an overloaded shopping cart with one broken wheel. She didn't walk as much as she staggered. She was a shapeless lump, an ambulatory heap of clothing, new layers added on top of the old, sweaters, sweat-shirts, torn coats, a blanket, another coat, the whole stuffed with old newspapers for insulation—she was an oblate spheroid of rubbish and rejection. Her swollen ankles made it difficult for her to move, even harder to push the cart. Her feet were wrapped in more layers of dirty cloth.

The woman's skin was leathery and lined, burned and scoured, eroded by the relentless weather. Her graying hair was a tangle of greasy ropes. If she'd ever had a name, she hadn't heard anyone speak it in years. Her eyes were rheumy and bloodshot—wherever she looked, she seemed to be staring at something on the other side of reality.

Several people passed her by, none of them saw her. She was invisible to them, not even scenery. Oblivious to her anguish and embarrassment, they hurried on about their business—exhaling puffs of breath like human locomotives, they chugged along the unbreakable rails of their lives.

The bag lady didn't care. She had more important matters to attend to. She did not often push her way onto this street, the business owners frowned at her, turned their hoses on her, chased her away with epithets and sometimes even threats of violence. But today—

She frowned, she sniffed, she looked up the street and back again. Something wasn't right. No, not here. Not there, but close. Something in the universe smelled wrong. And it wasn't her.

And then, she spotted it—

The dirty van, the dirty dark grey van. A panel van parked at the curb. No windows at the rear or sides. The front windows were tinted dark. No markings to identify the vehicle, no bumper stickers, no ads painted on the side. Just a featureless block.

It smelled wrong.

She looked down the street, all the way down to the end of the street, where a little girl in a pink winter coat had just come bouncing around the corner. A cherub, she glowed with innocence—the world was still bright and beautiful to her. She was singing and skipping, trailing one mittened hand across the frosty store-fronts, leaving sketchy streaks in the hoar-frost.

And as it always did, the moment clicked into clarity. The bag lady made a decision. She pushed her heavy cart forward. She put all her strength into the effort, squelching desperately forward.

Finally, unable to move any further, she stopped, her cart inconveniently blocking the passenger door of the van, her reeking body blocking the sliding panel door on the side. Someone on the inside made a noise, it sounded like a curse.

The bag lady grunted in sudden annoyance. She leaned against the panel door of the van for balance, her wrinkled hand sliding and leaving an ugly smear—and then a stream of urine ran down her left leg, puddling at her feet, steaming on the icy pavement.

The moment was perfectly timed. The little girl came dancing by, her song abruptly stopping as she glanced over. She made a face, an expression of disgust and disapproval, then she broke into a run and scampered on toward school.

The bag lady still leaned against the van, frowning, concentrating on something more than her own body now. The left tail light of the van abruptly shattered. No repair shop would ever be able to make it light again. Every police cruiser that noticed would pull this vehicle over to cite the driver for the broken light—but no, that wouldn't be enough. She needed to do more.

She muttered a few words—barely finishing the curse before the van pulled angrily away. The greasy handprint on its side would not wash off—not easily and not for a long time. But the handprint was only the smallest part of the spell. The van and its unseen occupant were now afflicted with a fetid malcharisma. They would never go unnoticed again—it might be enough. The bag lady couldn't be sure.

In the great grand scheme of things, this little shift of possibility was so small as to be infinitesimal in its reach—but to the little girl in the pink coat, the unknowing recipient of this reversal of entropy, it was an unknown coup, a victory of life-changing proportions—simply because she would live to see tomorrow.

But for the bag lady, it was going to be a very expensive triumph. The avalanche of entropy is unforgiving and the effort to shift it even a millimeter would cost her dearly.

Already, she was groaning with new pains. She grabbed onto the handle of her shopping cart to keep from falling. It was so heavily loaded it was an anchor to her sudden dizziness. For a moment, she did not know who she was or where she was. She knew only pain, the bottomless well of icy fire that gnawed at her gut, the first warnings of the waves of despair to come.

Somehow, she managed to make it across the slippery sidewalk to the nearest doorstep, where she sank down to her knees, collapsing in her rags, sagging against the frame of the door. She knew she couldn't stay here long. She knew the proprietor of this shop was an unforgiving tyrant, a small and petty excuse for a human being, interested only in the amount of commerce he could attract, never in the people he might serve. Soon, he would come bursting angrily out of his sacred warmth to chase her away.

But right now, she was overcome with the simple effort of breathing. In. Out. In. Out. She gasped for breath, strove to regain some sense of herself, but failing. This was going to be a bad one. Very bad. She couldn't help herself, she had to see. Still puffing, she began laboriously unwrapping the coils of cloth around her right leg, around and around, all the way down, until she finally revealed the mottled skin of her left foot. It was stippled with ugly blotches of green and yellow, blue and purple. There were new sores appearing, pus-filled boils, inflammations that grew even as she watched. Blood oozed from old scabs.

She searched desperately for the first telltale signs of gangrene, but was quickly disappointed. As eagerly as she hoped—no, not yet. This wasn't the one. Not even close. Not big enough. Not yet. She was going to survive. She was going to live another day. She wept.

She could remember another time—so long long ago—a time of naïve ignorance, but that was before the flashes began, before the smells and the flavors and the clamoring sense of wrongness overwhelmed her with a terrible compulsion to do something— *anything*—that might restore even a small balance to the world.

"It isn't fair! Why me?" she wept. "Why me? What did I do to deserve this—?"

But even as the words dribbled out of her torn mouth, she already knew the answer. Because. Because. Because she'd brought it on herself—with her own outraged scream of anguish at the universe. "Why doesn't somebody do something?"

And the universe had answered. "Why don't *you?*"

So tomorrow, just like today, just like yesterday, just like all the days and years before, freezing through the unrelenting winter, burning and baking beneath the heavy blanket of summer, nevertheless she'll lever herself up again, every day paying the ugly price of her compulsion one more time. She has no choice—

The bag lady will pull herself up from the unforgiving pavement, stumble to her feet, wheezing and groaning, her bones crackling resentfully, all stiff and resisting—racked with pain and hunger, driven by desperation, she'll go out and search the streets and the alleys, looking for the big one, hoping, always hoping—every day hoping that today will be the day she can finally earn her death.

Thank you for diving into this book.

If you enjoyed these stories and would like to see more of my work, you can find me at

www.facebook.com/DavidGerrold
and
www.patreon.com/DavidGerrold

About The Author

David Gerrold has been writing professionally for more than half a century. He created the tribbles for Star Trek and the sleestaks for Land Of The Lost. His most famous novel is *The Man Who Folded Himself*. His semi-autobiographical tale of his son's adoption, *The Martian Child* won both the Hugo and the Nebula awards, and was the basis for the 2007 movie starring John Cusack and Amanda Peet.

His latest novel is *Hella*, available on Amazon.